ARROYO ATTACK

"Stand fast, men!" Ingram shouted. "Form breastworks like Zack showed us!"

Several men began whipping the mules into a makeshift circle, and Ingram fired at the nearest Kiowa brave, killing his horse. The Indian hit the ground running and stopped a bullet as he was about to let loose an arrow.

Others along the line of mules opened fire as the Kiowas veered sharply around the lead mule and thundered past. A brave drove a lance into the lead mule, but Ingram gut-shot him.

"Stay down behind your horses!" Zack commanded as he rode into the din. He jumped off his horse, laid the barrel of his rifle across his saddle, and triggered. A brave hit the dust. Then, not bothering to reload his big gun, he jerked his two five-shot pistols from their holsters and started blasting away.

Faced with the deadly rain of hot lead, the Indians withdrew out of range.

"Get ready boys," Zack shouted, reloading. "They'll be back!"

SCALE TO THE HEIGHTS OF ADVENTURE WITH

MOUNTAIN JACK PIKE

By JOSEPH MEEK

#1: MOUNTAIN JACK PIKE	(092-8, $2.95/$3.95)
#2: ROCKY MOUNTAIN KILL	(183-5, $2.95/$3.95)
#4: CROW BAIT	(282-3, $2.95/$3.95)
#5: GREEN RIVER HUNT	(341-2, $2.95/$3.95)
#6: ST. LOUIS FIRE	(380-3, $2.95/$3.95)
#7: THE RUSSIAN BEAR	(467-2, $3.50/$4.50)
#8: HARD FOR JUSTICE	(502-4, $3.50/$4.50)
#9: BIG GUN BUSHWACKER	(530-X, $3.50/$4.50)

MOUNTAIN MEN
ON THE
SANTA FE TRAIL
JESS McCREEDE

PINNACLE BOOKS
WINDSOR PUBLISHING CORP.

*To my friend, Michael Martin Murphey,
for his music and for promoting all
things Western.*

PINNACLE BOOKS

are published by

Windsor Publishing Corp.
475 Park Avenue South
New York, NY 10016

First printing: March, 1992

Printed in the United States of America

CHAPTER 1

Zack McClendon stood at the river's edge as the lingering coolness of a new day receded with the shadows. The big trapper looked around at the milling crowd of eager, bright-faced emigrants whose wagons and campfires littered the meadow-dotted valley near Bridger's year-old post. Jim Bridger and Louis Vasquez had established the post along the Black's Fork of the Green River almost in the shadow of the high Uintas, to serve fur trappers and Indians alike, but with the waning beaver trade, the collection of mud huts and smithy became a sought-after haven for the westward emigration of men and women headed for Oregon or California.

McClendon turned back to the dark waters that rushed by him with dizzying speed as most of his life had done. Here he stood, at the crossroads of his life, reality staring him hard in the face. What was he going to do now? Start a trading post like ''Old Vaskiss'' and Blanket Chief? His problem, like most other trappers, was hanging on too long. And like most other free trappers who thought the shining times would last forever,

1

Zack was in no better shape to face an uncertain future than a green farmer with seed in the ground and no rain in sight.

Behind him, Zack could hear the eager voices of adults amid the cries of laughing children as they prepared to depart the post. Men had repaired broken wagons and swapped trail-weary livestock for fresh animals from Bridger or from Jack Roberson, who had a cabin down river a piece from the post. The womenfolk had taken a few days off to clean clothes and tidy up wagons, while relying on Mrs. Bridger's hot oven to keep the men fed and in a jovial mood.

Things had really changed in the last two seasons. Gone were the hell-raising, drunken times where money, whiskey and squaws were swapped as freely among the trappers as yarns around a campfire. When they broke camp back then, you *by God* knew, as did any Indian or critter within a hundred miles, that a rendezvous had taken place.

Zack watched as a lone red-tailed hawk rose from a naked limb across the dark river, screamed once at the human activity on the opposite shore, spread its bronze wings, and caught the early morning updrafts of heated air above Black's Fork. The big trapper watched the rising, circling bird of prey until the hawk floated away from the river and finally disappeared from sight behind a line of trees and rocks. He felt much like the hawk now searching for new territory and prey.

Since '32 he had preyed on this land of climbing, tumbling mountains and sheltered valleys with no other thought but to trap as many beaver as he could. Now these quiet streams were trapped out. There was no more beaver water. But unlike the hawk, who could move to new territory and resume hunting, Zack and the others had no such place to turn. Even if they had, it would make little difference now. A change in fashion had effectively killed the market for beaver fur and that was that.

Zack heard the quiet approach of footsteps and knew without turning who it was. Even in country where no apparent danger

2

existed, Peck Overstreet walked with the careful stride of a man long accustomed to trouble at every turn.

"Packed up and ready to go any time you got a mind," Overstreet said in his halting soft voice. He appeared ten years older than Zack McClendon, with hair the color of winterkilled sagebrush and as thick as his full beard. A leather patch covered his left eye, lost to an Arapaho arrow some years back. Zack was a good six inches taller than his friend, who drew up beside him and fished out a worn leather tobacco pouch and packed his pipe. Neither spoke for a few minutes as they gazed across the dark waters at nothing in particular. When it seemed Zack would not speak, Peck stepped in to fill the void.

"Shoulda pulled out last year like you wanted," Peck offered, his pipe clenched in his teeth. "Now we got to put up with the likes of them pouring into the country." Peck Overstreet swept his hand behind him to indicate the busy emigrants hitching up their teams.

Zack turned away from the river and looked at his friend of five years with eyes the color of sandstone. He reached up to scratch the heavy beard now streaked with gray. The skin around his face and hands were burned deep by the sun.

"All we been doing is scraping by, and from the looks of things half rations is what we can expect from here on out."

"Overheard this morning Big Jim Ainsworth and Clyde Beckett are headed out fer Canada. Says that's the place to go if a man wants room to grow and prosper." Peck looked up at the taller man with expectant eyes. Up to now, Zack had not mentioned the direction they were headed. Peck never gave it a thought they wouldn't be traveling together. They had done all right together for five years and had made good money when beaver were thick as hairs on a man's arm. Wherever Zack wanted to go was okay by him. They both had given up long ago on ever getting rich in this business.

"A sight of country up there. Ought to do well if they are careful of the Blackfeet and such," McClendon ventured.

"Maybe we shoulda taken up guidin'," Peck said, eyeing Broken Hand Fitzpatrick, who sat before a large tent drinking coffee with a portly individual like he hadn't a care in the world.

Zack looked over at Tom Fitzpatrick. "As I recall, Tom said that very thing to us two years ago when he came through with Father DeSmet on his way to carry religion to the Blackfeet over in the Bitterroot Valley."

"And now he's back with near a thousand pikers ridin' his coattails. Reckon what old Broken Hand makes, fetching them emigrants out here?"

"A sight more than we'll ever see from beaver again," Zack said, looking at Fitzpatrick again as he burst out laughing at something the fat man said. Fitzpatrick appeared relaxed and in good humor. As well he ought to be, Zack figured. He didn't have to worry about the price of beaver falling lower than a pound of coffee or lead anymore. Fitzpatrick had seen it coming as well . . . only sooner than *he* had, and it angered Zack that he too hadn't acted on his instincts. Like a lot of others, he and Peck had simply held on in the face of reality, hating to give up the easy, free-style way of living they had grown accustomed to.

They walked away from the river back to their camp.

With undirected anger riding his shoulders, Zack picked up his pack and strapped it to his mule, giving it a few tugs when he had it lashed in place to make sure it was riding properly. He surveyed the polyglot assembly of free-trappers, Indians, half-breeds who hung around Bridger's Post and concluded that what he was witnessing was a funeral for a way of life long past its day. It was just as well. There wasn't enough beaver water left in the entire Rocky Mountain District, no matter what they were paying for furs. He had personally worked the beaver trade since '28 and now here it was '43 and the only person still buying beaver even at dirt prices was Pierre Chouteau, who owned the American Fur Company back in St. Louis. Even then, a man couldn't make back expenses any longer. Zack had seen the gradual decline in beaver population since the mid-thirties. He had stayed too long . . . much too long, and he guessed this single fact was the whole cause for his anger now.

"Want the last swig a coffee afore I clean the pot?" Peck asked. Zack shook his head, not bothering to turn around. Peck Overstreet emptied the last of the dregs into his cup, shrugging his shoulders. He wasn't one to waste nary a drop of coffee; the memory of going without for the last two months was still fresh with him. He scattered the coals about and walked down to the river to rinse the pot, his mind turning to the immediate future—something Peck rarely thought about. After hooking up with Zack, he had been more than glad to let the quiet man do the thinking so long as there was plenty coffee and good beaver water at hand. A man could spend too much time worrying about something he had no control over in the first place. And Peck knew what was eating at Zack. Had known it for the last year of trapping. Like everybody else, Zack had been caught with his drawers around his ankles over the sinking price of beaver pelts this season. Together, they barely had fifty pounds to show for this year's work. And they had to work hard to find that many. Most of the other trappers were no better off, nor the Indians who came to the post to trade skins for goods. With prices standing at three fifty a pound, they had little money to show for their efforts. He wondered again what Zack had in mind to do now.

"You going to wash that pot all day, old man?" Now that they were leaving, Zack was anxious to get on with it.

"Expect you'll want it clean come sundown and they ain't no coffee to warm yore innards, 'cause I got to find enough crick water to wash it." Peck gave the pot one last swish of water and turned back to camp. The usual banter between them helped to relieve tensions in an unsettled world where danger existed at every turn along a trail. And, Peck concluded, they had taken the wrong trail of late.

Seeing they were ready to leave, Thomas Fitzpatrick sauntered over.

"Decided on a direction?" he asked mildly. His lean frame bore the mark of a lifetime of wilderness living. Fitzpatrick looked a good ten years older than he was, with a head of gray hair that was the result of an incident with Gros Ventre Indians. He had been riding in advance of a pack train he was guiding West in '32 when he ran into the Indians at South Pass. He was pursued hard as he raced towards the mountains. For several excruciating days he remained hidden in a crevice where he had crawled, piling rocks and leaves about the opening while the Gros Ventres camped nearby. He escaped, and for five days he struggled west towards the rendezvous at Pierre's Hole. He escaped a wolf pack, lost his rifle and powder to the Snake when he tried crossing it, and cut strips from his leather hat to tie around his bloodied feet. He was near death and unable to walk when two other trappers found him a few miles from his destination. After he recovered from the ordeal, his hair turned completely white. But his eyes were still as lively as ever and they seemed to dance in his head as Fitzpatrick watched Peck stow away the coffeepot and cup.

Zack looked at his friend of a dozen years across the back of his saddle. Beyond, several men were busy tearing down the fat parson's tent.

"Looks like we not the only ones pulling out," Zack said, not wanting to answer Fitzpatrick's question.

Broken Hand Fitzpatrick smiled slowly and looked behind him for a second. "Hell, you know how it is with preachers, Zack. They ain't happy less they ranting and raving to a receptive crowd and ain't none of these old coons wanting to listen to such crap."

"Cain't worry none 'bout the soul when yore belly is thinner than sheet ice at first winter," Peck snorted.

The famous frontiersman laughed. "Right you are Peck, but don't tell the parson. They paying me handsomely to guide

6

them to Oregon country so they can preach to the heathens unheeded.''

''May as well try changing the course of the Green. Ain't never seen an Injun yet where religion has taken and stuck.''

''I'm of the same opinion, but as I said, all I'm doing is acting as guide. Don't intend to listen to the sermons.'' Fitzpatrick looked keenly at the silent-faced McClendon. ''You and Peck could do a sight worse than guiding. The money's good and there's thousands of green emigrants back in Missouri chomping at the bit to head West. We are going to see a major change out here in the next few years. These emigrants will give some stability to this open land and help build it up in ways we never done with all our traipsing about. They going to need solid men like yourselves who know every trail, rivers and passes in these Rockies to push civilization forward.'' Fitzpatrick paused briefly, looking at the two men. He couldn't tell if he was making an impression on them or not. ''Course, you could do a little scouting for the Army. Pay won't be nearly the same as for guiding though.''

''Something to think on,'' Zack replied, not knowing what else to say to his friend.

''Well, you boys watch your topknot and if you do decide to take up guiding, look up Howard Smith. He owns a mercantile in St. Louis and supplies most of the trains making up to head West.'' The trio shook hands and Fitzpatrick stepped back as Zack and Peck stepped into their saddles.

''Thanks for the information, Tom,'' Zack said. ''Best keep an eye peeled for Blackfeet. They may lift your hair not knowing you've turned over a new leaf and taken up proselytizing.''

Fitzpatrick laughed heartily. ''I would if there was enough money in it,'' he called to the departing horsemen. Zack waved a hand without looking back and turned south as soon as they were deep into the thick timber. Like a wary wolf, Zack had no intention of broadcasting his direction of travel to those remaining in camp, particularly the sullen-faced Indians who had fared no better than the trappers this year. They had little to barter with other than their squaws, and even they were in poor demand by the trappers. The dying market had killed a lot of desires and the need for a squaw was low on a sober-eyed trapper's list while his immediate future looked so clouded. Most was holding tight what little money they had, hoping something would come along to replace beaver.

As Peck brought up the rear with the pack mule, Zack picked his way across rough ground, over a stretch of valley dotted with tall grasses and low shrubs. Keeping Black's Fork on his left, they angled away from the river, all the while drifting in a northeasterly direction towards the Wind River Mountains. With nothing but hoofs on stone and the creak of leather to break the silence, Zack had time to think. And right now he felt empty and unsure of himself. Maybe Fitzpatrick was right. Guiding seemed to be the coming thing and a sure bet for making money. Yet as he thought this Zack knew he would rather not fool with a bunch of green people who knew absolutely nothing about how to care for themselves when trouble came along. And trouble would come along, it always did.

They stopped for a quick lunch of coffee and cold biscuits Peck had saved from breakfast. They ate the biscuits in silence while the coffee boiled over a low fire. The animals were picketed on a shaded grassy slope that got its moisture from a nameless creek that fought its way down from the higher slopes to the east, searching for the distant Green in which to empty.

"We headed fer South Pass, I take it?" Peck asked after he managed to get the last of the dry bread down. He looked at the pot on the fire longingly, but the coffee was nowhere near ready.

"Once we cross the Little Sandy. No better place to get through this rocky wall and you know it."

Peck Overstreet eyed his quiet companion before he spoke. "All depends."

Zack looked up from the fire at Peck. "On what?"

"On where a fellar is headed. You could drop straight south. Course, doing that we got to cross the Red Desert and there ain't nothing out there but alkali, scrawny greasewood and winds that feel like they're blowing up from the very gates of hell. And if you're dumb enough to survive it, there's still the benchlands you got to deal with, not to mention the grief them Utes can dish out along the way. No sirree, I'll keep to the high country long as I'm able."

Zack grinned at his friend, knowing what he had on his mind. He held out his cup. "Pour me some, otherwise I'll never get the rest of this biscuit down." Peck poured them both a cup of the black liquid.

"Once across South Pass, then what? I take it we ain't headin' north?" Peck asked, not wanting to play the waiting game any longer. Some of the others had asked him last night and again this morning. But none had asked the tall silent McClendon. Most trappers regarded McClendon as unapproachable most times and about as dangerous as a rattler if provoked. Stories of his prowess with the big knife he carried at his belt or the big muzzleloader strapped to the saddle horn had gotten around over the years, and those that hadn't heeded his warning felt the sting of his blade or the bite of his bullet.

"Going to head south," Zack said, washing down the last of the dry biscuit. "We'll follow the Sweetwater until we can work our way south once we reach the Platte."

"Just fine by these old bones. Little sun might get these hinges of mine working proper. What we gonna do when we get there?"

"Take up trading," Zack said, watching Peck's reaction across the rim of his cup.

Peck Overstreet looked up blankly at his friend. Zack didn't say much, and when he did it was no more than necessary to convey the thought or message. Most times it wasn't enough for most ordinary folk. Peck had learned long ago to patiently pull the information from Zack like an embedded arrow.

"This child ain't made for no tradin' post life."

Zack looked sharply at Overstreet, as if to say he couldn't understand how he had missed what was being said.

"Not trading post. Trade goods. Figure we could make a good living hauling goods from St. Louis down to Santa Fe. Way I hear it, a man can clear six hundred dollars per wagon."

"What you planning to use fer cash to buy these trade goods with?" Peck asked, noticing the grin on Zack's face.

"We got nearly a thousand saved between us and I figure if we can haul something back to St Louis for somebody, then we got a chance of loading out a few more wagons if we get this Howard Smith to go a loan or partner up with us for one or two trips. We keep doing this until we got enough wagons hauling goods to really make money." Zack's eyes came alive as he talked and his normally quiet voice filled with an energy he had rarely displayed before. Peck looked at the tall trapper with eyes wide.

"Zacharia McClendon! You ain't said that much at one spell in two seasons."

Zack grinned sheepishly at his friend, his eyes dancing. "What do you think?"

"Well, we both ain't seen Taos in quite a spell. I remember that little thing you took a shine to. Let me see . . . what was her name now?" Peck pretended to think while scratching his scruffy beard.

"Rosita," Zack cut in, "not that you was going to be out-done. It was me, you remember, that pulled you away from that big-breasted woman in Juan Ortega's cantina. Expect you would be there still, with three or four little half-breeds running around underfoot. Most likely, I saved your life."

Peck snorted loudly at such tripe. "Be Jasus, you was as moonie-eyed over that skinny gal as any man that ever laid his pod in a furrow."

Midafternoon saw them across the gentle swell that marked the break in the rocky spine of the Continental Divide, first

10

discovered by Robert Stuart and his Astorians some thirty years before as an easy way through the Wind River Mountains.

Three miles below the windy summit a dozen Indians rode out of the thin willows bordering the Sweetwater and cut north to head them off. They were Cheyenne and riding what looked to Zack like played-out winter horses. Could be they had it in their minds to add two good ones to their group.

Zack lifted the heavy percussion rifle from his saddle horn just in case. It looked much like a Leman or Hawken, but it was a sixty-caliber rifle made especially for Zack by Sam O'Dell of Natchez. The only modification Zack had made to the gun was to file off the projecting spurs of the trigger guard so it wouldn't snag his clothes when in a hurry. Other than that, the gun was solid, dependable . . . and quite deadly at long range.

Without speaking, Peck spread the distance between his horse and Zack's, his rifle still in the crook of his arm where he had placed it since lunch. Peck wasn't one to be caught with his pants down. Both men pulled up in unison, letting the Indians come to them. Cheyennes could be as unpredictable as Sioux, especially if they figured they might hold the advantage. As they rode slowly forward, Zack recognized the short, stout-built leader as Blue Wing, a minor war chief of the Colorado band of Cheyennes. The trappers had clashed with the flat-faced Indian a few years back when they were working traps down on the Middle Fork of the Little Snake. Blue Wing had finally decided to ride away from the deadly men after six of his warriors fell beneath their guns. Word got around after that to ride a wide circle around the tall hazel-eyed trapper with the deadly thunderstick. Since then, the Cheyennes dubbed Zack "Straight Arrow," for never missing his mark. And now Blue Wing was back to even old scores.

"Ain't that square-bodied Injun prancing 'bout Blue Wing?" Peck asked, squinting his eyes against the cold wind.

Zack nodded. "Him all right."

Suddenly Blue Wing reined his horse to a stop just beyond rifle range. Zack and Peck watched as the Cheyennes conferred with one another. By the gestures, it looked to Zack as if Blue Wing was having trouble convincing the others to attack regardless of the odds.

"Guess they done figgered out who they dealin' with," Peck said, holding the pack rope tight in case they had to make a run for the trees.

Zack was thinking the same thing and he decided to help the Cheyennes make up their minds.

Chapter 2

The roots of the tiny settlement of San Miguel del Bado, shortened simply to San Miguel by passing traders, reached deeply into the eighteenth century. Founded by Christianized Indians and later joined by Spanish herders and farmers, San Miguel grew at a steady pace. In 1806, the Indians built a stone church under the direction of Padre Jose Francisco Leyba. Its stone walls were three feet thick, and stood twenty feet high, and its bell contained gold and silver donated by the faithful.

One of those who had given freely to the creation of the bell was Carlos Vermejo, a man of sixty who now enjoyed his position as alcalde, or mayor, and the official in charge of the customhouse. Although a religious man, Vermejo was not above accepting small gifts of money or small items of trade goods from the St. Louis traders as they passed through the customhouse. Only then could they continue on to Santa Fe.

For twenty years, Alcalde Vermejo had collected duties from the increased trade with the United States and had grown rich from the small bribes. He was the most powerful political figure in San Miguel. His town was the first place the Texans were first brought after the ill-fated Santa Fe Expedition. Vermejo himself watched from his office window, horrified, as two Texans were led into the plaza and shot for trying to escape. Governor Manuel Armijo's right-hand officer, Captain Damasio Salezar, had carried out the sentence. The sadistic Salezar then marched the remaining three hundred prisoners to Mexico City, shooting those not able to walk the distance. Vermejo heard that Salezar, on his return to Santa Fe, had presented five sets of Texan's ears to Governor Armijo as proof of the Tejanos deaths. Nothing but trouble would come of such actions, Vermejo knew, but like others who were afraid to garner Armijo's wrath and face the cruel Salezar, he had kept his opinions to himself. And now trouble had come to San Miguel. In fact that very morning. Bright blood once more stained the dusty plaza street, and this time it was not Texan blood, but that of Pedro Salinas, one of Salezar's men.

Vermejo lifted a pudgy hand to his temple and quietly massaged the ache within. He did not feel like dealing with the unstable Salezar, yet tomorrow he would have to explain in great detail how it came to be that one of his men was shot down by an American trader.

But Vermejo didn't have to wait that long. At the news, Salezar and ten of his men left Santa Fe immediately. By ten o'clock that night they walked their lathered, trembling horses into the plaza. Salezar sent at once for the Alcalde while he had a drink in the cantina. A few minutes later, Vermejo appeared, looking disheveled and puffy-eyed, having been awakened from a troubled sleep.

"Ah, Señor Vermejo, my friend. Come have a drink," Salezar said, waving the Alcalde over. Salezar smiled coldly as the portly Mexican took a seat, staring at the full glass before him. His stomach wanted nothing to drink, yet his brain told him he had better. To insult a man like Salezar was tantamount to signing your own death warrant.

"You did not expect to see me so soon, hey, amigo?"

"That is true," Vermejo said, lifting his glass and taking a small sip. "I knew you would come tomorrow for sure."

"I would come no matter the time or circumstances the minute I hear of a murder of one of my loyal soldiers." Salezar's dark eyes fairly flashed.

Trusted spy and thief you mean! Vermejo thought, but did not say. They were all thieves and Armijo was the biggest. The fact was, Salezar did not trust anybody, especially those handling money for Governor Armijo . . . and Vermejo handled a lot of money. That alone made him uneasy around Salezar.

"It was most unfortunate, Capitán," Vermejo said quietly, keeping his eyes on the table. To stare directly into Salezar's eyes was like baring his soul to the man. And that Vermejo did not want to do.

"Yes, in that you are correct." Salezar turned and spoke quickly to one of his officers. The lieutenant bowed slightly and left with two other soldiers. Vermejo knew Salezar had sent for the American who had shot Pedro Salinas.

Vermejo lifted his glass, his hand trembling slightly, and took a deeper drink, feeling the fire race downward. It was going to be a long night, and he needed to steel himself against what he knew was coming. Vermejo felt the stares from the other patrons quietly drinking as they watched the proceedings. Even those playing monte had quit the game, waiting to see what Salezar's next move would be.

In a little while, the officer and two soldiers were back, prodding the white-faced American with the end of their bayonets. A swarthy-faced constable brought up the rear, looking as official as he could on such short notice. The soldiers halted the prisoner before the table occupied by Vermejo and Salezar. Vermejo would not look at the gringo for fear he would discover the truth behind his eyes. Salezar had no such fears and stared boldly at the visibly shaken man.

"So, you are the one who murdered brave Pedro Salinas," Salezar began. The American's jaw dropped open and he stared hard at Salezar.

"Weren't murder. The man tried to run me through with his bayonet when I refused to pay him *mordia*. I had already paid duties to Señor Vermejo." The prisoner pointed to the mayor, whose face sought his glass and stayed there. "I won't bribe anyone, soldier or citizen." The American had gotten his nerves under control and his voice was steady and hard-edged.

Salezar's face flamed and he banged his empty glass hard on the table. "Lies! The military of Mexico do not ask for favors from gringos." One of his men refilled his glass and stepped back.

"Why don't you ask the alcalde what happened. He was there and witnessed the shooting."

Salezar rose from his seat, trembling with rage. "Do not tell me how to conduct an investigation! You are a prisoner and on Mexican Territory. You have no rights here. I alone hold your miserable life in my hands. Do not anger me further." Salezar eased back into his chair. Several patrons looked around at their friends. Their faces reflected a desire to be elsewhere, but they lacked the courage to leave. None wanted Captain Salezar to focus his sudden anger on one of them.

The American blanched, but did not waver before the verbal attack. Vermejo seemed to sink further into his chair at the mention of his name and for a moment he had difficulty breathing. He did not know if he could tell an effective lie with this gringo staring down at him in an accusing manner, but he knew he must . . . or he might well take the place of the gringo before the firing squad. One never knew with Salezar.

Without looking up, Salezar spoke quietly to the prisoner. Those at nearby tables could not hear what was being said, but there was no mistaking the effect it had on the gringo, whose face drained of all color.

"You . . . you can't do this," the American whispered, his

16

confession in half and sticking it in his coat pocket. The officer nodded slightly at the constable, who stepped forward and replaced the handcuffs on Walker. Walker looked from Salezar to Vermejo and back again.

"I thought—"

"That is the trouble with all you gringos. You do not think well," Salezar said sharply. A vicious gleam flared deep in his eyes.

"What the hell! I did what you asked." Rough hands jerked Walker from his seat. He felt the prick of bayonets once more.

"Yes you did and it sealed your fate," Salezar said coldly. "Carry out your orders," he commanded the young officer.

"Why you lying greaser!" Walker shouted as they dragged him to the door. "I'll see you in hell, Salezar," he screamed over his shoulder.

"Sí, sí," Salezar replied off-handedly. He was already thinking of how much money could be translated from the traders goods. Tomorrow he would have a closer look at them. He poured himself another drink, looking for the first time at Vermejo who continued to stare at Walker's empty glass.

"Do not worry, *me amigo*," Salezar said. "We have his confession and a roomful of witnesses." He waved his arm about him and laughed loudly at the joke he had played on the gringo. "If only he had known we were going to shoot him anyway." He laughed even harder.

"Are we to turn the others loose, then?" Vermejo asked.

"Yes of course. But without weapons, mules or provisions. They will be lucky to reach the Arkansas alive. And if their bones are found later on, *quein sabe*?" The crack of rifles filled the night air and a roar of approval rose up from those in the cantina. None present saw how Vermejo flinched at the sound, and he sagged further in his chair, bringing the glass to his lips. He quickly drank its contents and poured himself another. The demons would not rest easy tonight and Vermejo determined to get himself very drunk to keep them at bay. In spite

19

of the celebration, Vermejo had a dark foreboding that what happened here tonight would come back to haunt Salezar and himself down the not too distant road. He closed his eyes and drank deeply, shutting out the sight of a lone glass before an empty chair.

CHAPTER 3

Zack let out a blood-curdling yell, raised his rifle above his head and dug his heels into the startled horse. Not to be outdone, Peck was only a jump behind him.

The astonished Indians broke off their deliberations as the charging trappers bore down on them. Blue Wing immediately answered Zack's challenge, calling for his brothers to follow him as he whipped his pony forward. But his fellow Indians wanted nothing to do with Straight Arrow's medicine and they fled to the safety of the Sweetwater, leaving Blue Wing to face McClendon and Overstreet alone.

After a dozen yards, Blue Wing glanced behind him and was astounded to find he was all alone. His men were fleeing like old women. Without adequate support, Blue Wing had no other choice but to veer off and follow them.

"Look at 'em run!" Peck cried. After a few more yards of hard riding, Zack pulled his horse to a stop. The dark bay stood with sides heaving from the high altitude run. Peck rode up beside the big trapper, his eyes blazing with excitement. Zack hung the big rifle around his saddle horn once more.

"Figured they weren't up to a fight the way Blue Wing was carrying on," Zack said. "Just the same, we best put some distance between them and us before nightfall. Blue Wing is going to be hard to live with for the next few days. He'll harangue his men for turning tail, get them worked back up and pay us another visit if we ain't shet of this country by then."

They camped that night in deep timber a few miles above the Sweetwater. It was dark and cold in the thicket of trees, and snow was still deep in sheltered spots the sun never touched.

Although it was late spring, the distant Big Horns still lay under a bed of deep snow, with Cloud Peak jutting upward, its hoary mantel rising into the brilliant blue sky like some proud sentinel. To their immediate south lay the Green Mountains, half the height of its northern neighbors. Little snow remained on its rounded, wind-blown peaks.

"Tomorrow we'll take the gap I know through the Greens and skirt the Seminoes until we hit the Platte."

Peck stared at his friend over his coffee for a full minute. "Don't recollect no notch between them two mountain ranges."

"Came through there one summer with a band of friendly Arapahoe. It's there all right. Save us a few days and might just throw Blue Wing off our scent."

After a quick supper of cold biscuits and more coffee, Peck outed the fire. There was no use making it easy for Blue Wing to locate them in the night. Except for the ever-present wind through the big trees and the occasional stamp of a horse, the night passed quietly.

When Zack rolled out of his blanket an hour before dawn, he wasn't surprised to find it snowing. He had smelled a change in the air late yesterday. The tiny flakes gathered over objects like a hoary frost, and, by the time Peck shook off the thin covering of snow, Zack had the fire going and was slicing meat

22

into a skillet. Peck eyed the younger trapper critically from his covers, running his fingers through his beard where it was flat on one side from having lain on it during the night.

"Tired of cold biscuits," was all Zack said on the subject, as he added coffee to the pot of water he had gotten from a nearby creek.

Three nights later they camped between the folds of a sheltered draw that overlooked the North Platte as it cut its way through the Medicine Bow Range between the Sierra Madre Mountains. Shadows of dark green conifers and rivers of silver-trunked aspen, still naked from winter's grip, marched away from the narrow valley and up the flanks of both mountain ranges. In the lengthening shadows, the Platte reminded Zack of a huge shining snake as it curved its way across the quiet meadow.

Situated some three hundred feet above the valley floor and near Sage Creek, their camp provided a commanding view of snowcapped Medicine Bow Peak to the east.

Zack walked to the edge of the timber, breathing deeply of the mountain air laced heavily with the smell of spruce. Far below, he watched as a bull elk stepped from the edge of the forest and made its way down to the Platte for a drink. Zack stayed there until all light left the valley and the mountains were nothing more than dark masses against the purple sky. He lost himself in the fullness of this peaceful place, yet he knew that somewhere out there now Blue Wing and his band were silently trailing them. They were deep in Sioux and Cheyenne country, and they would have to be particularly careful. A full moon rose as if by magic above Medicine Bow Peak and flooded the valley. The moonlight reminded Zack of Mexican silver. His thoughts turned to the dark-eyed Mexican beauty in Taos. Distance and time had probably erased any memory of him from her mind, yet even the Arapahoe squaw he had wintered with for the past two seasons had not dimmed his memory nor his desire for the fiery little Mexican. He turned back to camp, his mind still toying with the subject.

Was she the overriding reason for his decision to take up trading with New Mexico, and not the money? It was something he had not stopped to consider, yet now that the image of her floated freely in his head once more, Zack had to admit that both money and seeing her again was two important reasons for heading south. Peck was still gone when he stepped into camp and added a few pieces of wood to the fire. A few minutes later, Peck emerged from the shadows carrying a fat rabbit he had managed to snare.

"Purty country 'round here, Zack. Man could live here and be happy. Plenty game, and the river is brimming with fish too. I drank outa a mountain stream so cold and sweet, I'd swear the headwaters musta started in heaven."

"Guess that's what lured old Henry Freeb and Bridger to build a post the other side of this mountain to the west. Can't be more than fifty, sixty miles from here."

"You don't say," Peck said, laying the rabbit across a small boulder. "Now you ain't going to tell me you done been there 'cause I know fer a fact they didn't settle in 'til '37, Zack McClendon, and I been with you fer the whole time 'afore that."

Zack smiled as he watched Peck expertly skin the rabbit with his knife. Fresh meat would be good for a change, even if it wasn't elk or black-tailed deer.

"Bridger told me about the place when we came through Brown's Hole last year." Zack was referring to the post, David Crockett, more commonly called Fort Misery, a huddle of log and mud chinked huts erected at an opening in the deep canyons through which the Green pounded its way through the Uinta Mountains.

"Ain't no better'n Fort Misery, don't reckon this child'll go crossing rough country fer a peek." Peck spoke without looking up from his skinning job. In a few minutes he was through and stuck the rabbit on a green willow branch to roast over hot coals. He sat back from the fire with a cup of coffee Zack had handed him.

24

"Got an uneasy feeling 'bout this place, Zack."

"You too?"

"Injuns. I can smell'm."

Zack nodded and looked around at the moonlit objects. "I expect this would be a good night for a visit, way things stand out in this light." The moon had cleared the dark outline that marked the Medicine Bows. It was brilliant white in a sea of black. There was no hiding a camp tonight.

"Figger Blue Wing is chafing fer a chance to send us under and a man couldn't ask fer a prettier night to pick fer such doings."

"Best drink all the coffee you can hold, old man. We gonna have us a cold lonely night."

"Been cold before," Peck said, reaching out to turn the rabbit. "Danged if that don't smell fittin'."

"Expect Blue Wing and them hollow-ribbed braves of his thinks the same as close as they are to us."

"When you figger they'll make their play?" Peck asked, handing Zack his cup for a refill. Fresh coffee again was something not to take lightly where Peck was concerned. He took the steaming cup from Zack and sipped it, breathing in the aroma. Push come to shove, he figured coffee held just a tad edge over a woman . . . but not by much. And then he thought of the buxom Mexican down at Ortega's and his pulse quickened. Talk about draining a man.

"Blue Wing will wait until this moon is about to slide down the backside of the Continental Divide behind us. That way, if things go wrong, they stand a better chance of escaping in the dark." Zack smiled tightly. "And things *will* go wrong for them."

Later, both men hobbled their horses and the pack mule, rolled their blankets by the fire and stepped into the soft moonlight to await the Cheyenne. They settled down some distance apart, yet not so far that they could be hit by dangerous crossfire. Both had a clear view of camp and the horses. Away from the inviting fire the night air grew cold, and Zack wished he

25

he had the coat now draped over his blanket. To fool Blue Wing, everything must appear just right to the wary Indian. Zack had picked the more open ground to watch the camp, figuring Blue Wing would make his approach from the more densely wooded area hugging the mountain. Peck simply found a slight depression and flattened himself to the ground.

Blue Wing and the others came up from the valley floor across soft meadow grass, dodging from rock to bush, their eyes glued to the circle of fire in the distance. Blue Wing had warned the others about Straight Arrow and his strong medicine. Like the cunning wolf, he could move silently and strike with deadly speed. But this time, Blue Wing was not doing what was expected of him as he halted thirty yards away from the glowing fire.

With raven eyes he probed the thin shadows where the moonlight failed to touch, searching for objects that were at odd angles to the natural surroundings. His eyes had not lingered over the quiet camp where the two blanketed objects lay close to the fire. Straight Arrow and the other white called Peck would not be there, yet two of his men pressed ahead, stalking the camp against his orders. Blue Wing felt the sudden rush of anger at the two men. If the whites failed to kill them, he promised himself they would die by his knife. They were stupid. The two they faced were not some soft-bellied whites fresh to the mountains. In spite of the need to go slow, Blue Wing pressed forward, afraid that, because of the two braves, the element of surprise would be lost at any moment and with it their advantage.

The only part of Zack McClendon that moved was his eyes, and they never stopped sweeping the area in front of him. Wedged between a wagon-sized boulder and a pine, Zack crouched beyond the probe of the moonlight. Trouble was, if he was forced to counter an attack from his rear, Zack would expose his big frame to the moonlight and to a possible bullet or arrow. Twenty feet away, Peck hugged the shallow depression, facing the fire. He was fully exposed to a sudden attack from the open meadow if they chose to attack from that direction. It was then a tiny nagging doubt crept into his brain where Blue Wing was concerned. The two Indians stalking the fire from the direction of the meadow made Zack realize just how wrong he had been about Blue Wing.

Zack barely had time to shout a warning to Peck before the two Indians let out war whoops and charged the camp. They had not seen the hidden trappers. Bullets from both men cut short their charge, one falling near the edge of the camp, while the other, a few steps beyond, hit the rocky ground and rolled across Zack's bedroll, coming to rest with one leg in the fire. Neither Indian moved.

Zack rose up from the boulder with a roar as the others rushed forward from the meadow. He smashed the nearest Indian in the face with the butt of his heavy rifle, hearing the bones crunch as the Indian screamed and then fell silent. Dropping the rifle, Zack pulled his five-shot Patterson and killed an Indian who had come up behind him. Zack leaped to the defense of Peck, who was rolling around on the ground locked in hand-to-hand combat with a big Indian. Zack shot the Indian through the head and Peck came up from beneath the dead man, holding a bloody knife in one hand and a pistol in the other.

Something burned his side and Zack staggered backward, almost falling. A dozen yards away the moonlight highlighted a crouching Indian. A hasty shot by Zack caused the Indian to drop the rifle and jump behind a small boulder before Zack could fire again. In better lighting, the Indian might not have missed his mark, but the moon was slipping behind the dark mass of rock to the west, taking with it the waning light.

Suddenly it was over as quickly as it had begun, leaving Zack and Peck standing back to back, their pistols at the ready.

They watched silently as blackness filled the valley. The only sound was Peck's ragged breathing from his hand-to-hand fight with the large Indian.

"So much fer them coming down the mountain," Peck whispered as he put away his pistol. He felt around on the cold ground for his rifle, but couldn't locate it in the dark.

Zack felt his cheeks redden. Blue Wing had outwitted him, there was no use denying it. He touched his burning side and his hand came away wet. He thought of the crouching Indian and wondered if it had been Blue Wing. Another inch and he would have paid for his mistake with his life.

"You found your rifle yet?" Zack asked softly.

"Right here. Danged Injun jerked it outa my hands."

"I'll get mine. We can head back to the fire now. They ain't likely to come back, but I'm not promising," Zack said, thinking where Blue Wing was concerned, anything was still possible. He walked over to the large boulder and felt around the base of the tree. Zack sensed rather than felt the presence of the attacker and he flattened himself out on the ground as rushing air passed over his body. Zack came away from the ground with his big knife gripped tightly in his fist just as a solid body slammed into him. He heard Peck shout something as he tumbled to the ground with the Indian on top of him, seeking to slash Zack with his knife. Zack plunged his knife into the dark where the Indian should be and he felt a steel hand close around his wrist. He managed to twist his body to one side just as the Indian thrust his knife downward. The knife struck rock and Zack quickly drove his knee into the groin of the Indian, who gasped loudly at the pain. It was all Zack needed; he tore his knife-hand free and drove the blade deep between the attacker's ribs—once, then twice. Zack felt the body go limp. He rolled from beneath the Indian and staggered to his feet.

He found Peck standing over him with his pistol in his hand. In the dim light from the nearby fire, Peck had been unable to use the weapon for fear of hitting Zack.

"You okay, boy?"

Zack gasped for air, his burning side now bleeding heavily. "Got . . . to . . . be . . . Blue Wing." Zack stood breathing deep for a few moments before continuing.

"Danged near had you too."

They built up the fire after pulling the charred leg of the dead Indian from the bed of coals. Peck made a poultice from trade tobacco and applied it to the six-inch gash on Zack's ribs before wrapping it tightly with strips torn from an old shirt. Zack put his leather shirt on again, ignoring the drying blood.

Peck took a burning piece of wood and went out to check the dead Indian. He had a grin on his face when he came back.

"That puts an end to old Blue Wing," he said to Zack, who sat nursing a cup of coffee. He had thrown a blanket about his shoulders for added warmth. "You did good, boy." Peck tossed Blue Wing's knife before Zack.

Zack stared at the ten-inch blade with open curiosity. The handle was wrapped with rawhide and streaked with blue lines. He wondered what, if anything, the lines represented. He had a strange feeling, looking now at the weapon that had almost murdered him. He picked it up, turning it slowly in the palm of his hand to feel the edge. The knife was as sharp as his own. Peck hunkered down next to Zack and poured himself a cup of coffee.

"You keep it, old man," Zack said, handing it to Peck. "I don't need a reminder of how close I came to going under."

Peck grinned and slipped the knife into his belt. "Near as I can figger, we kilt six of them, counting these two here." The sweet smell of charred flesh hung heavy over the little camp. Peck had not bothered to remove the dead Indians.

Zack looked around the death camp. "Let's get the hell out of here, Peck," he whispered softly. "We can follow the Platte, now the stars are out again. They could come back if they find more brave souls out there to join them."

"Suits me to a tee. Ain't hankering to sleep no way with dead men lying 'bout."

"Couple days we ought to be out of Cheyenne country. Then we can push on south to the Arkansas."

"All we'll hafta worry 'bout then is 'Raphoes er Utes," Peck reminded him dryly.

Zack grinned at his friend. "You rather have Sioux and Cheyenne on our tail?"

"You got a pint, boy," Peck said, getting up to break camp. "Still set on St. Louis?"

Zack watched as Peck Overstreet rolled up his bedroll. For more years than he cared to remember, they had tramped up and down this rugged country, fighting hunger, mountain sickness, and wild Indians while trying to earn a living, only to have their livelihood taken from them by a change in fashion a continent away. Never again would he allow something so fickle to control his life. All they had to show now for their years of hardship, toil and swollen joints was a thousand dollars between them. At forty, Zack felt each and every year the mountains had put on him. This beautiful wild country also extracted a physical price from a man, and he was through paying for it.

"Now more than ever," he said softly.

CHAPTER 4

Keys rattled in locks, bringing the prisoners to their feet, groggy-eyed and disheveled. Dawn was still a good hour away. The men looked at one another, wondering what was happening. It had been a long time before either of the three men had returned to their beds after Simon Walker was led away. Their furtive glances held what each already knew to be the truth. The fusillade of gunshots that echoed across the plaza wasn't caused by a group of drunken soldiers firing their guns in merriment. Their friend, Simon Walker, was not coming back, and now it looked as if they were to be treated to a similar fate. The largest of the trio squared his shoulders and stepped through the open cell door. On the other side stood four grim-faced Mexican soldiers with the swarthy constable who motioned them forward.

Bull Stanton led the others from the cell, looking the soldiers square in the eyes as he passed. Unlike the others, Stanton was rawhide-tough and had spent the last ten years trapping beaver north of New Mexico. He had given up trapping after the last rendezvous on the Green back in '40. Finding himself in St. Louis without a way to support himself, Stanton had turned to the only skill he had to offer, and that was guiding traders across the vast plains.

In a way, Stanton felt responsible for Walker joining the pack train in the first place. After Walker showed up driving a broken down wagon and six worn-out oxen, Bull had helped the man dispose of the sorry wagon and those possessions he didn't need on the trail. Next, he had made sure Walker was properly outfitted with a good wagon and a team of fresh oxen and saw to it Walker bought trade goods most needed in Santa Fe rather than what the merchant was trying to push on him.

"What have you done with Walker?" Stanton demanded of the constable.

"Do not concern yourself with such matters, Señor Stanton, move along." The constable waved his hand forward. Bill Taylor and James Mann followed Bull Stanton's broad shoulders, finding comfort in the big man's presence.

The soldiers led them out into the cool morning air and across the plaza. A dog began barking from the shadows of a nearby adobe. One of the soldiers cursed the animal in Spanish which only caused the dog to bark even louder.

"*Caramba!*" one of the soldiers swore, turning to the constable. "Can you not shut him up?"

"What'cha afraid of Mex? You ain't fixen to do something these folks shouldn't know about, are you?" Bull Stanton asked in a loud voice. The Mexican gave him a look of warning.

The constable yelled at the dog, and a lamp was lit in the tiny house. The constable swore under his breath. His nerves were frayed from being up all night, the shooting, and now this. He promised himself he would kill Jose Lamas's dog the first chance he got . . . maybe tomorrow if Captain Salezar left for Santa Fe. He was a little more than frightened of the crazy soldier and of the power he possessed. A sharp word from the house silenced the dog as the small procession passed by.

Stanton fully expected to be executed as he knew Walker had been, but the soldiers prodded them into the smoky cantina, which was now filled to capacity. Stanton thought it a little strange for such a crowd to be still up at this hour, but he saw the reason when they were halted before a table where the alcalde and a Mexican officer sat drinking and smoking.

Salezar looked up at the big man with piercing eyes and saw no fear in their depths. Here was a man that would not frighten easily. His smoky eyes trailed to the other two men with him and saw no resistance there. Vermejo slumped forward in his chair, a spilled drink before him. Unlike Salezar, the mayor of San Miguel could not hold his mescal. The cantina was quiet as the desert at night.

"So you are . . . ?"

Stanton looked down at the Mexican officer and said in a loud voice, "Stanton, Bull Stanton."

"I can see why they call you Bull, Señor," Salezar smiled broadly. The alcohol had relaxed him and his mood had grown better over the last few hours. "You are *mucho hombre*."

"What have you done with Simon Walker?" Stanton demanded.

The smile faded from Salezar's face and his flashing eyes narrowed. He was beginning to dislike gringos as much as Armijo.

"Señor Walker was executed for the murder of Pedro Salinas," Salezar said crisply, watching Stanton for effect. He saw no surprise in Bull Stanton's eyes. The other two white men's gasps were audible in the silent cantina.

"Walker killed your man in self-defense, and you know it." Salezar jumped to his feet angrily. Even the drunken alcalde was roused from his stupor.

"Silence! I represent the Mexican Government through Governor Armijo. None of you have any rights in my country, yet when one of you murders a soldier, you expect to go free." The red-faced Salezar paced back and forth in front of Bull

Stanton, but the attempt at intimidation was ineffective against the tough mountain man, who stood head and shoulders above the prancing officer.

"Bull, maybe you best keep quiet, least 'til we find out what they intend on doing with us," James Mann said in a timid voice.

"Hell, Mann, can't you see what they intend to do?" Stanton shot back. "We'll be shot just like Walker."

"Lordy, lordy," Bill Taylor whimpered.

"Shut up, Taylor!" Stanton said harshly. "You and Mann knew what could happen if things went wrong down here. Comanches ain't the only ones can skin your hide."

A vicious gleam appeared in Salezar's eyes while a cold smile touched his lips. "You are a brave man, Señor Stanton. I like that. Another time and place we could have been . . . *simpicatio*, no?"

"Not in ten lifetimes."

Salezar roared with laughter. "Perhaps then, you will use up those ten lifetimes crossing the desert without your boots, water or food, eh, Señor?"

"Piece of cake," Stanton replied in an unemotional voice.

"Then you can start by removing your boots," Salezar said, looking delighted. Mann and Taylor looked at one another and at the Mexican.

"Us too?" Mann asked.

"No, only your friend here. He is the tough one. But maybe you watch yourself out there amigos. Señor Stanton may cut your throat for your shoes after a day or two in the sun." Both men seemed frightened by Salezar's words, and they shrank back from Stanton, who was busy removing his big boots.

"What about our wagons and trade goods?" Stanton asked.

"They have been confiscated by the Mexican Government. Consider yourselves lucky to be leaving with your lives."

A thin smile creased Bull Stanton's features. "Not giving us much . . . three maybe four days in the desert."

"Nevertheless, I give you your lives. What you do with it

is up to you." Salezar turned and picked up his hat from the table. "Now if you gentlemen will excuse me, it has been a long night and I am going to get some sleep."

"What about other traders coming to New Mexico? You going to give them the same treatment?" Stanton called as he was being herded to the door.

"This changes nothing, unless they resort to murder. The word will soon spread as to what happened to your friend Walker and to you three as well." Salezar tapped his coat pocket, "I have Simon Walker's signed confession and a roomful of witnesses. There will be no further trouble," Salezar assured the angry man.

"You can bet on the word spreading. I intend to survive to see that it does and to hell with your signed confession," Stanton replied grimly as the soldiers shoved him through the door. Behind him, Salezar laughed loudly.

"Good luck, gringos!" Salezar called after them. "And be thankful I send you off in the cool of the morning rather than the heat of midday." Salezar laughed again, and the others in the bar broke into a chorus of guffaws over the plight of the Americans.

The soldiers mounted their horses while Stanton and the other two traders stood by silently.

"Go!" one of them said, pointing his rifle toward the northeast. They marched the three Americans out of town, followed by the barking dog. It was light enough to see as a pink glow to the east spread across the cloudless sky.

"Going to be a hot one," Stanton said to Mann and Taylor.

"No talking!" the Mexican said, bumping his horse into Stanton deliberately. Stanton looked back at the soldier and gave him an evil grin. The Mexican did not like what he saw in the big man's eyes and pulled his horse back in line with the other two soldiers.

They stumbled across the Pecos, and Stanton deliberately fell face down in the water to wet his clothes and take a long drink. The soldiers laughed at him as he got up and continued forward, limping across the rocky-bottomed river on bruised feet.

The soldiers pushed them hard all that day and well into the next before turning back after they had marched them fifty miles to the east of the small Mexican community of Las Vegas. The soldiers warned them that if they turned back they would be shot on sight. Their only hope of survival was to find a passing trader, and that meant heading east for another thirty miles across burning desert to intersect the Cimarron Cutoff on the Santa Fe Trail. They had a chance if they could last until they reached the Canadian River. There were still roving bands of Comanches to avoid even if they somehow survived the trek.

Bull Stanton stood there in the heat and dust, watching the soldiers disappear in the distance. As the sounds of their horses faded away, an oppressive silence filled the heated air. They were truly alone now. Stanton realized it would take everything he knew about wild country and a lot of luck if they were to survive this. Mann and Taylor, who were smaller and in poorer physical condition, looked ready to throw in the towel. Even with boots, both men had formed blisters on their feet that burst and filled their shoes with a bloody mixture. Stanton had long ago chosen to ignore his lacerated feet that left a bloody trail across the hot sand as he walked.

"Give me your hat, Taylor," Stanton said. The hollowed-eyed man looked at Stanton with fear and apprehension.

"My head'll bake in this damn sun."

"I need it to make shoes for my feet," Stanton explained patiently.

"Ain't giving it up. You know I ain't got no hair. My head won't be nothing but one big blister if I do. Take Jim's."

"Mann's won't do. It's cloth where yours is leather. Now give it here."

Both Mann and Taylor looked at Stanton's swollen and cracked feet. "You ain't going to walk much further as I see it anyway," Taylor said, holding unconsciously to his wide hat with one hand. "Me and Jim might stand a chance, but not with you dragging us down," Taylor said.

Stanton looked from one to the other of the two men. "That the way it is, then?"

"Bull, we got no choice. Once we find help we can come back for you," Jim Mann said.

Stanton sat down on the burning sand and looked at his feet for the first time since leaving San Miguel. They looked bad . . . real bad. He reached down and extracted a curved thorn from his heel. A watery-bloody mixture followed the thorn out. There was no pain and Stanton marveled at this. Even with strips of rawhide, how much further could he really go? he wondered. He looked up at the two men.

"Best get going if you're leaving. Longer you stand here, the less ground you cover and the more water you lose."

"Sorry, Bull," Taylor whispered, turning away.

"Keep an eye peeled for Comanches. You get thirsty, chew prickly pear. Not much moisture in the pulp but it should help some," Stanton called after them. Taylor waved at him while Mann left without a further word.

Stanton took stock of his situation. First he had to bind his feet with something and he took off his coarse Hickory shirt and began cutting strips from the lower part with a small knife he had kept concealed from the Mexican guards. Once that was done, he put the shirt back on, the bottom part of which was now several inches above his pants. Would be cooler now but he would pay for it when the temperature plunged tonight. He got to his feet and looked around him at the distant horizon, noting the lay of the land. What he had to find soon was water, but now wasn't the time to go looking. Stanton marked the direction he intended to travel in the sand, crawled beneath a thin greasewood shrub to rest until sundown, and promptly fell into an exhausted sleep.

CHAPTER 5

Zack McClendon and Peck Overstreet saw no more of the Cheyennes after they forded the Colorado River and rode through the broad, sweeping Blue River Valley where they had trapped beaver years before. Zack liked the thirty-mile-long valley of deep meadow grasses and sloping mountains, their folding flanks covered by forests of dark green conifers and slashes of aspen groves. The innumerable streams that flowed out of these mountains had given them one of their best trapping seasons ever. Zack could see that this rich, river bottom country would be settled someday by ranchers, but for now the lush grass provided excellent grazing for the mule, deer, and elk that came down out of the thickly timbered slopes to feed.

As they entered the narrow-walled canyon of Ten Mile Creek, a drenching rain laced with ice pellets blew across the peaks to the west. The narrow split created by the tumbling waters of Ten Mile Creek was overshadowed by high, ragged mountains that formed an impenetrable wall to the east, their granite sides above timberline still heavy with snow. Zack and

Peck walked their horses into the gloom, the sunlight barely penetrating at this hour of the day. A cold wind whistled through the narrow canyon, adding greatly to the misery of the cold rain. They found a small clearing where the creek had cut away part of the underbelly of the mountain eons before, leaving a sheltered cave that was eight feet high and twenty long. It was here they made camp. There was signs others had used this spot to camp in the past. Zack picked up a broken arrowhead from a blackened campfire. Ute.

"Grab a pot of water from that crick while I get a fire 'a going," Peck said, his teeth shivering from the icy rain. He and Zack were wet to the bone.

Zack tossed the arrowhead to Peck and headed off to the nearby creek with the pot. "What do you make of that?" he called over his shoulder.

"Hellfire, boy, ain't got time fer this when I'm standing here freezing. Besides, it's Ute and you know it." Peck threw the arrowhead to the ground and concentrated on building a fire out of what little dry wood was left in the cave. What he needed in the worst way right now was a hot cup of coffee to ward off the ague. It was then the sleet turned to snow.

They continued their climb up Ten Mile Creek and across the high pass until they struck the East Fork of the Arkansas. This they followed to a broad high valley framed to the east by the ragged peaks of the Mosquito Range that marked the Continental Divide and the Sawatch Mountains to the west. Through this pine-studded flat lying between these two mountain ranges ran the Arkansas, just beginning its voyage to the Mississippi River, some eleven hundred miles to the east.

Zack pulled his horse to a stop, taking in the beauty of the place. Out of the Sawatch rose two snow-covered, massive mountains, over four thousand feet higher than the valley floor. The sight was breathtaking, and it took Peck's nudge to refocus his mind.

"Somebody's camped looks like," Peck said, pointing to the rising smoke that curled up in the distance among dark pines. Zack studied the location for a few minutes. Judging by the smoke, Zack calculated the campfire was near the river.

"Guess we'll know who it is soon enough," Zack said, nudging his horse forward, "since we got to pass right by." Automatically, Zack reached for his rifle and Peck did the same. Until they knew who they faced, they didn't figure on taking any chances that weren't necessary. Neither had forgotten this was Ute country.

"Could use some coffee," Peck said, looking around the cold mountains.

"Needing coffee is going to get you killed someday, old man."

"It's when I *don't* get it you better look out," Peck called softly to Zack who was leading the way.

They eased through the timber with caution, the smell of wood smoke strong in their nostrils. Rather than a hunting party of Utes, what they found was a lone man, frying fish in a skillet. He was so startled by their appearance he came close to dropping the skillet in the fire.

"Zack McClendon," Zack spoke up to reassure the man they meant no harm. When the man didn't speak, Zack introduced Peck.

"Name's Silvester Houseman," the man finally said. There was obvious relief in his voice. "Thought you were those Indians, coming back to finish me off."

"Mind if we get down and have a cup?" Peck asked, looking for but not seeing a coffeepot.

"Step down, but I ran out of coffee more than a week ago." The two trappers secured their rifles and dismounted.

"Got the makings," Peck said, turning to the pack mule. "Boil us up some in a jiffy." The man's eyes brightened.

"Mighty cold for early summer," Zack said, offering his hands to the fire, while his eyes swept the camp. He saw no sign of pack mule or horse and the man appeared sickly on close examination. Zack judged him to be in his early twenties. He wore a scraggly red beard, his clothing was thin and badly

40

worn, and strips of rawhide held what was left of his shoes on his feet. The man had obviously been through some rough times.

Houseman went back to frying his fish. He squinted his eyes to the sharp wind and looked up at Zack.

"Only got this one piece of fish, mister. Took me most of the afternoon to hook it," Houseman said, apologetically.

"We got food. You go on an eat," Zack said.

"How come you in Ute country alone?" Peck asked, dumping coffee into the pot of water he had hauled up from the river. Zack suppressed a smile. Peck was not one to beat around the bush once his curiosity was aroused.

Houseman turned the fish over and set the pan on a bed of glowing coals he had raked aside with a stick from the fire. Peck sat the pot on the opposite side of the fire.

"Wasn't," Houseman said quietly.

"How's that?" Peck asked.

"Tom Lankford—that was my partner—got himself killed by Indians more than a month ago. We was over in Eagle River country. We both got lost," Houseman said sheepishly. "They took our furs and our horses. Tom's leg was badly shattered in the attack and gangrene set in . . . it was something awful." Houseman looked at the two trappers for understanding. "Wanted me—no—he begged me to shoot him. He hurt that much." Houseman took a deep breath. "I just couldn't do it. One morning I woke up and he was gone. Did the best I could, covering him with rocks and all." Peck reached over with his big knife and flipped the forgotten fish to keep it from burning.

"You did the best you could, boy," Peck said soothingly. "Shooting a man even when he's dying ain't no easy thing."

"I'm grateful you fellows came along. Been looking for those Indians to come back and kill me any time. I've been walking for three weeks. About done in."

"Now you don't worry none, boy. I'm going to fix up a real supper. Here you drink some of this coffee and eat that fish, while we tend to things." Peck went over to get more things

41

from the pack mule while Zack fetched more wood for the fire. He watched as Houseman finished up the small fish. Something wasn't adding up here, yet Zack was unable to say why.

"How long you and this Tom been out here?" Zack asked casually.

"This was our first season."

Zack was completely taken back. "Haven't you heard about the beaver trade?"

Houseman wiped his mouth across a dirty sleeve. "What about it?" Zack stared at the hollow-cheeked man for a moment.

"Gone to hell, that's what."

"You trappers?"

"Was. Ain't nothing now." Zack still found it hard to believe the man didn't know about the beaver industry. Something kept nagging at him about this whole setup. Houseman wasn't telling all of it. Although Houseman acted the tenderfoot, he didn't look it on close scrutiny. For one thing, his clothes reflected those of a man who had spent more than a single winter in the mountains. And he wore Ute leggings and that meant a squaw was figured into this someplace. Zack wondered what other clothes he was carrying in his pack.

It was during the evening meal that a dozen Utes rode out of the timber undetected, the hoofs of their horses muffled by the spongy lush grass that grew across the flat. Even still, Peck and Zack had their weapons at the ready before the horsemen had cleared the timber by more than a few yards.

"Don't look like a hunting party to me," Peck said quietly, noting the black faces and painted yellow stripes across their chests. "They hunting a different kind of game."

"Just stand ready," Zack said, never taking his eyes from the tall leader who drew up before the tiny camp. His black eyes swept over the men and rested on Houseman for a moment before moving back to Zack. Zack stole a glance at Houseman. The man looked as though he had seen a ghost. Strange. He wondered how Houseman fit into all this. He didn't have long to wait for his answer.

The dozen Indians made a half-circle around the white men, with their leader in the center. Some had old muzzleloaders, but most carried bows with an arrow fitted to a string. There was no mistaking their grim looks, they meant business.

Zack made the sign for friendship which the leader ignored. Houseman looked ready to bolt.

"Steady, man," Zack whispered. "We start running and that will be the end."

The tall Indian looked at Houseman, pointed his finger and beckoned him forward. Houseman stood rooted.

"Best do like he asks," Zack told the reluctant Houseman.

Houseman shook his head. "I can't. They will kill me." Zack took his eyes from the Indian and looked at Houseman sharply.

"What's that you say?"

"I haven't been entirely truthful with you," Houseman said.

"You better explain quickly, before the shooting starts. They don't look like they came here to dicker."

"Weren't in Eagle River Country," Houseman stated quietly. "Me and Tom been over to the Yampa for three seasons. Done pretty good too. Beaver was thick 'til this year."

"How come we never seen you at any of the rendezvous?" Zack asked. He could see the Indian was growing impatient.

"Never came. Tom always took the furs. I . . . I stayed back in the mountains." Houseman turned his pleading eyes on McClendon. "I'm wanted for robbery back in Philadelphia. Was afraid someone would see me and turn me in."

"But that ain't got nothing to do with what's happening now," Zack reminded him. As far as he was concerned, what a man did before he came West was his worry. It was what he did once he got out here that counted, and Zack had known a few murderers in his passing, all good men. It hit Zack now what had been bothering him about Houseman. Something so

43

obvious, he was surprised at himself for overlooking it. The man had no weapons other than a small knife. And a man out here all alone and without a gun was a dead man.

"This Indian," Houseman pointed to the tall leader, "Yellow Weasel, should be dead. I saw Tom shoot him. He fell from his horse and went over the edge of a steep cliff." Zack saw the Indian's eyes brighten and he knew he understood what was being said for he now seemed less inclined to make a hasty move. Zack figured it may have had something to do with the guns he and Peck had trained their way.

"Yellow Weasel found out his squaw was visiting Tom in the middle of the night. We had stopped over at their encampment on the way to our winter trapping grounds. Tom was always one with the ladies . . . even Indian women. Yellow Weasel and six of his men attacked us once we left their camp. We fought them as best we could. I killed Red Leaf and Tom shot Yellow Weasel out of the saddle, but not before Tom had his horse shot out from under him. Put him up behind mine. Didn't know at the time how bad he had broken his leg. The others chased us for miles. I managed to kill Little Snake before my horse was shot out from under us. We lost our rifles in the fall and had to take to the brush to escape. Later, I crept back and got what few belongings they had scattered about and didn't want."

"That it?" Zack asked.

"That, Mr. McClendon, is the honest-to-God truth."

"It better be," Zack replied grimly. Zack looked back at Yellow Weasel. "Does he speak the truth?" This he spoke slowly in the way of the ancient Ute language.

Only Yellow Weasel's eyes betrayed his surprise that the white man could speak fluent Ute. "It is as he says," Yellow Weasel finally acknowledged.

"Then there is nothing more for you to do," Zack said. "The one you seek has died, this you already know. This man only defended himself and helped a friend. No less than what you would do."

44

"He has taken the life of Little Snake and Red Leaf. He admits this. He must pay." Yellow Weasel's voice had grown colder and more belligerent. Zack could see trouble coming. He said something he hoped would have a meaning to this White River Ute.

"I am called Straight Arrow, brother to Lechat, war chief of the Tabeguache Utes."

"I have heard of you, Zack McClendon," Yellow Weasel replied in English.

"Then you also know we will not give up this man without a fight." Yellow Weasel's features did not betray the anger that welled up inside him. Zack continued, "And you, Yellow Weasel, will be the first to die . . . this I promise. And after that most of your braves before we ourselves are killed."

Yellow Weasel looked deeply into Zack's eyes and saw the truth reflected there. Straight Arrow was a great warrior. Yellow Weasel knew the white man was not making idle threats. The White River Utes shared a common border with their Tabeguache brothers to the south and Yellow Weasel was reminded of the last encounter his people had had with this white man along the Roaring Fork Valley. Three of his fellow warriors died that winter day trying to steal Straight Arrow's horse and furs when they caught him alone in camp. Many of the young men with him now did not know the big trapper; otherwise they would not be so willing to embrace certain death.

Several Indians moved their horses forward in a threatening gesture, and instantly the two trappers brought their guns to bear. Zack centered his big gun on Yellow Weasel's broad chest. Both trappers stood their ground coolly, ignoring the taunts. Houseman looked as though he was going to be sick.

Slowly, Yellow Weasel held up his hand, and the other Indians calmed down but kept their bows tightly strung. For all the cold, Zack found himself sweating. Had there been one wrong move, it would have been over except for the dying.

Yellow Weasel spoke, first in Ute and then in English so

45

there would be no mistaking his intentions. His clear voice never wavered and he spoke with authority.

"We are brothers to Lechat and all Tabeguache. We do not wish to make war with you, Zack McClendon." Several young warriors grunted their disapproval and Yellow Weasel spoke sharply. Although silenced by their leader, their eyes flamed with hatred for the white men.

"Yellow Weasel is a wise leader," Zack spoke up. "We wish only to leave your country in peace. And we will take this man with us so there will be no further trouble." For a long moment, Yellow Weasel judged the depth of Zack's determination to stand beside Houseman. He found no give in the trapper's frank eyes.

Yellow Weasel make the sign of friendship, his eyes never leaving McClendon's face. And then he looked at Houseman and his face betrayed his displeasure at the white man. He looked back at Zack.

"We leave you in peace, Straight Arrow. But you," and he pointed his lance at Houseman, "must never again return to the Smoking Earth River." Abruptly, the Ute warrior wheeled his horse around and with his men at his heels disappeared into the line of timber to the west.

Houseman let out an audible sigh of relief. "That was close." He looked at the hard-faced McClendon who stood there staring after the Utes. "I don't know how to begin thanking you, Mr. McClendon. And you, Mr. Overstreet."

Zack finally looked around at the grateful man. "Just make sure you do like he says. You ever venture into White River country again, Yellow Weasel will see you never leave."

"All I want is away from this godforsaken place," Houseman vowed. "Hope to never see another Indian."

"Most likely will," Peck said, stirring up the coals beneath the coffeepot. "Expect we'll be dogged by dang Indians plumb to Missouri."

"You can travel as far as Bent's Fort with us," Zack said. "After that, you're on your own." Zack had caught the ex-

46

change between Yellow Weasel and Houseman and a vague uneasiness settled over him. But it wasn't his worry . . . not yet anyway. He went over to check on the horses while a cold wind funneled across the broad valley, bringing with it the smell of new snow. Zack pulled his coat next to him. Dang if he wouldn't be glad to get down Taos way again. He planned on sitting in the warm sun for days, just so his aching joints could soak up the healing rays. Like Peck and other veteran mountain men who had spent years trapping beaver, Zack suffered the same malady of premature arthritis from spending too much time in frigid mountain waters and sleeping on frozen ground.

After supper, Houseman couldn't seem to settle down. He continued to stare nervously towards the timber as if expecting the Utes to reappear at any moment.

"Hour or two daylight left. Don't you think it would be a good idea to move further down the Arkansas and make camp in case they decide to come back?" Houseman asked.

Zack looked steadily at the worried man and it was here he decided Houseman was not telling them the complete truth. He cut off a piece of trade tobacco and offered it to Houseman, who shook his head. Zack worked the tobacco around in his mouth for a minute, getting it wet before he spoke.

"This is good a place as any to camp," he said casually.

Peck removed his pipe from his mouth and pointed the stem at Houseman. Zack waited for the trapper to add his two cents.

"If you frettin' about Yellow Weasel and his men returning later on during the night, don't. Unlike some low-down whites, Utes and a few such tribes won't go back on their word."

"But Comanches are something else again," Zack interjected. He picked at a tobacco stem between his teeth with a fingernail. "They'll drink your whiskey, smoke the pipe with you and bury an axe in your skull as soon as you turn your back." He knew of a few white men would do the same, Zack thought and he passed the night in uneasy sleep with Houseman just a few feet away.

CHAPTER 6

"What do you think, Lafe?" a man squatting by the fire asked. Lafe Ingram shook his head and bent down to pour himself coffee. Ingram was a broad-shouldered individual nearing forty, and his deeply lined face showed the strain of the last few days. He wore no hat, and the only hair on his head was the large drooping mustache that completely covered both lips. With two half-grown kids and a wife back in Independence, this trip was to give them the nest egg they needed to continue their travel on to Oregon country, where Ingram intended to stake out a farm. Now Ingram wasn't so sure anymore.

Charlie Marsh lay in his blankets, felled by a high fever that had kept him there for five days now. Without Marsh, they stood a poor chance ever reaching Santa Fe. Yet with each passing day, it looked more and more like they were going to have to try. Lafe looked about the camp at the silent-faced men. Like him, none had ever been west of the Missouri River.

Without a man like Charlie to guide them, their chances of success were slim indeed. But Charlie was beyond going.

"What we gonna do, Lafe?" the man by the fire persisted. His voice betrayed the mixture of fear and uncertainty the silent group of men were not yet willing to voice. They were in danger of losing it all and they looked to Lafe Ingram as their unspoken leader. This added burden for Ingram was evident in his stooped shoulders.

"What choice do we have, Haney?" Ingram said rather sharply. "We got no choice but to push on south and hope for the best. Could be we will meet others on the trail."

A slab-sided individual came over to the fire. He had nervous eyes that matched the color of the coffee, and a face that reminded Ingram of a chicken hawk. Jamie Edwards had been nothing but a thorn in everybody's side since leaving Missouri over two months ago. Ingram knew that Edwards was about to say something nobody wanted to hear, but the man had a right to his opinion. He was the kid of the group and had the least to lose.

"I hate to say it again, Lafe," Jamie Edwards started in, "but we most likely wouldn't be in this fix if we had taken the Cimarron cutoff like them other fellars. People moving up and down the trail all the time."

"That's all well and good, Jamie," Ingram snapped, "but as you can plainly see we are camped somewhere on the Arkansas next to this mountain range and that's that." The kid shrank back under the harsh words, and Ingram instantly regretted the outburst. He rubbed his tired eyes, feeling the pressure in his skull increase.

"Didn't mean nothing by it, Lafe," the kid whimpered. That was another thing he didn't like about Edwards. He would ride you until you snapped back and then Edwards would break down like some sugar-tit kid needing his momma's comfort.

"Okay, okay. It's all right, Jamie." Then Ingram addressed the group. "You men know the predicament we face. We going to need to make a decision if Charlie Marsh dies. If Charlie lasts another day, I'll be surprised. When that time comes, we got to move or all what we have done to this point will have been in vain." The tight group looked at one another, murmuring among themselves.

"We got to follow your lead, Lafe," a tall man in the center of the group spoke up. "Most of us got our life's savings tied up in this trip. It's root hog or die. Ain't that right boys?" The rest of the traders nodded their heads.

"Figured you men would say that and I'm in complete agreement," Ingram responded. "As you know, I'm betting on the same thing as you. Get enough money to homestead a proper farm in Oregon country. I've been doing some thinking once I saw Charlie Marsh slip farther and farther into the fever. In the morning, I figure to saddle my horse and ride back to Bent's Fort and see if I can hire us a new guide. Seen a few men back there looked like they would know rough country. Could be one of them may know the way through these mountains to Santa Fe."

The kid started up again. "But what if you don't find anyone, Lafe, what then?"

Ingram studied Edwards for a while and saw the kid was really scared about the outcome. His reply was tempered with compassion.

"Expect I'll ask one of the Bent brothers to draw me a map of some kind and we'll push across on our own. Regret not asking old Charlie more about the trail we were facing before he fell into a deep fever." With nothing more to be said, Ingram finished his coffee in silence. Before he turned in for the night, he checked Charlie Marsh's condition and found his fever even higher. The man was laboring to breathe. There was a rattle in his chest that had not been there this morning. Charlie Marsh, mountain man, trailblazer, and guide would not last the night, Ingram predicted. He thanked God that whatever fever Marsh had contracted, it didn't appear to be contagious.

During the night a gentle breeze swept across the steep ridge behind the little camp, stirring the dying coals of the fire, and, when it moved out across the open prairie, it carried along the soul of Charlie Marsh.

Nothing moved in the vastness of dying heat that stretched before Bull Stanton. He watched as the setting sun slowly bled the sky of color before turning back to face the northeast again. There wasn't much to mark the distant horizon. The purple outline of Turkey Mountain to his left seemed nearly flat from where he stood. Nothing but hot broken country unfolded before him to his right, yet he knew he would find a trickle of water there in some rock crevice if he could only hold out. He stood motionless until it grew dark enough to see the stars. Bull marked his location and started off again, his body aching with every step. He had stopped looking at his feet for fear of what he might find. They had stopped hurting, yet they were badly swollen and cracked open from the heat. As he stumbled along, it never failed to amaze him how fast the curtain of heat lifted from the desert at night. He would need to find water before daylight or face the possibility of dying. He had gone without water for three days now, and he could no longer close his mouth for his protruding tongue. The driving need to survive pushed him beyond most men's endurance. When he wasn't thinking of water, which occupied his waking moments more and more now, he focused on the swarthy face of the alcalde and the Mexican soldier, Salezar. Burning hate for these two men was the fuel that moved him forward, one teetering step at a time.

A coyote broke out in song in the cool distance, and, as Stanton passed by, things scurried away in the darkness. He no longer thought of Taylor and Mann. They were the lowest form of men to Stanton's way of thinking for leaving him behind. He hoped he never saw them again.

A distant rumble brought Bull out of his trance. He looked to the northwest and saw jagged lightning split the night sky.

few seconds passed before he heard the answering thunder. He calculated the storm was at least ten miles off and most likely would peter out long before any of it reached him. But it was something new to think about. Bull actually increased his pace slightly. He could imagine how the taste of cooling rain would feel to his swollen tongue. Suddenly the ground disappeared from beneath him and he found himself tumbling down a steep rock-faced gully. Something smashed him in the head and as blackness descended around him, Bull heard the cries of a Lark Sparrow dislodged from the clump of gumweed where it had settled in for the night.

"We ain't gonna make it, Bill," Jim Mann croaked through parched lips. They had stopped for the night just as Bull Stanton was beginning his. They lay on their backs too exhausted to move. Like Stanton, neither man had come across water in the baking sand. Every draw they stumbled across had been bone dry.

"Shut up!" Bill Taylor fired back. Both men were the worse for wear, having wandered aimlessly in the desert heat with no forethought the second day after leaving Bull Stanton behind. Now no matter which direction they struck out for, it all looked the same after a while.

"Wish now, I had stayed with Bull," Mann mumbled. "At least he was good at keeping his direction. All we done is gone off and got ourselves killed in this damned heat."

"Told you to shut up, Mann!" Taylor warned, not that he had any strength to do much about it anyway. Like Mann, Taylor had just about used up his remaining strength today. Without water, by this time tomorrow they would be like pieces of dry leather, good only for the coyotes to gnaw at.

Both men fell silent for a time, and Mann closed his aching eyes. Between the white-hot sun and gritty sand, his eyes felt like they rotated in their sockets using sand as rollers. He wondered what had happened to Stanton and regretted it deeply that he had listened to Taylor. It wasn't right. He could see that now.

Suddenly Mann sat up and sniffed the air like some desert animal. He hadn't been dreaming after all. He did smell wood smoke. Mann turned to Taylor.

"You smell that, Bill?"

"Christ! what is it now?" Taylor was half-asleep and didn't want to be bothered.

"Wood smoke."

Taylor opened his eyes and concentrated on the smell. A faint odor of burning wood clung to the cooling air. He rolled over quickly and got stiffly to his feet. Mann did the same.

"What we got to figure is where it's coming from," he said to Mann.

"We find them, Bill, and we find food and water," Mann said with tears in his eyes that Taylor couldn't see. The liquid burned his scratchy eyes, but he was too happy over the prospect of being rescued from certain death, that he ignored the pain.

"First we got to find them, so let's get to looking." They surveyed the surrounding desert but failed to detect a campfire.

"Got to be around here someplace," Taylor said. "Most likely built in a depression of some kind or maybe some of this damn greasewood's blocking our view."

"Think it's coming from that direction," Mann pointed.

"Which way? Can't see a damn thing in this darkness. Any other time there'id be a moon to go by."

Mann reached out, touched Taylor's arm, and turned him the direction he wanted him to face. "Now, don't you feel that slight breeze on your face?" Mann asked.

Taylor stood for a moment trying to feel something, but his face was so badly cooked from the sun it had lost all feeling. Mann's face was saved by the large floppy hat he wore.

"Got to take your word for it, Jim. It'd take a snow for me to feel anything again."

"Well, follow me close and I'll lead the way."

53

"Just watch out for the damn cactus. Got enough spines in me that it'll take six months of picking to remove them all."

Taylor stumbled along as close to Mann as he could, wondering if they both weren't going around the bend and the smoke was nothing more than hallucinations of dying men too long in the desert. They walked what seemed like hours, but in reality was less than two minutes. Mann had not spoken since taking the lead.

"It's getting stronger," Mann finally whispered over his shoulder. Taylor roused himself long enough to sniff the air. It did seem the smoke smell was more pronounced. Maybe they weren't hallucinating after all.

Somewhere up ahead a horse whinnied, and both men nearly collapsed from joy. Taylor pounded Mann on his back, sending the desert dust flying.

"By grabs, Jim, you were right," Taylor exclaimed.

"If I had the strength, I'd run the rest of the way," Mann said, responding to Taylor's rising enthusiasm.

"You see the campfire yet?" Taylor asked, pushing around Mann.

"No, but it's close by and well hidden. We just gotta keep walking in this direction."

"Okay, okay. Let's get to it," Taylor said, slightly irritated at having Mann resume the lead again. He would rather have been the one who led them to safety.

They continued on once more, the wood smoke now strong in their nostrils. Even Taylor thought he could locate the camp now, but he let Mann continue to lead. They were surprised to find themselves standing before a large gash in the earth without realizing it. By sheer luck or dumb blundering, Taylor and Mann had stumbled across Aqua Chiquito Canyon. Both men could smell water and they saw the flickering campfire several hundred feet below the sand cliffs where they stood.

Taylor let out a shout at the sight of the fire. Both men hugged one another, not daring to take their eyes from the yellow flames for fear it would disappear.

"Told you I smelled smoke," Mann said to Taylor. "Next time maybe you'll believe me."

"Never doubted you for a moment, Jim," Taylor cried. Both men knew that was a lie. But who cared, they had found water and other humans. The crisis was over.

A sudden movement next to them on the cliff caused them to look around at the shadowy figure that seemed to have appeared out of thin air. There was just enough light for them to see the outline of a man.

"Lord, are we glad to see you," Taylor blurted out. "We been lost—" his voice faded as three more figures emerged in the darkness.

"Dear God, Bill, we are doomed," Jim Mann whispered. "These men are not traders at all. They're Indians." Taylor was horrified and he sank to his knees making incoherent sounds. Mann just stood his ground and waited the fate he knew was coming. His only regret was not tasting cool water again. His whole being craved it . . . but in a little while even that would go away.

CHAPTER 7

In the early morning light, Lafe Ingram was busy saddling his horse. Behind him, he could hear shovels scraping bare rock as two men dug a shallow grave for the body of Charlie Marsh. The activity covered the approach of the three horsemen who entered the camp quietly from upstream. Ingram was as surprised as the other traders upon seeing the three white men. They looked rough and half wild to Ingram. Two of them were dressed in grease-stained leathers, full beards and sported big guns. He saw how their eyes swept the camp with quiet appraisal, lingering over the wrapped body of Charlie Marsh and the fresh dirt. The smallest of the three looked like he had seen better times and he sat on a pack mule like it hurt him to ride.

Lafe Ingram found his voice first. "Good morning. Light and have breakfast with us." The tallest of the three turned his piercing eyes to Ingram. They appeared friendly yet cautious.

"Somebody die?" Zack McClendon asked.

"During the night. Had a fever for five days. Pneumonia

most likely," Ingram said, looking over at the body. "He was Charlie Marsh. Guiding us to Santa Fe. As you can see this is as far as we got."

"So old Charlie's gone under," Peck Overstreet said, amazed, as if he never expected anything like this happening.

"You knew Mr. Marsh?" Ingram asked as the three men stepped down from their horses. Others in his group gathered around them to hear what was being said, the half-dug grave momentarily forgotten.

"We sure do," Peck returned. "That old coon's been in this country a sight longer than all of us put together."

"He was rather old," Ingram admitted. " We never thought something like this would happen. Would you know where Mr. Marsh was from? I'd like to notify the next of kin when we return to Missouri."

Peck responded immediately, "East of the wind and west of the prairie. Hell who knows. Old Charlie was like us, a thistle blown from one mountain range to another. Wanderlust finally killed him. I expect the same'll happen to us one day."

Meanwhile, Zack was taking note of the men and the two dozen or so mules they had staked to a grassy area near the Arkansas. These men were doing exactly what Zack intended, except he planned on taking the Cimarron cutoff. It was level and better time could be made with loaded wagons. Raton Pass was hell on wagons.

Lafe Ingram introduced himself and several of the others, standing nearby. The two men returned to the task of digging Charlie's grave. Sylvester Houseman was all eyes, but up to this point he had said nothing.

"You men welcome to coffee. Could get Nate here to whip up a little breakfast," Ingram said hospitably.

"Coffee's just fine, Ingram," Zack said, watching Peck hurry to the large blackened pot that hung on a metal hook above the fire. "What are you men planning on doing without a guide?"

Lafe looked keenly at the big trapper, noting how slabs of muscle rippled beneath the tight leather shirt. He also noticed the dried blood on the side of his shirt. From head to toe, Zack McClendon was a man to reckon with in a fight, Lafe determined.

"I was getting ready to ride back to Bent's and see if I could hire another guide. Don't suppose you gentlemen would know the way through these mountains and over Raton Pass, would you?"

Peck handed Zack a cup of the strong liquid and answered for them. "Hell, me and Zack been over the hump a time er two." He winked at Lafe Ingram. "Fact is, old Zack here is hankering to get back down that way fer more than just tradin' goods." Zack gave Peck Overstreet a look that could freeze a lake in July.

Lafe looked with growing interest at the big trapper. "You taking trade goods down Santa Fe too?" he asked Zack.

"Well, that's the plan, but we first got to get back to St. Louis before that happens." Zack glowered at Peck, who seemed not to notice he had spilled their plans to strangers. It was one of the reasons Zack had deliberately postponed telling Peck until they were away from Bridger's Post; he hadn't wanted it scattered about. And Peck was the best at scattering news . . . good or bad.

Lafe Ingram looked at his fellow traders, and several men nodded their heads. Lafe cleared his throat. "Mr. McClendon, I can see where we might be able to benefit from each others help."

"How so?"

"We are in need of a guide who knows this country. We can pay you, say, two hundred dollars to guide us to Santa Fe. That way, you got extra money for supplies back in St. Louis. What do you think?" Peck looked at Zack with glowing eyes. Two hundred dollars could go a long ways in making up the poor trapping season this past winter.

Zack studied on it for a moment before speaking. "I can see

your point, Mr. Ingram, but Santa Fe is over three hundred rough miles and all in the wrong direction for us.''

Ingram stared intently for a moment at Zack McClendon, trying to decide if the trapper was merely holding out for bigger stakes since he had them over the proverbial barrel. But the trader saw nothing of the sort in the big man's eyes.

''Would you excuse me for a minute, Mr. McClendon.'' Lafe Ingram went off to the side with the other traders. Zack and Peck watched them talking in earnest tones, but couldn't understand what was being said.

''Coulda asked me,'' Houseman said with hurt in his voice. Peck looked down at the half-drawed-up man with a critical eye.

''Got to be honest, Houseman, you don't look to be worth a hunert dollars, much less two.'' Houseman's face flamed.

''Maybe so, but I could do the guiding just the same.''

''You been down New Mexico way, have you?'' Zack questioned.

Houseman looked flustered for a moment. ''No, not exactly, but I've heard enough talk about the trail to know I could find it,'' he said defensively.

''Same talk these traders have heard, most likely. Talking and doing is a world of difference, Houseman. It can be dry this time of year. You got to know where to look for water and where to cross the Sangre de Cristo Mountains. There's places where a body could get lost for months.''

''I'm not afraid. Me and Tom made out all right for three seasons.''

''Thought you was hell-bent on getting out of this country,'' Zack retorted.

''Didn't know I was under a time limit,'' Houseman shot back. Zack shrugged his shoulders and turned away. A man still that green after three seasons in the mountains couldn't be talked to. Zack had seen men like Houseman in the past. Men who pushed their shallow knowledge of the country to the limits and usually lost. Even those with vast experience and broad understanding of the mountains and Indians came to grief from time to time. Damn few ever lived to see Charlie Marsh's age.

The two men digging the grave stopped after they had hollowed out a place in the rocky soil nearly three foot deep. Both were sweating heavily even though the air moving down the Arkansas drainage was cool. Zack watched as they lifted Charlie's body and placed it gently in the fresh earth. One of them called to Ingram as they stood there with shovels in hand. Ingram waved for them to wait.

"Got a feelin' they fixen to raise the ante," Peck whispered, helping himself to more coffee.

"Be careful they don't charge you for all the coffee you been drinking," Zack said. "They are traders you know." Peck couldn't tell if the big trapper was funning him or not, and he debated for a minute before refilling his cup for the third time.

Ingram broke away from the group and came over to the fire, his face a serious study. "Mr. McClendon, we have talked it over and in order to save us time, with me having to ride back to Bent's place, we're willing to give you three hundred dollars and five more from the trade goods on each pack mule. That's another hundred and forty dollars. What do you say?"

Zack scratched his thick beard, thinking extra money would go a long way in buying extra supplies in St. Louis. Peck's eager eyes sought out Zack's. It would only take fifteen, twenty days. It still gave them plenty time to head east and be back that fall with trade goods to sell.

"You've made the offer mighty tempting, Mr. Ingram."

"It's worth it to us. We got over ten thousand tied up in these trade goods and believe me, Mr. McClendon, our very lives are riding on the outcome of this venture. We've lost nearly a week with poor Mr. Marsh."

"Expect we best get old Charlie buried so we can get on to New Mexico then," Zack said.

Relief flooded Ingram's face. "That takes a load off my mind, Mr. McClendon."

"Call me Zack," McClendon said softly.

They had Charlie Marsh buried and the mules repacked and ready to ride inside of an hour. The mule skinners were excited to be getting underway once more and to be leaving this camp of death. Peck fashioned a crude cross from dead cottonwood limbs and, while Zack looked on, pushed it into the fresh earth and packed dirt around it.

"Probably more than we'll ever get done fer us," he said to Zack, who held the reins of both horses. Some distance away, Houseman sat on the mule, looking unhappy. Zack had offered to let him use the mule and ride on to Bent's, but Houseman wouldn't hear of it. Said he didn't want to be beholden to any man. For a man hell-bent on leaving this country, Zack was mystified that Houseman was willing to travel to Santa Fe rather than accept his offer.

Peck stepped back and surveyed the grave site. "Now that's better."

"Mount up, Peck. Let's get going," Zack said, swinging a leg over his horse. "Charlie ain't going to care one way or the other whether he has a cross." Zack looked back at the strung-out pack mules, twenty-eight in all, waiting for his orders to start.

"Maybe so, but I feel better." Peck climbed into the saddle and looked at Houseman. "He coming too?"

"What the man says," Zack replied, kicking his horse in the ribs. Peck followed close behind, wondering what it was about Houseman that disturbed him so.

Bull Stanton first realized he was still alive when he was awakened by noise. Close by, a dipper sat on a rock going through his bobbing, up-and-down ritual. Stanton watched the bird for a few minutes while he gathered his thoughts. His head hurt like hell, and there was blood on the rocks where he had lain through the night. Suddenly he remembered falling during the night. He managed to sit up. The bird was still performing his peculiar dance. Stanton studied the bird for a minute before he realized it was a water ouzel. And where there was a water ouzel, there had to be water.

Stanton looked around at the steep-sided draw. Nothing but rock and dust except for a small juniper here and there whose roots twisted between boulders, searching for what moisture could be found beneath. Stanton touched the hot sand where he sat. There had been no water in this place for a very long time. Yet an ouzel was living proof that water existed . . . and not too far away. Bull struggled to his feet, feeling dizzy. He touched his head and felt the swollen area and dried blood along his face and jaw. Once on his feet, the bird did his crazy dance for the last time, and flew off down the draw. Stanton tried to follow the bird with his eyes, but the small animal was soon lost from sight among the rocks.

Stanton knew he had failed to cover much ground last night and now faced another blistering day. Without water this day, he would never survive the night. It was all he could do now to stand on his feet without falling over. Bull squared his shoulders and started off down the narrow draw after the bird. The only thing that pushed him to try anymore was his hatred for Salezar.

Two hours later the winding draw gradually opened out into a canyon. Juniper was more abundant here, and he saw a flickering movement. It was the bird again. Stanton locked his eyes on the dancing bird and stumbled towards him. The dipper allowed the man to come within a few yards before flying away. Just as before, the dipper continued up the canyon. Bull Stanton had no choice but to follow. Somewhere up ahead he would find either water or a place to die.

A different sound made itself known to Stanton, yet even then it took a few minutes before he acknowledged it, so intent was he on the bird.

Rocks rattled in the distance followed by guttural laughter. Stanton froze. He looked around the fifty-foot-high walls of rock, trying to decide if the noise came from somewhere within the canyon or atop the burning desert floor.

Another rock clattered down the canyon wall and he knew then that whoever was there rode along the rim. Instinctively, Stanton knew they were Indians. No white man in his right mind would be this far in the desert from the main trail. Bull hurried forward as best he could on legs almost beyond going, all the while scanning the rock walls for a place to hide.

He could hear the horses coming closer. Desperately, Stanton searched the rocks above him and spotted a depression beneath a broken ledge of rock that jutted outward into the canyon. The area beneath the ledge was shaded and might offer some protection from the approaching riders. It was his only hope.

A horse snorted close by, and fear for his life drove Bull Stanton scrambling up the wall on hands and knees. It took his remaining strength to pull himself into the small depression where he sank into the shade. Another minute and six mounted Indians broke into view from around a bend in the canyon wall.

Stanton froze in position, trying not to breathe. The Indians were laughing and making gestures at a big Indian who was wearing a broad, floppy-brimmed hat . . . Jim Mann's hat! The realization that Mann and Taylor were dead sank slowly into his tired brain. It left Stanton feeling strangely alone. He couldn't identify the emotion, but it wasn't sadness for the two dead men, for in truth, had he met them again Bull would have tried to kill them with his bare hands for leaving him behind. And then another thought entered his mind. What if they had told the Indians about him? Was that the reason the Indians were here now? A chill of fear raced through him, for he realized had he not stumbled into the draw last night, but continued on, the Indians would have cut his trail and hunted him down.

The lead Indian appeared more serious and paid little attention to his fellow braves as he concentrated on reading the surrounding terrain like a lobo wolf. Stanton felt the Indian's eyes sweep over where he lay, and instinctively he drew deeper into the shaded depression. Something moved at his back and he heard the short warning rattle of a snake. Fear from a new source of danger clutched him. Again, Stanton froze. To move further invited being bit in the back by the rattlesnake or drawing the Indian's attention. Either way was certain death. In the end, Stanton chose to stay with the snake, knowing the Indians would see he died a hundred times over.

Bull barely breathed as he watched the Indians continue on out of sight, but still he did not move from his position for over an hour, fearing they might return. When he finally did move, Stanton literally threw himself headfirst from the depression. He tumbled down the rocky face and landed heavily on his wrist. There was a sharp snap followed by stinging pain and Stanton knew he had broken his arm. He lay there, exposed to the broiling sun for a long time, the pain nearly more than he could bear. Dazed from the fall and hurting badly, Stanton realized how much he still wanted to live. And it had everything, yet nothing to do with seeing Salezar dead.

It took great effort to sit up, but he knew if he lay there much longer, he would never move again. As much as he tried to protect his arm from further damage, he managed to hurt it whenever he moved. Finally, he simply let it hang by his side, gritting his teeth against the throbbing pain. On his feet once again, Stanton lurched off down the canyon. *Had the Indians found water somewhere up ahead?* Could be that was their reason for riding by the canyon and not searching for him after all.

The canyon narrowed once more and finally divided. One branch headed off to the south and appeared to be choked with rocks, while the other continued to the northeast. For a moment, Stanton stood there, swaying, sucking in lungfuls of hot air and undecided the way he should go. Chasing a dry canyon was certain death for he simply didn't have enough strength left to backtrack. He closed his burning eyes to the scene before him. It seemed all his life he had been faced with difficult decisions that had a way of turning out wrong. Coming to New Mexico was living proof of his continued inability to make sound judgements in the things that mattered. He was so tired that all he really wanted to do was lay down an let death come. But a tiny spark of life still remained, and he resisted the urge by opening his eyes once more.

Stanton half-expected to see the little ouzel pointing the way for him. All that greeted him was bare rock and silence in the heated stillness. Not really knowing why, he stumbled into the canyon that threaded across the baking desert to the northeast like an open wound.

An hour later he was lying face down and delirious. Something stung him on his cheek, and he used his good arm to brush away a big-headed red ant. It was enough to bring him out of his heat-induced stupor. He sat upright without thinking. Stanton found his swollen feet covered by the big ants, working at the cracked and blistered places. The strips of cloth he had bound up his feet with were dirty and covered with dark, dried blood. Stanton brushed half-heartedly at the ants, noticing his blackened toes, and finally realized he could go no farther. His strength, something he had always been proud of, was gone as well. Slowly he lay back in the burning sand and rolled over on his side to wait for the end.

And then he saw it, a small patch of green and red in the distance. Stanton fought back the dullness in his brain as he concentrated on the spot. Gradually the blooming prickly pear came into focus. He was astonished. No plant could bloom in dry country unless there was water. With a sudden burst of renewed strength, Bull sat up and began to crawl the twenty yards to the plant. He ignored the bursting pain every time he moved his broken arm, concentrating instead on the prickly pear. He left behind him a trail spotted with fresh blood from skinned knees and hands. It seemed a lifetime passed before Stanton drew near. The flowers were not flowers at all, but the swollen, ruby fruit of the cactus.

Ignoring the protective thorns, Stanton tore at the succulent flesh and mopped his blistered lips with the fruit. Nothing in his life had felt so good to him. He tried forcing some of the fruit into his mouth around his thick tongue, but it was impossible. The only thing that would do was water. He looked around for the water source the cactus was using, but other than damp sand, there was no visible moisture anywhere.

Furiously, Stanton clawed at the sand around the cactus with his one good hand. There was wetness there, but nothing that would sustain life. The well-nourished cactus seemed to mock him for his feeble efforts and Stanton felt sudden rage at the plant and at circumstances of life that put him here in the first place. They were the thoughts of a man beyond rational thought. No longer aware of his injured arm or his surroundings, Stanton took his rage out on everything in sight; the cactus, rocks, anything to vent his fury.

Disturbed rocks at the base of the cactus caused others to be dislodged from above on the wall which crashed down on Stanton. He barely felt the thudding blows. What came down next was a pencil-thin stream of cold water let loosed by falling rock. Stanton stopped his raging and looked up in amazement at the stream of life wetting the rocks around him. He felt like crying, but no tears would come. All he could do was lay with his head in the inviting trickle of water while deep sobs racked his body.

CHAPTER 8

Through the umbilical cord known as Camino Real, "the Royal Road" first established in 1598 by Don Juan de Oñate, the colonies of New Mexico were sustained by companies of soldiers, traders with goods from Mexico City, bands of Franciscan friars and colonists that trudged the road leading north from El Paso, across ninety miles of barren, waterless land known as La Jornada del Muerto—"the Journey of Death." The Camino Real rejoined the Rio Grande Valley at Paraje de Fray Cristobal and shot north to Santa Fe.

Situated at the foothills of the Sangre de Cristo Mountains, and founded on the ruins of an ancient Tanoan Indian village, Santa Fe was already two and a half centuries old by the time Manuel Armijo became Governor for the second time.

In the Palace of the Governors, a walled fortress built to house the seat of government, were located a guardhouse, military chapel, the resident of the governor and various official offices. To the rear were the patio, servants' quarters, stables, and a parade ground.

Manuel Armijo sipped a fruit drink while a cooling breeze stirred the leaves of the trees shading the patio where he sat with Captain Damasio Salezar. The day was pleasant, and Armijo was in an especially good mood, for lying on the table before him was a leather bag containing over three thousand in gold and silver coins—his share of the goods appropriated from Bull Stanton, Simon Walker, and the other gringos. Salezar had held back—with Armijo's blessing—five hundred dollars to distribute to the Alcalde at San Miguel and several of the soldiers.

"And the men you turned loose in the desert, they will not survive?" Armijo questioned his loyal officer, remembering the Texas rebellion and what trouble it had caused him. Rumors were still being circulated that the United States was considering invading New Mexico because of the harsh treatment dealt the Texans.

"They cannot," Salezar stated flatly, lighting a thin cigar the color of his eyes. The breeze carried the curl of blue smoke away from his head. Salezar removed the cigar and a smile creased his cruel face. "Had they been Tijanos, I would have been forced to shoot them instead." Both men laughed over the joke, but deep down, they held to the same opinion that Texans were a tough breed, and not to be compared to those Americans that came to New Mexico to sell trade goods.

Armijo smoothed back his dark hair with a pudgy hand where the breeze had dislodged it. A large, florid man running to paunch, Armijo was also a vain man who loved to dress in a flashy blue uniform with gold epaulets and a white ostrich plume in his helmet. When away from the Palace, he either rode in a grotesquely carved and gilded coach, dubbed "the wheeled tarantula" by his subjects, or else he strutted about on a huge white steed. Armijo boasted he owned the fastest horse alive in all New Mexico. It was not an idle boast, for he had ordered a doctor to poison a racehorse owned by his nephew in order to attain that distinction.

Damasio Salezar was just the opposite of Armijo. A rather tall thin man, Salezar was trail-tough and battle-scarred and steered clear of showy clothes or grand performances. When not in military uniform, Salezar preferred common pants and cotton shirts to the gold-and-silver-embroidered Chaqueta jackets that most men of substance wore. But both Armijo and Salezar shared several common traits: they were greedy, brutal to man or beast, and completely unprincipled. Also, both men loved good food, fine champagne, and women of every stripe. Tonight, Armijo would visit his mistress, the gambler Doña Gertrudis Barceló, once she tired of dealing monte. Doña Barceló, better known as La Tules, had become wealthy from gambling and was a social and political force in the small community of Santa Fe.

Salezar turned more serious as he studied the end of his cigar for a moment. "I have heard from my men that arriving white traders do not like the five hundred dollars duty imposed on each wagon of goods. There is talk they will unite with the gringos living here and start a rebellion. Is there anything you wish me to do about this, Governor?"

Armijo waved his hand as if to dismiss the rumors. "They make a fuss when paying the taxes, but after their profits are realized, they are happy once more, Capitán Salezar. I do not see there is cause for concern . . . still it would not hurt to keep an eye on things."

Salezar understood and quickly stood up. "Excuse me Governor. I wish to see to my troops and visit the plaza. If we have trouble it will develop there."

Armijo nodded his head, and the straight-backed Salezar crossed the patio and entered the military barracks on the opposite end of the fortress.

Armijo watched as his officer disappeared from sight. He hefted the bag of coins and smiled to himself. Tonight he would play a few hands of monte with Doña Barceló before retiring to her room. He lifted the glass of pale lemon and orange juice and sighted through it before drinking it down in one single swallow. At that moment, far to the east in a lonely canyon another man drank the life-giving waters from beneath a rock.

Zack McClendon, with Peck Overstreet by his side, led the way up a series of steep switchbacks that marked the beginning ascent to Raton Pass. Piñon and juniper trees dotted the folding foothills of the Sangre de Cristo Mountains along with sagebrush and cactus. Higher up, the black trunks of taller pines stood in sharp contrast to the tawny landscape of rock and blue sky.

Peck glanced back at the slow-moving laboring mules, each loaded with four hundred pounds of trade goods. They were making poor progress up the rocky face of the mountain.

"Rate we travelin' we ought to make Santa Fe by Thanksgiving," Peck said gloomily.

Zack turned in the saddle and looked back to judge for himself. Peck was right, they were moving awfully slow, even for mules. He figured they had barely covered a half mile in the last hour. At that rate it would be well after dark before they reached the summit and Zack hadn't counted on stopping there for the night. Nights could be miserably cold at the pass the way the winds blew constantly from the snow-draped rugged peaks to the west.

But here between the pleated foothills, the dust and the stink of sweating mules were stifling in the dry heat. The constant cursing of the traders and the braying of mules added to the din and Zack had to question his decision to take up pack trading for a living. Maybe Peck was right. Could be he was only doing it to legitimize his desire to see the Mexican Señorita once again. It was something to consider. A piercing scream broke in on his thoughts and Zack jerked around in the saddle.

A mule skinner was fighting desperately to hold the lines of a mule that was slipping over the edge of the trail after its pack had shifted. But the shifting load was too much for man or mule, and everyone watched helplessly as the mule tumbled end over end down the rocky precipice and smashed into the rocky bottom. When the mule hit, the pack flew apart, scattering goods in every direction.

Peck shook his head. "There goes five dollars of our money," he said sadly.

The mule train became a mass of confusion in the excitement, and several stubborn animals turned tail and raced the way they had come, kicking and braying loudly. It was all the men could do to keep the other pack mules from either being pushed over the edge or from joining the retreat. Men cursed even louder while more loads shifted in the confusion and dust.

Zack looked on in disgust at the turmoil for a minute, deciding right then and there to use wagons and let oxen to do his hauling.

"We best go round up those crazy mules, else we'll wind up owing them money by the time we reach Santa Fe," Zack said to Peck.

They never even come close to reaching the pass by nightfall. By the time the runaway mules were brought back, the pack train calmed down and straightened out, and what goods weren't broken retrieved from the dead mule in the bottom of the deep ravine, it was midafternoon.

Lafe Ingram, sweating heavily and looking the worse for wear from the experience, asked McClendon if there wasn't a less dangerous route across these mountains.

Zack smiled faintly, knowing the Missourian was serious. Peck only stared in open-mouthed astonishment at the trader.

"Unless you want to head back east until you reach the great bend in the Arkansas and take the Cimarron cutoff, this is it."

Lafe Ingram squirmed in the saddle. "Don't mean to doubt your word, Mr. McClendon, but some of the men kinda figured the trail that angled off back a ways looked to be a lot easier than the way you taking us."

"That what they think, do they," Zack said coldly. "That's an old Ute trail and it is a lot easier. Only trouble, it wanders deep into the mountains for ten miles or so until it hits Long Creek and there it turns north again to Cucharas Pass. You won't ever get to New Mexico that way."

Lafe Ingram was uncomfortable confronting the big trapper and it showed. "I apologize for questioning your intentions Mr. McClendon, but a fellow can't be too careful."

"The question was fair enough," Zack responded with a little more warmth in his voice. "Back East, you don't have a monopoly on dishonest men. We have our own share of unscrupulous scoundrels, cutthroats and thieves. A man can't be too careful with whom he strikes bargains and should stay completely away from those who speak in a free and easy manner."

"Will the trail get any easier?" Ingram was looking ahead at the twisted rocky trail that wound upward out of sight.

"It's going to get a lot tougher than it already has before we clear Raton Pass. And I ain't promising you better on the other side. We still got to cross a sizable stretch of dry country and another mountain pass before we reach Santa Fe. If you still got any doubts about me and Peck's intentions, you best spit it out so's we can ride on off now." Zack's voice seemed cold and distant.

Lafe Ingram dropped his eyes under Zack's glare. "We didn't mean no offense," he mumbled under his breath. "We agreed to hire you and I stick by that."

"Then let me do my job. Now let's get these damn ornery mules moving." Zack wheeled his horse away and Peck followed, but not without glaring back at several of the mule skinners with his one good eye.

Lafe Ingram sagged in the saddle as he turned to the waiting men. "You heard the man, let's get'm moving." Ingram waited for the pack train to stretch out again and operating smoothly before he rode to catch up with Houseman. "I'll not tolerate further talk with my men about alternate routes, Mr.

Houseman. It's upsetting and only tends to slow us down and shakes our confidence in Zack McClendon.''

Houseman shrugged his shoulders. ''Thought that might be an easier trail is all.'' He offered nothing further in the way of apologies.

Now that the question had been settled about the other trail, there was a noticeable increase in forward speed by the mules even though the trail was becoming steeper and more torturous as it snaked higher and higher towards the pass.

Bull Stanton had no idea how long he had been laying there with his head resting under the trickle of water, but the canyon now rested in a cooling shade. He sat up and realized for the first time how hungry he was now that his need for water was not so great. Although his lips were cracked and bleeding in places, Stanton found he could swallow without difficulty and the swelling in his tongue had gone down enough that he could close his mouth. While the shadows grew longer, Stanton ate the swollen fruit of the prickly pear and surveyed his surroundings with clear eyes and brain. At best it looked bleak. The rocky-walled canyon now in deep shade seemed foreboding and lonely. No other life moved in the cooling stillness. For the first time, Bull Stanton felt truly alone. The silence pressed in on him like a bad dream he couldn't escape. He shook off the feeling and concentrated on his predicament.

Stanton ran his hand over his arm, feeling for the break. Stinging pain brought a cry to his damaged lips when he came to the broken bone, midway between the wrist and the elbow. He closed his eyes to shut out the hurt. Of all the blasted luck, he thought.

He opened his eyes again and was surprised to see the dipper perched on a nearby rock doing his crazy dance as if for him alone. Stanton felt joy at the bird's presence. It tied him to the rest of the world he knew was out there and got him to thinking again where the water source for the dipper was located. He watched the bird until it grew too dark to see him anymore. Stanton held to the belief the ouzel was still sitting there, performing to please himself.

Stanton bathed his feet and thought he detected some feeling in his toes. He only had three pieces of fruit left, and tomorrow he would have to find water further along the trail; otherwise he would starve in the end. He drank more water, curled up on the still warm sand, and dropped off into a peaceful sleep.

CHAPTER 9

They were two days south of Raton when the Kiowas rode out of a dry wash leading away from Eagle Tail Mountain. The pack train was spread out over a quarter mile along the Canadian, now little more than a rusty streak of wet earth under a mid-July sun.

Zack was a mile in the lead more out of the need to be free of the constantly braying mules rather than to scout the trail. At this point the trail had seen a lot of use and where it swung close to the river. Ruts were two feet deep in places. From here on out, even Lafe Ingram would have no trouble staying on track. It was the unseen dangers and the unexpected problems that required experienced men like Zack McClendon and Peck Overstreet to see a pack train safely through.

Zack wheeled his horse about as the first distant shots echoed across the flat stillness. The faint cries of the Kiowa reached him as he dug his heels into his horse and unhooked the big rifle from his saddle horn. He could have used an experienced gun like Peck's, but the one-eyed trapper had ridden off towards the western foothills, searching for game.

Lafe Ingram did his best to rally his men against the charging Kiowas, but several men bolted for the wooded draws in the distance, leaving their mules to run wild.

"Stand fast, men!" Ingram shouted. "Form breastworks like McClendon showed us." Several men began whipping the mules into a makeshift circle. Ingram drew his pistol and fired at the nearest Indian, but killed the horse instead. The Indian hit the ground running and let loose an arrow that came dangerously close to Ingram, who sat there amazed anyone could have stayed on his feet, much less keep a bow strung, after tumbling from a dead horse. Ted Wyman killed the Indian as he restrung his bow, and called for Ingram to help gather the mules close.

Others along the line of mules opened fire as the Kiowas veered sharply around the lead mule and thundered past. A brave drove his lance into the lead mule. Ingram killed him with a quick shot. The free-running mules were taken in hand by the Indians while five Kiowa pursued the whites into Springer Arroyo, which fronted Crow Canyon.

Zack raced up, shouting orders above the loud cries of the Kiowas and the noise of popping guns. The two dozen Indians were already tightening the circle around the small group of inexperienced men, looking quite confident of the outcome.

"Stay down behind your horses!" Zack commanded as he rode into the din of dust and noise. He dismounted, laid the barrel of his rifle across the saddle, and squeezed the trigger. A grotesquely pained Indian flew from his horse. The coarse roar of Zack's muzzleloader sounded like thunder. Not bothering to reload the big gun, Zack jerked two five-shot pistols from their holsters and started blasting away in a methodical fashion. A number of Kiowa were knocked into the dust, and the Indians withdrew out of range to study the situation. Someone among the group was deadly accurate.

Zack quickly reloaded his pistols and rifle, all the while

studying the Indians, who continued to shout taunts and make obscene gestures at the white men.

"Get ready boys, as soon as they work themselves up again, they'll charge," Zack shouted, never taking his eyes from the Indians. A big Indian with a chest as wide as his own seemed to be working the other Kiowas up to a pitched frenzy.

Lafe Ingram appeared at Zack's side, hatless and with blood streaming down his face. "Are we all gonna die, Zack?" Ingram asked, his voice cracking.

Zack took his eyes from the milling Indians for a moment and looked at Ingram's bloodied face. A sheen of glistening sweat covered the man's bald head. Zack saw concern, but no fear in the man's eyes.

"Expect we'll know that shortly, won't we." Zack looked around at the small group of worried mule skinners. "Don't try to shoot them while they are behind their shields. Even bullets bounce off. Wait for them to expose their sides or their backs. Understood?" They nodded their heads silently. "For those of you real handy with a gun, you can just go on and shoot them in the head," he said dryly. There was a nervous laugh or two among the tense group. There wasn't a man among them had any experience at killing anybody, much less blood-crazed Indians but they were determined to do their best.

The Kiowas charged them again, this time in the shape of a V with the big Indian riding point. He carried a large bull shield that was colorfully decorated behind which he hid.

"Hold your fire 'til you hear me shoot and then count slowly to five," Zack warned. The others wondered what he meant by that until they saw the dark smoke belch from Zack's rifle and the big Indian throw up his hands and tumble from his horse. The mule skinners were amazed at the distance the Indian was killed and most forgot to count in order to allow the remaining Indians time to get within shooting range.

The charge petered out with their leader dead and two warriors rode back and picked up the big Indian whose brains still dripped from half a skull. To the west could be heard the distant sounds of shooting. Zack figured the three mule skinners had been cornered by the five Kiowa. He could only hope they gave a good account of themselves.

After a few minutes of debate, the Kiowas, with their dead leader held in front by one of the warriors, recrossed the Canadian and disappeared behind a thin screen of willows that marked the boundary of the wide river.

Lafe Ingram breathed a great sigh of relief while the others checked their pack animals, tightening loose loads and cutting away packs from those brought down by Kiowa arrows. In all, counting the three mules taken by the Indians, the traders had lost seven. Three of the mule skinners had arrows pulled from their bodies and bandaged up as best could be managed.

Zack walked around counting Kiowa dead and came up with five, plus the leader. Lafe Ingram with his head bandaged came out to where Zack stood over a dead Indian. Zack was holding a large floppy hat in his hand and examining it carefully.

"Need a hat?" he asked the bareheaded Ingram.

Lafe Ingram peered closely at the hat. "Didn't know heathens wore white men's hats."

"An Indian will wear most anything and at other times nothing at all. Just depends on their medicine that day." Ingram tried on the hat and found it a little snug with the bandages, but it was better than letting his bare skull bake in the sun.

"How do I look?" he asked the big trapper.

"Like a Pilgrim from Canaan." Ingram laughed in spite of the death around them. Zack always found it a good sign when a man could still find humor in life after a particularly harrowing experience. It meant he was learning to survive in spite of the harsh ways.

"Look," Ingram said, pointing towards the deep arroyo to the west. Two men appeared, one dressed in full leathers.

"Looks like them Kiowa run into old Peck," Zack remarked. As they drew close, Zack recognized Houseman. He had completely forgotten about the quiet man. It didn't surprise him to learn he was one of the three that had ridden away the first sign of trouble.

"Where's Harry and Sydney?" Ingram asked as they rode up.

"Dead," Peck said matter-of-factly. "Managed to kill two of them heathens before they took off. Zack noticed the fine black-tailed deer lying across Peck's saddle. "Never did find their horses. Expect them Injuns taken off with them. What they was after in the first place."

Zack turned his burning eyes on Houseman, who had a sheepish look on his face. "You sure you didn't run off and leave your partner to them Utes?" The words stung Houseman and his face colored deeply. His eyes sought the ground and stayed there.

"Ain't being paid to get myself killed over no pack goods," he managed to say quietly. Zack and the others looked at the man with open contempt.

"First town we come to will be Nuestra Las Vegas, Houseman. That's where we part company," Zack said. "Won't have a man riding with me I can't depend on."

It took them over an hour to redo shifted packs and distribute what goods they could from the dead mules. Zack rounded up three Indian ponies and pressed them into pack service, which helped the load considerably, while Peck, Lafe Ingram, and two other mule skinners went off to bury the remains of Harry Weems and Sydney Calhoun.

Zack knew that Kiowa sentinels watched them from Eagle Tail Mountain that rose proudly above the desert floor for several thousand feet. He could feel their dark eyes probing their weaknesses, wondering if they would make another attempt to overcome the small group of whites.

Peck lit his pipe looking back at the closely bunched mules. Houseman had been made to share in the work load now they were short by two mule skinners. It was obvious the man disliked the work, but the stern countenance on Zack's face kept him quiet. McClendon was in no mood for back talk.

"Them Kiowas rounds up a few more braves, they just might make another try."

"It's possible, if they find a few Comanche brothers to join them," Zack allowed.

They camped that night two miles up river on the Vermejo, which drained a large portion of the mountains to the northwest of them. Unlike the sluggish, dirty-red water of the Canadian, the Vermejo was rushing, sweet and cold. Zack had chosen a good place to stop for the night. There was ample knee-deep grass for the animals and shelter from prying eyes for a campfire. The smell of cooking venison, bracing air and calmed nerves lifted everyone's spirits even though a watchful presence was maintained throughout the night by Peck and Zack. Three hours before dawn, Lafe Ingram relieved Zack so he could catch a couple hours sleep. When he rolled into his blankets, Peck, who had stood watch earlier in the night, was snoring loudly nearby.

It was full morning before anyone realized Sylvester Houseman had slipped away on an Indian pony during the night. The tracks pointed south.

"I'm sorry, Mr. McClendon," Ingram apologized. "I guess he slipped off without me knowing about it."

"Not your fault. Besides, man had a right to leave if he wanted and the Indian pony didn't really belong to anyone." Zack was thinking ahead and taking bets on how long a lone man riding an Indian paint horse would last in the desert with Kiowa watching their every move.

"What do you make of that?" Zack asked Peck. They were sitting their horses close to where the Cimarron River joined the Canadian. Peck scratched his beard softly, sucking on his unlit pipe. They were both staring at a set of lone horse tracks that pulled away from the Canadian and headed west along the Cimarron.

"He's headin' fer rough country, fer a fact," Peck said, relighting the pipe. Zack looked west at the low-slung foothills that rose steadily to embrace the higher ridges of the Sangre de Cristo Mountains. What Zack kept wondering was, had Houseman planned on doing this all along? More than that, why? It was nearly fifty rugged miles through the Cimarron Range to Eagle Nest Lake and another thirty across Palo Flechada Pass to Taos. It was rough country to travel through with a group and near impossible to do alone. Why Taos? It was nothing more than a huddle of mud huts and poor Mexicans and dirty Taon Indians.

Zack shook his head at such foolishness. "I've seen a few dumb pilgrims in my time . . ."

Peck removed the pipe from between his teeth, his eyes dancing. "Could be this Houseman fellar couldn't be caught in Santa Fe fer some reason." Zack let this turn over in his mind for a few minutes. It still didn't make any sense to him.

"That the case, why didn't he ride on to Bent's Fort?" Peck looked stumped. Clearly, he had not thought that far.

"Don't know," Peck finally said, clearly confused by the man's actions. "You're the thinker in this group." They had settled nothing as to Houseman's intentions when the mule train caught up with them and they spent the next half hour helping them ford the shallow, rocky-bottomed Cimarron. Zack had a deep abiding feeling they had not seen the last of Sylvester Houseman . . . or whoever he was. But why did he think that?

Bull Stanton awoke to the feel of early morning sun in his face. He sat up groggily, and it was a few seconds before he gathered his thoughts and realized where he was. His stomach growled loudly, and he quickly ate the last pieces of fruit. His tongue had lost most of its swelling, and he could actually taste the bitter-sweet flesh of the prickly pear. It was then he noticed his swollen, reddened hand on his injured arm. When he tried closing his fingers, pain raced up his arm and exploded in his brain. Stanton let out a howl. He waited until the pain settled into a dull ache before moving again. He turned on his good side to get a drink of water, and was horrified to find no water trickling down the rocks. Frantically, Stanton clawed at the rocks with his good arm, trying to relocate the tiny stream of life once more. After an hour of digging and shoving rocks aside, he collapsed with despair in the hot sand, breathing heavily and fighting off the wave of suffocating loneliness that threatened to overwhelm him now. With water there was still a tiny ray of hope he could cling to. Without it, there was nothing.

Finally, he sat up and stared stupidly at the prickly pear. Wherever the water had disappeared to, the cactus would most likely die from being deserted as well. Taking his pocketknife, Stanton shaved the spines and green leather covering away from the plant and sucked at its moisture. He spit out the chewed pulp and watched as a solitary ant scurried over and probed the mass with his antennae before picking up a piece. With nothing better to do, Stanton watched the ant with the oversized load struggle across the hot sand. Right now he felt like the straining ant, fighting impossible odds. Only difference, the ant knew where he was going and Stanton didn't.

The sun grew to a molten mass in the overhead sky, and still the man in the rocky gulch did not move. Stanton had finally given up on life and was waiting for death to come and take away his pain.

CHAPTER 10

The small group of mule skinners, led by Zack McClendon and Peck Overstreet, met a wagon train of twenty near the large rock formation that marked the rejoining of the Santa Fe Trail with the Cimarron Cutoff. Zack was relieved by the sight, for on several occasions, he had seen Indians shadowing the pack train. One of those Indians looked down on them now from the large rock formation on their left. And now, since joining up with the twenty wagons and thirty-two men, Zack figured the Kiowas might well forget about attacking such an armed group of men.

A bulbous-nosed individual who rode a large white mule headed up the wagon train. Benjamin Delaney considered himself a veteran of the Santa Fe Trail, having successfully negotiated it twice before without mishap. This was to be his last trip, for he expected to clear enough money from the goods in ten of the wagons that belonged to him to retire for good. Pompous and overbearing, Delaney was approaching fifty and it showed in the puffy eyes, dropped jowls and the expanding girth provided by his successful Mexican trading. Even in the heat of New Mexico, Delaney wore a suit of white linen and a Panama that failed to cover his large head of flowing gray hair. Delaney reminded McClendon of someone trying to be what he felt people expected him to be, rather than the midwest shoe drummer he had been for twenty years. But whatever his faults, Delaney possessed a keen intelligence. When he learned of the going trade with New Mexicans, Delaney sold everything he had accumulated over a lifetime, against the protestations of his wife and two children, bought two Murphy wagons, loaded them with everything from needles to farm implements, and set off to find Santa Fe with three hired hands.

So successful was that first trip, that the following year, Delaney loaded out six wagons. Now he was hauling enough goods in ten wagons to make him a rich man. Confident and forever smiling, Delaney was just days away from realizing his dreams, and he wanted everyone he came into contact to know it. He wasted no time informing the mule train that he expected them to follow along behind the wagons, as he would continue to do the guiding.

Zack wondered how someone with such little knowledge of western country and of Indians had managed to survive previous trips. Peck merely shook his head at the fancy dressed white-suited Delaney, reserving his comments until he could formulate an appropriate response.

As the two groups came together to water their animals at a drying waterhole, Zack asked Delaney if he or his men seen any sign of Indians. Delaney wasted no time in responding to the question.

With an uproarious laugh that shook his broad belly, Delaney looked McClendon and Overstreet up and down.

"You gentlemen seem to be appropriately dressed and properly prepared by the looks of your pistols you carry in your belt, but you sound as if this is your first time ever in this part of the country. This is my third trip West, gentlemen, and I've yet to see a single Indian." If Delaney expected his pronouncement to cause McClendon or Overstreet to blush and squirm for having asked such a foolish question, he was disappointed. What he got, instead, was a cold-eyed look from McClendon that made Delaney realize he might have been a little hasty in judging the two men.

Peck couldn't resist firing a volley. "Well, Mr. Delaney, your are purty sharp and a good judge of character, yes siree. Told old Zack here, we couldn't fool the likes of a man like yourself when you rode up on that purty mule of your'n." Delaney smiled broadly, looking around to see if others were taking all this in. "Expect you seen through us right off," Peck said, packing his pipe. Zack just sat his horse, knowing what was coming and knowing he couldn't stop it if he wanted . . . which he didn't. Delaney was still smiling.

"You say this your third trip out?" Delaney nodded. Peck dipped his head beneath his floppy leather hat as if this explained everything, blowing a lung-full of smoke skyward. "And you ain't seen no Indians, correct?" Again Delaney nodded. "Well, Mr. Delaney, if you will look over your shoulder, at that rock kinda looks like one of your covered wagons, expect you'll catch a glimpse of your first Comanche."

Delaney's jaw dropped open as he turned to stare at the big rock. For all his looking, he saw no Indian.

"You must be jesting, sir. I see no such Indian," Delaney remarked, gathering himself together once more.

Peck scratched his head in mock embarrassment. "Now I know me and Zack only been out here since '28, but I swannee they was an Indian 'mong them rocks last time I looked." And then quick as a flash, Peck brought his old muzzleloader to his shoulder and fired at the rock, some eight hundred yards away. Those nearby were stunned by the belching gun and the sudden appearance of an Indian who scrambled away in the rocks.

Peck's movement had been a blur and Delaney sitting comfortably in his saddle was launched over the big white mule's head as the animal came off the ground, bucking wildly. Zack caught the mule and brought him back to the deeply embarrassed Delaney who stood brushing the dust from his linen coat and mustering as much dignity as a duped man could under such circumstances. Peck grinned down at the chagrined man.

Delaney never said another word nor did he object as the mule train pulled out front of the wagons with McClendon and Overstreet leading the way when they left the water hole.

"You mighta put Mr. Ben Delaney in his place, old man, but that Indian most likely will bring back all his cousins in a little while," Zack said, trying to keep from laughing at the situation.

"You know well as I do, that Injun was just before riding off and gathering up his clan. Expect they'll come outa them Corduno Hills er the Turkeys late today like piss ants runnin' from boiling water."

Zack looked at the dry, chalk-colored hills to the east. "More likely the Turkeys," Zack said, indicating the piñon-covered mountains they had to pass by, some five miles distant. "Good water and forage in there and plenty shelter for cover. You best ride back and warn the others while I check around for sign."

Peck grinned, "I'll do my best, but don't know if I can convince them wagon drivers er not."

Zack rode off with a wave of his hand. Three miles out he crossed the Gallegos, nothing more than a wet smear in the dust. Veering northwest with the river, Zack crossed several dry washes and had started up a shrub-covered ridge to gain view of the country when he came across tracks of thirty to forty unshod horses. He dismounted and scanned the tracks up close. There were no insect trails across the indentations, and little sand had fallen back on itself. He marked their passing at one to three hours, all riding at a slow easy gait. Zack followed the tracks through the stunted brush, gulled ground carefully until he was satisfied as to their direction, and rode hard for the pack train to prepare the men for a fight that wouldn't be anything like the last one. Mr. Delaney was about to have his first experience fighting Comanches. Zack only hoped the man and the rest of his crew would stand fast and not buck and run. There were four hours of daylight left when the grim-faced McClendon rode up to the waiting white men.

They were nearing Mora River and beyond the Turkey Mountains and still the Comanches had not materialized. Several men driving wagons grew more confident with each passing hour and in the end felt no attack would ever come. One even had the temerity to tell McClendon that what he had seen was nothing more than a hunting party looking for game. McClendon had only smiled tightly and ridden off without commenting. Lafe Ingram overheard the comment and as soon as McClendon was out of hearing, he told the burly driver that he better keep his rifle handy, for McClendon had yet to steer them wrong. The driver glared hard at Ingram and laid a whip across the backs of the straining mules as if giving his answer where McClendon was concerned.

As if on cue a line of feathered warriors appeared along a bare ridge to the west of them. Heat waves shimmered between the plodding mules and the motionless Indians. Zack fixed their number at forty-four. As things stood now, they outnumbered the Indians by several men. Still if a leader had powerful medicine, he might convince his braves to fight.

Immediately, the wagons formed a defensive circle while the pack mules were driven inside. Zack looked back at the tight circle of wagons and knew if the Indians chose to fight they would pay dearly for the privilege.

Overstreet and Ingram rode out to confer with McClendon, who sat his horse on a slight rise a hundred yards from the wagons. No one failed to note that Benjamin Delaney had prudently remained with his wagons.

"Think they'll fight?" Peck asked McClendon. Zack was studying the Indians beneath a shielded hand. The heat was unbearable, and Zack longed to ride over to the Mora and wade waist-deep into its cold waters.

"Could go either way," Zack said quietly. "Still an hour before the sun sets. Lot of men could die in that amount of time."

"Amen, to that," Peck said, solemnly. Lafe looked nervously from the line of Indians, to the wagon corral and back again. Zack thought the trader would be more comfortable back with his men and asked Ingram if he would rather wait with the others.

Ingram looked a little sheepish, as if knowing what McClendon was trying to do, but the trader shook his head. He squared his shoulders and gripped his rifle even tighter, but he never made a move to return to the wagons.

"I'll stay here if you don't mind. It's more my affair than yours," Ingram said tightly.

Four Indians broke away from the main group and rode slowly down the ridge towards the waiting white men. Their leader wore a single feather in his hair and plain deerskin shirt. The only thing extravagant about him was the red and blue marked leggings and lance decorated with otter fur he held upraised.

"Looks like they want to parley," Peck remarked. "Sure sign they don't like the odds they're facing."

Zack thought the same thing as he studied the stocky warrior. He seemed familiar. When they were less than a hundred yards out he recognized the Indian the same time as Peck.

"Why that's old Kicking Bear," Peck exclaimed. "Thought that old rascal done got too old fer such parties." Peck and Zack had visited the old chief some years back when the Comanche was in Colorado hunting buffalo. Kicking Bear looked to be in his seventies then.

"Whatever happens, Ingram, sit tight and say or do nothing," Zack warned the trader.

The four Indians rode within twenty yards of the group and stopped. Zack could see recognition in the old chief's eyes, but Kicking Bear never let on that he knew McClendon.

Zack made the sign for peace and friendship while noting

the condition of their ponies. The dry summer had been rough on the Comanches. Kicking Bear did not respond to Zack's overtures. They waited in the hot sun for the Comanche to make the next move. Zack saw their sweeping glances as the Indians took in the armed men and the wagons in the distance. Next to Kicking Bear rode Blue Horn, war chief, and next in line as chief of the Kotsotekas. The big Indian had been unfriendly back during their stay in Colorado, and it seemed nothing had changed as Zack looked into his cold eyes.

"Straight Arrow no longer hunt flat tails?" Kicking Bear asked Zack in halting English.

"Beaver not any good, trading with Mexicans instead," Zack said, knowing the old chief understood to some degree the economics of white men's ways, even if it didn't make much sense from a Comanche's point of view.

"Wagons cross our lands. No ask Comanche."

Zack understood what the old chief was really driving at since traders had used the Cimarron Cutoff since '22. Crossing Comanche and Kiowa lands was nothing new. The chief was asking for a graceful way out of a fight he knew would be disastrous for them, and Zack thought he knew of a way.

"Traders willing to give Kicking Bear tobacco and blankets to cross lands," Zack told the old chief, never mind that they were no longer in what was considered Comanche territory. Zack turned to Ingram.

"Ride back there and tell Delaney to break out twenty pounds of trade tobacco, blankets and coffee for the chief. If he gives you any trouble tell him when the fighting starts, I'll personally make sure he's out front to meet the charge." Ingram nodded his head, backed his mount slowly away from the group and cantered back to the wagons.

Zack glanced at Blue Horn; he didn't seem all that pleased by the gifts, yet even a war chief knew there was a time to fight and a time to accept things as they were. He said something to Kicking Bear in Comanche, too low for Zack and Peck to catch.

"Need guns, powder too," Kicking Bear said to McClendon. McClendon knew then what Blue Horn had whispered.

Zack shook his head. "We carry no extra guns or powder except for our own use." Zack really had no idea what was in the wagons, but he was not about to equip Comanches with guns that could be used on them or other traders headed down the trail. There was a heated exchange between the old chief and Blue Horn whose eyes flashed a burning hate at McClendon. Kicking Bear did not repeat the request. A few minutes later, Ingram and two other traders returned with the requested supplies. Kicking Bear motioned two of his men to pick up the goods.

"When Straight Arrow hunt buffalo with Comanche?"

Zack smiled at the old chief. He had a feeling that he better never be caught inside a Comanche camp as long as Blue Horn was around.

"Someday, maybe," Zack answered Kicking Bear. The wily chief nodded to McClendon and with the three Comanches retreated to the rocky ridge where they paused for a minute before disappearing down the other side.

Ingram was the first to speak. "I for one hope to never have to face that tall one in a fight. Did you see his eyes?"

"Name's Blue Horn," Peck told the trader. "War chief. He wanted to fight instead of settling for a few trinkets."

"Suppose they'll come back?"

"Not long as we hold the advantage," Zack cut in as Benjamin Delaney came riding up on his big mule. His eyes blazed at McClendon, his mouth drawn in a straight line.

"McClendon, I hold you personally responsible for the cost of those goods we were forced to give those ragtag bunch of heathens."

Zack turned cold eyes on the puffed up man in his fine clothes, thinking what a splendid picture he would make running for his life from a man like Blue Horn. Zack felt his anger rise at the pompous trader who couldn't seem to let things alone.

"You do, do you? You still got time to ride over that ridge and take them back. What was prevented here, Delaney, was a lot of bloodshed. And that, only because I knew Chief Kicking Bear personally, although that wouldn't cut no ice if the odds had been different."

"We could have whipped them. We are better armed and outnumbered them," Delaney pressed.

"You are right when it comes to guns and numbers, but never having been in a fight with Indians, you don't have the slightest idea how ferocious and deadly Comanches can be with just bows and arrows. While we're busy reloading our guns, a good warrior can get off twenty arrows with telling effect."

"Mr. Delaney," Ingram spoke up, "I can testify that recently, the Kiowas gave us a good fight even though we outnumbered them as well. Even then we lost seven mules, two dead mule skinners and two more wounded. If Mr. McClendon says these Comanches are worse than the ones we fought, then I want nothing to do with them. As for the goods, my men and I will split the cost of those items or give you the goods from our share."

Delaney seemed somewhat mollified by Ingram's generosity. "That would be most honorable of you, Mr. Ingram," Delaney said in a quieter tone, although he still glared at Peck and Zack as if they were the reason the Indians were here in the first place.

"You best get the wagons across the Mora before dark," Zack broke in. "Come hard rains in them mountains to the west and you may lose a lot more than a few boxes of tobacco and coffee." With that, Zack wheeled his horse away from the group and headed for the Mora. Peck caught up with him, all the while scanning the ridge to their right for Comanches. The rushing waters of the Mora was everything McClendon expected, and he allowed his horse to take a long drink while he dismounted and did the same. The water was so cold it hurt his teeth.

Zack stood up. Water dripping from his full beard wet the

front of his sweat-stained, dust-caked shirt. He took off his boots and hung his pistols on his saddle.

"Keep an eye peeled, Peck. I'm going to cross and ride out a piece." Without waiting for a reply, Zack plunged into the cold waters. The icy waters were indescribable on his parched skin; McClendon sunk down to his armpits and finally pushed his head under as well. He came up feeling greatly refreshed and led his horse across the three-hundred-foot river in what looked to be the best place for the wagons.

Peck watched the crazy McClendon from the far bank. "You going to catch your death someday doing that," he shouted at his partner. "And don't expect me to nurse you back to health."

"You just get them wagons across, old man," Zack called back as he clambered out on the other bank, pulled on his boots, and mounted his horse. With a wave of his hand he disappeared over a gentle rise, leaving Peck glowering at the empty stillness.

He had no idea how long he had lain there before the evening shade crept into the canyon and cooled his face. Bull Stanton rubbed his burning eyes and sat up. His movements were slow and awkward, his mind dulled by the heat and the need for water. He figured it to be late afternoon and was surprised to see he still lived. Stanton picked up the remaining portion of the prickly pear and slowly chewed the pulp for moisture. His movements were mechanical, as if he no longer had control over his own body. There was a sudden flutter of gray wings, and three feet away sat the little dipper again. Stanton tried to smile, but failed.

The small bird cocked his head from side to side as if wondering why the man did not move, and he began his curious dance for Stanton. Still Stanton did not move.

Stanton stared at the bird until he realized its feathers were still wet and that mud clung to its tiny feet. Stanton's mind began to slowly process this bit of information and it roused him from his half-stupor. If the bird's feathers were still wet, it had to mean water was close by; otherwise they would have dried in the desert air.

"Which way to water, little friend?" Stanton croaked. It was the first time he had heard his own voice in days and it sounded strange to him.

The dipper stopped his dancing and cocked his head at Stanton. Slowly, Stanton forced himself to his knees, trying not to scare the bird, but the dipper burst from the rock at full speed, flying directly over Stanton's head and this time out of the canyon to the north. Stanton pondered over this for a minute. All the other times, the bird had gone up the canyon. Bull looked up the rocky slope at the rim, some three, four hundred yards above him, and suddenly he made up his mind. He began climbing over the loose rock, slipping and sliding, yet always upward. Stanton ignored the pain every time he bumped his broken arm or scraped his hands on the rocks. If he was going to die, he wanted it to be on top of the ground, not in some hole.

The western sky was a blaze of red, the back-lit Sangre de Cristos a mantle of deep purple, when Bull Stanton shoved his head above the canyon rim. He somehow managed to drag his beaten body the rest of the way out of the canyon with much of his remaining strength. He lay there for a few minutes while he steadied his breathing, wondering what to do next. He raised his head and looked around at the low shrubs and scattered rocks for signs of the bird. Nothing moved, and he let his head sink back to the still warm sand. A cooling breeze drifted down from the foothills and revived him.

With nothing but will left, Stanton pushed himself to his useless feet and stood there, swaying like some giant snag in the wind. He wanted to take a look at the world standing up, for he knew it would be his last. What he saw brought astonishment to his face. Less than a mile away lay a thin blue ribbon of water, but what caused him to shout with tears of joy, was the big buckskinned rider coming dead at him. Stanton shouted hoarsely, took two steps and crashed heavily to the desert floor.

Zack saw his horse flick his ears forward, and he wondered if a few Comanches were out there trying to cut him off from the rest of the group. He thought he detected a slight movement directly in front of him. Zack checked his rifle and pulled one of his five-shot pistols from his belt as he rode forward cautiously. He wouldn't put anything past Blue Horn, knowing how the Indian felt about him.

Something thrashed about in the brush ahead of him and Zack cocked his pistol and rode slowly forward, scanning the area as he went. Zack was amazed at what he saw as he rode up to the figure of a man sprawled in the sand. Quickly, Zack dismounted and tied the reins to a low greasewood and lifted his canteen from his saddle.

Zack eased down beside the man, whose face, blackened by days of exposure to the desert sun, seemed as dried up as cowhide. He was still breathing, though, and Zack lifted his head and allowed a trickle of water to run into his mouth. It was then he recognized the big-framed man whose gauntness allowed his tattered clothes to hang from him. Zack looked at the cloth-bound feet and knew Bull Stanton was through walking.

"Bull, what happened, man?" Zack asked of the semiconscious man.

Stanton thought he was dreaming as the cooling water splashed against his lips and he drank greedily.

"Whoa, now. Not too much, Bull," Zack said softly. Stanton opened his eyes and appeared to be having trouble focusing them on the apparition bending over him. He tried to speak but no sound came out.

"You just lay there, Bull," Zack said, easing the man's head back to the ground. "Get some help."

Zack stood up. Taking the reins of his horse so he wouldn't be spooked, he fired off a round in the air from the Patterson. The sound was flat and harsh in the hot stillness. He watched as Peck looked his way and Zack waved his arm. Peck came on a dead run covering the distance in less than a minute.

"What is it?" Peck asked, bringing his horse to a halt in front of Zack. He carried a pistol in his big fist, and the faded deerskin patch over his right eye caused him to look like some wild desperado.

"It's Bull Stanton. Looks like he's been out here for some time."

"Reckon what old Bull is doing out in these parts on foot? Looks to be dead," Peck said, peering hard at the prone Stanton.

"Ain't a minute from it. You hightail it back and bring over a wagon. Delaney starts to—"

"Ain't seen the day, I cain't handle a duded-up feller like Delaney, McClendon," Peck cut in as he wheeled his horse around and galloped back to where the first of the wagons were emerging from the Mora.

Stanton mumbled something. Zack knelt, putting the canteen back to the man's lips. Stanton took a long drink and looked at McClendon with clearing eyes.

"You seen a little bird hereabouts?" Stanton managed to ask, thick-tongued. Zack was surprised by the question.

"No, I haven't, Bull," Zack replied.

"That you, Zack?" Stanton asked incredulous.

"It's me, Bull. And old Peck is here too."

Stanton tried to smile but failed. He closed his eyes for a second and seemed to have drifted off to sleep.

Zack took a closer look at Stanton's feet while he waited and caught the odor of rotting flesh. Bull's feet were beyond saving, if not his life. Peck came riding back with a heavy wagon lumbering along behind.

"It's going to take all three of us to get him loaded," Zack said as they came to a stop. The driver of the wagon peered down at the blackened corpse, but made no move to climb down while Peck dismounted and tied his horse beside Zack's. Zack gave the driver a hard look.

"Hamilton isn't it?" the trapper asked.

The sandy-headed driver nodded. "Peter Hamilton."

"You want to get down off that wagon and lend a hand with this man or do I have to shoot you from that seat?" Zack had lost all semblance of patience. Hamilton scrambled down from the wagon.

Zack and Peck took Bull's head and shoulders while Hamilton managed his legs. Together they were able to lay the injured man atop the fully loaded wagon.

"Watch his arm there, Peck," Zack said. "Think it's broken."

Hamilton wrinkled up his nose. "Ask me, this man is dead." Peck looked down at the blackened feet that seemed ready to burst. He lifted a pant leg and saw the discolored areas.

"Afraid, Pete's right. Ain't much we going to do fer Bull 'cept make him comfortable."

"And that's just what we are going to do. Now, Mr. Hamilton, get back up there and ease this wagon over to the river. May as well make camp there now, bein' it's getting so late," Zack said, untying the reins of his horse.

"He say anything?" Peck wanted to know as they rode slowly behind the wagon.

"Asked about a bird."

"A bird?" Peck said. "Pore Bull, most likely plumb off his rocker by now. You seen his legs?"

Zack shook his head. "Don't need to, his feet says it all."

They rode the rest of the way to the river in silence as deepening twilight settled across the cooling desert. Bull Stanton moaned occasionally whenever he was jostled by the wagon. Far off, Zack heard the high-pitched cry of a hawk looking for a meal.

CHAPTER 11

Zack had Stanton placed by the fire and covered with some of Delaney's new blankets. The wagon leader had the good sense not to protest. Peck brought over a cup of coffee for Bull, who was propped against Zack's saddle. Stanton was feverish and seemed to be having difficulty breathing. Zack had gotten nothing from Bull concerning the circumstances of his ordeal.

"Try sipping some of this, Bull. My coffee's good for what ails you." Peck held the cup to his lips.

"Never thought I'd taste anything that good again," Bull Stanton said weakly.

"Just you wait, got a skillet of meat frying fer you right now," Peck said, leaving the cup with Zack and going back to the fire. Zack had stabilized Stanton's broken arm so at least it wouldn't hurt so much when he moved it. Lafe Ingram squatted on his heels nearby, listening to Stanton tell McClendon what had happened.

Several yards off, Delaney and his crew had established his own camp, while Ingram and his men shared their fire with

McClendon and Overstreet. Zack had posted sentries around the camp and ordered the mules fed and placed inside the circled wagons for protection. Comanches would try to steal animals whenever they got the chance.

Stanton stared at Ingram for the first time. "Jim Mann had a hat like that," Stanton said, "until I saw an Indian wearing it a day or two ago . . . I forget." Zack and Lafe exchanged looks.

"McClendon shot a Kiowa out from under it, yesterday," Ingram said, removing the hat so Stanton could take a closer look.

"That's Jim's all right," Stanton said.

"Well, I think he got what he deserved, running off and leaving you that way," Ingram said.

"Somehow it don't really matter now, and maybe not even if Mann and Taylor had stuck by me. Looks like we all going to wind up dead."

"Aw, you don't know that," Ingram said, putting the hat back on his head. "I've found out, old Peck is a pretty good cook. He'll have you up and going before you know it."

"Wish that were true, but it ain't and Zack here can tell you the truth of it." Bull Stanton spoke with conviction, his voice tinged with sadness. "Legs are gone as well, I can feel the poison moving up." Ingram looked at Zack for confirmation. Zack dipped his head slightly as he put the cup to Stanton's lips once more.

"What I could really use right about now is a bottle of whiskey."

Ingram sprang up. "Got a bottle of Irish whiskey in my bag," he said and hurried off to fetch it.

"You just be careful like I said, when you get to San Miguel," Stanton told Zack. "And especially so, when you get to Santa Fe. This Salezar is Governor Armijo's right-hand man and carries a big stick, otherwise, he could never have had Simon Walker executed and us turned out into the desert."

"We'll be careful, Bull, appreciate the warning," Zack said.

Ingram was back with the bottle and he passed it to McClendon to open. Zack cracked the unopened bottle and poured a good measure into the coffee cup. Stanton took a long swallow, closing his eyes.

"Best whiskey I've ever had the pleasure of drinking," he said to Ingram who smiled.

"Anybody we can contact back home for you and the others in your party?" Ingram asked.

"Already told Zack all that." Stanton took another big swallow. "Lord, the pain is easing already." Zack refilled the cup. He touched Stanton's brow. His fever seemed to be rising. Stanton's breathing was irregular and ragged now. At best, Zack figured he had a few hours.

Bull Stanton died peacefully an hour later, without ever tasting the food Peck had prepared for him. Zack stood up from the body, recorked the nearly empty whiskey bottle and passed it back to Ingram.

They buried Stanton under a full desert moon with coyotes yipping in the background. Ingram said a short prayer. Afterward, some went to their blankets while others relieved those on guard duty. Delaney and his men had stayed away from the entire proceedings, which was just as well as far as McClendon was concerned. A man that thought only of himself and money all the time was not someone to put a lot of trust and faith in. Delaney did have the good sense not to ask for the blankets back, for Zack had wrapped Stanton's body in them for burial.

The night passed without incident, and they were underway by the time the sun cleared the low peaks to the east. That night they camped within sight of Las Vegas. Ingram came over to McClendon where he sat on his bedroll cleaning the big muzzleloader. Zack saw the serious look on Ingram's face.

"What you got on your mind?"

"You know, Zack, we can make it on from here without any trouble. The road is wide and well traveled. All we got to do is follow along with Delaney."

"Trying to squeeze us out?" Zack said, grinning.

"You know better than that. Just thought you might like to start back for Missouri. Form your own wagon train. You see, me and the others talked it over and well . . . here," and Ingram handed Zack a wad of bills. "It's all there, paid in full, even the packs we lost. If it weren't for you and Peck we'd still be stuck in those mountains or most likely killed by Indians."

Zack shoved the money back into Ingram's protesting hands. "When me and Peck sign on to do a job, we see it through and that means Santa Fe . . . nothing less." Ingram started to say something but Zack held up his hand. "Furthermore, we ain't accepting pay for what was lost or stolen by Indians."

"That your final word?" Ingram asked.

"That's it," Zack said firmly. Ingram smiled, putting the money away.

"Told the others you wouldn't go along with the notion but we had to try."

"Admit I got another reason for going on to Santa Fe. Bull Stanton was a good friend," Zack said, tight-faced. "Aim to see this Salezar pay for what he done."

"You better be careful around that Mexican," Ingram warned.

"It's him best be careful," Zack said, ramming a new charge down the long barrel of his rifle.

By late afternoon of the next day they had skirted Starvation Peak and the broad mesa that rose nearly twelve hundred feet above the valley floor and entered the customhouse at San Miguel after crossing the shallow Pecos.

McClendon warned Delaney again about the troubles Stanton and the others had gone through and for him to keep his men in line. But Delaney was a consummate salesman, and he joked with the Mexican soldiers, presenting each with a few items that caught their interest and the necessary cash to see his wagons came through the customhouse without a hitch. Unlike Simon Walker, Delaney knew when to pay up and smile while doing it. When it was all said and done, Delaney brought his wagons through for less than a hundred dollars in addition to the few items he handed out to the officers. It helped to mention to the officers that he was a personal friend of the alcalde, whom he had entertained the last two trips.

Lafe Ingram's pack mules followed close behind, having cost them less than twenty-five dollars each to clear the custom-house.

They camped two miles north of town on the Pecos River with the mule skinners and wagon drivers in high spirits, eager to ride back into town to visit the cantina.

McClendon advised against it, but Delaney let eight of his men leave camp, whooping and racing their horses. Delaney himself had changed to a powder-blue suit he had brought out of a trunk he carried in one of his wagons. He looked as fresh and as stylish as anyone from the city.

"Do not concern yourself, Mr. McClendon," Benjamin Delaney said, striding over to his mule and mounting. "Mayor Vermejo and I will be having dinner tonight. My boys will get into no trouble that I cannot extract them from."

Peck and Zack watched the pompous Delaney ride off.

"Don't he beat all," Peck said.

Zack shook his head as if Delaney defied logic. "Delaney is a prime example some men are born more equal than others."

"It's a fact, I don't have anything near purty as them suits he wears. We still ridin' over to the cantina and wet our whistle?" Peck asked.

"Only if you're buying."

McClendon and Overstreet were used to rough Mexican saloons with dirt-floors, thick smoke and precious little else in the way of amenities. Ingram looked around him at the drinking Mexicans playing Spanish Monte and wondered how anyone could spend much time in such a foul-smelling place. Thick clouds of harsh Mexican tobacco stung his eyes and burned his nostrils.

An hour later, they met Delaney and the alcalde in the plaza, and the trader made a big show out of introducing the mayor to them. To Zack the Mexican looked worried rather than pleased at having run into the trappers. He wondered if Delaney had told Vermejo of finding Bull Stanton in the desert yesterday. Zack felt his anger rise, wondering how he could stand by and let three men be sent to certain death in the desert.

"Would you gentlemen care for a drink? We were headed for the cantina to check on my men," Delaney said, yet his voice reflected the insincerity of his offer.

"Just leaving," Ingram said, speaking for them. "Need to get back to camp and relieve those on duty." Zack never acknowledged the alcalde, or Delaney for that matter. He was afraid he would wind up having words with the Mexican over the treatment of Stanton and the others, and Zack owed it to Ingram to keep quiet. Maybe sometime in the future, when it was just him and Peck around, they could settle the score for Bull.

The backbone of the spiny Sangre de Cristo Mountains glistened in the early morning light amid a backdrop of deep blue sky as the cavalcade started up the narrowing valley they would climb for twenty-five miles to the summit of Glorieta Pass. From there it was a relatively easy twenty miles to Santa Fe, most of it downhill. At this point, the Santa Fe Trail paralleled a steep-walled, flat mesa on their left that shot westward towards the pass. Dark shades of green clung to the upper reaches of the foothills along the canyon while small piñon and juniper dotted the rocky mesa. It was here the Pecos pulled away from the mesa and cut its way through the heart of the mountains to the north.

Zack was glad to be entering the cool of timbered slopes once more. Desert living wasn't something he cared to do for long.

The next day they looked down on Santa Fe after stopping at the Canoncito Trading Post where the trail entered Apache Canyon. The adobe ranch house was the last stop on the trail before they reached Santa Fe.

* * *

The Santa Fe that Benjamin Delaney had known the year before was no more. There was a tenseness to the town as the heavily loaded wagons rolled up and stopped before the customhouse. Mexican dragoons marched across the plaza in perfect step, their red sashes and plumed helmets reflecting the sun back into the eyes of the wagoneers.

Their approach to town was observed by silent-faced Mexican men, women and children, none crying out to the traders as in the past, *"Los Americanos! Los Carros! La entrada de la Caravana!"*

"Place don't seem none too friendly," Peck observed as he and Zack hitched their horses in the main square. They stood beating the dust from their clothes, using the opportunity to look the place over. They had sold furs here four years ago, furs they had taken out of the Sangre de Cristo Mountains before the Mexican Government made it illegal for Americans to trap beaver in New Mexico. A few trappers either took Mexican wives or formed partnerships with other Mexicans to get around the law. McClendon and Overstreet simply left altogether. Back then, Santa Fe had been bustling with activity and friendly people. Zack wondered if Salezar had anything to do with the change. The plaza was still full of people coming and going, but they cast furtive glances at the two buckskinned men as if they expected trouble at any moment. Dark-eyed, half-clad women still smiled at them from darkened doorways, but their gestures seemed mechanical and lacked warmth and sincerity.

La Villa Real de la Santa Fe had been born out of strife and revolt and had often subjugated to dictatorial governors such as Armijo and his chief henchman, Damasio Salezar. These two were simply the last of a long line of persecutors that had its beginning with the Franciscan priests, two hundred fifty years before. And the people, both Mexican and Indian, could accurately recall the number of times they had revolted in those turbulent years against iron rule. The names of those governors who were either killed or fled for their lives during these revolts could be counted on one hand: Antonio de Otermin fled the city, leaving the Indians in charge for twelve years; Don Santiago Abreu killed by having his hands, tongue and eyes pried out; Colonel Albino Perez decapitated by a mob and Jose Gonzalez put to death by the current Governor, Manuel Armijo. The people were still waiting to pass judgement on Armijo . . . they were people of great but not endless patience.

The two trappers waited outside the customhouse while Delaney and several of the mule skinners stepped inside to pay their duties. McClendon heard loud voices coming from inside the customhouse; suddenly a rear door banged open and a soldier rushed out, mounted his horse, and galloped for the Palace of the Governors.

"What you reckon set his tail on fire?" Peck asked. Zack wasn't sure, but he guessed the soldier was probably going after help. And that was a sure sign things were not going well.

"Maybe we should mosey in and see what's holding them up," Zack said casually.

"Lead on, old coon," Peck said, putting away his pipe. "Sooner we get through here, the sooner we get our money. And I got myself two kinds 'a hankerin', boy."

When they stepped into the building, Zack was confronted by a red-faced Delaney snorting fire. A short, lazy-looking individual in a dirty uniform was receiving all of Delaney's wrath. The Mexican never wavered under the onslaught, and Zack figured the man endured such treatment every time a caravan of goods arrived in town. Only thing is, his eyes betrayed his true feelings, and Zack saw the hatred buried there.

"Outrageous! Five hundred dollars a wagon will ruin me!" Delaney shouted.

"But señor, that is the duty," the Mexican said quietly. "I cannot change the law." Delaney looked around for help and spied Ingram waiting his turn.

"What about them mules? You charging five hundred as well?"

"No, señor, only two hundred. They do not carry the goods your big wagons do." Ingram's face came alive with interest.

"I was told in St. Louis, the duty for mules was fifty," Ingram cut in. Zack knew now why the soldier had left in such haste.

"Governor Armijo has established the duty at five hundred for wagons and two hundred dollars for pack mules," the Mexican custom official replied, his voice beginning to show anger.

"Well, by damn! I'm not paying such out and out thievery," Delaney said. "I'll just take my goods on to Albuquerque or clear down to Chihuahua if Santa Fe doesn't want them. I hear they bring a better price down there anyway."

The Mexican flushed, his eyes flashing anger. "You cannot proceed south unless you pay the duties now. After that, I will give you papers to travel to those places if you do not wish to sell your goods here." The Mexican was openly hostile now.

"Would it do any good talking with this Armijo?" Zack spoke up.

The Mexican turned his angry eyes on the big trapper and in an insolent tone said, *"You* or none of these other gringos are allowed to speak with Governor Armijo. It is not permitted." There was a thunder of hoofs outside and McClendon knew the fat was in the fire.

A tall well-dressed Mexican officer entered the customhouse, his manner authoritative and commanding. Six soldiers with fixed bayonets entered behind him.

"What is the problem here?" he asked the customs official, who appeared meek in the officer's presence. The two conversed rapidly in Spanish for a few brief minutes. As the customs official spoke, the officer looked from Delaney to Ingram and finally to Zack who lounged against the wall. Zack saw the officer did not fail to notice the brace of pistols and the big knife at his belt. The man finished explaining the situation to the officer, who stood motionless for a few minutes before speaking. He looked directly at Delaney as he talked.

"I am Capitán Damasio Salezar. As Juan Ortega has fully explained to you, a duty must be paid to the Mexican Government before Americans are allowed to sell goods in this country. That is the law, there are no exceptions."

Zack studied the infamous Salezar, finding a certain cruelness about the man's face and curt demeanor. So this was the Mexican who, with Armijo's blessings, had put Simon Walker to death and banished Bull Stanton and the others to die a slow death in the desert. His dislike for the swaggering Mexican was instant and total. Zack pushed away from the wall and headed for the door, already knowing the outcome here. There really was never any choice. Delaney was simply crying foul when he himself would impose such duties if it benefited him, and Zack was certain most of the money wound up in Salezar's and his boss's pockets. If anyone was the loser, it was the poor people of New Mexico, made poorer by such high-handed affairs.

"Do not move!" Salezar shouted at McClendon, who stopped to look at the Mexican officer. The trapper stood six inches above the tall Mexican who seemed infuriated by McClendon's attitude of indifference. Zack looked the Mexican square in the eyes.

"We only acted as guides. Don't have any trade goods of our own," Zack said, indicating Overstreet, who stood near him. McClendon spoke clearly, there was no give in his strong voice.

"No one leaves until all duties are paid," Salezar replied. "You gringos act so independent, as if you are still in the United States. And you trappers are the worst of the lot." The slander stung McClendon and his features grew hard, his eyes never wavering from the Mexican.

"We came in here as free men and by Christ we'll exit the same way," Zack said softly. The Mexican should have read the sign, but with six of his men backing him, Salezar was overconfident. He was used to dealing with men who couldn't deliver beyond mere words when under pressure.

Without realizing it, Salezar had pushed McClendon into a corner from which there was no way to escape gracefully. Yet Salezar was too proud to admit such shortcomings, for deep down he hated all Americans. If it were not for the money they brought, he would have put an end to this trade business long ago.

As if anticipating their commander's next move the six soldiers brought their rifles to bear on the trappers, their bayonets less than ten feet away. The clicks of their rifles were ominous in the stilled room.

"Then you leave me no choice but to place you under arrest." The words were barely out of Salezar's mouth before McClendon lunged at the nearest Mexican, who was not prepared for such an instant reaction. With one hand on the soldier's rifle and the other holding his pistol, Zack laid the barrel alongside the Mexican's left ear. The man dropped without a whimper.

Salezar shouted orders, but by then things were a mass of confusion in the suddenly too tight room. Somewhere behind him, McClendon heard Delaney pleading for calm. McClendon was almost to the doorway when he felt something prick him in his side the same time a smashing blow sent him crashing to the floor. After that, there was nothing but darkness all around him.

CHAPTER 12

The first thing that made Zack realize he was still among the living was the stench assaulting his nostrils. He opened his eyes to a world of filth, rolled over on the hard mat and sat up with great difficulty. The movement caused a sharp pain in his side. He looked down at the dark, caked blood on his leather shirt, and suddenly everything flooded back in sharp focus. He looked around the stinking cell and caught sight of a fat Mexican asleep in a corner. From the looks of him, Zack figured the Mexican had been brought in during the night for drunkenness. McClendon smelled the staleness of alcohol about the sleeping man.

"You finally among the livin'?" a familiar voice asked from an adjoining cell. McClendon looked over his shoulder at the one-eyed man, who stood there holding the cell bars with both hands, grinning down at him.

"Head feels like a blacksmith been using it for an anvil."

"You can thank that slimy Mexican, Salezar fer that. Tried

to stop him but two of them soldiers had me pinned to the wall with them pig stickers so's I couldn't move.''

Zack shook his head. ''That was a stupid thing I did. Could have waited until Delaney and Ingram were through.''

Peck chuckled. ''No you couldn't and what's more we both know it.''

''Who dressed my wound?'' Zack asked, feeling the lump of a bandage beneath his shirt.

''Somebody call's hisself Doc Rameriz but if you ask me, Rameriz's had one too many tequilas. He was half-drunk and looking like he might die hisself.''

Zack managed to get to his feet by holding to the bars in his cell. The sudden shift in pressure brought more pain to his head. He touched the swollen place behind his right ear, thinking that someday he would have the courtesy of paying Salezar back.

''Delaney and Ingram?''

''While old Doc Rameriz worked over you there in the customhouse—guess Salezar didn't want to see you bleed to death before he hung us—Delaney coughed up the money from a roll big enough to burn a wet mule. Ingram paid up as well, but listen, there's bad trouble brewing around here.''

Zack smiled faintly. ''Think we may be part of it.''

The Mexican in the corner rolled over to his back and began snoring loudly.

''Give that greaser a good kick,'' Peck said, scowling with his one good eye at the dirty Mexican. ''Bastard's probably a spy.''

''What you need is coffee, might settle your nerves some,'' Zack said.

''I ain't the nervy jasper got us in this fix.''

''I concede the point, old man,'' Zack said a little sheepishly. ''Now what's this talk of trouble?''

Before Peck could launch off, the inner door opened and a big swarthy Mexican with long greasy hair and a thin mustache that trailed down over his lower lip came through the door.

Behind him came Lafe Ingram. The jailer eyed the two trappers half-expecting them to reach through the bars and tear him apart. Ingram stepped around the wary Mexican.

"Good morning, Zack . . . Peck," Ingram said cheerfully. He was clean-shaven and had changed to a brown suit, white shirt and string tie. To the trappers, Ingram looked even more citified than his usual self.

"Get us some coffee, Mex," Peck bellowed at the jailer. "Ain't you people got no manners?" The jailer backed up a step and put his hand on his pistol.

"Do not call me that, señor," the Mexican warned the one-eyed trapper.

"Oh, you real brave ain't you, Pedro. I don't get my coffee real soon, I'm gonna tear hell outa this flimsy hoosegow."

Ingram headed off a confrontation. "Can't you please get them coffee? I have no weapons to give them and the pot is in plain view through the door."

The jailer hesitated, glaring hard at the big trapper who seemed not to care that he was the one who had the gun. He backed through the door and poured them coffee, his eyes on them the whole time. He handed the cups to Ingram and stepped back. Peck reached a beefy hand through the bars and took his cup from Ingram. Zack did the same.

"Can't we be alone?" Ingram asked the Mexican. "I want to speak to them in private."

"Are you their representative?" the jailer asked.

"Why yes, I guess you could say that. I'm the reason for them being here in the first place."

"Stay back against the wall so I can see you through the open door."

"Thank you. I will do as you say," Ingram replied and put his back against the wall. The jailer took a last look at the pair in the jail and backed out of the room.

"I am trying to arrange your bail, but the judge is in Albuquerque and isn't due back for three days. I've tried to talk with Salezar but can't get past his lieutenant."

"Figured as much," Zack said, sipping the muddy strong coffee.

"The word is all over town about how you stood up to Salezar."

"Didn't do such a hot job," Zack said, trying to think what to do next.

"Listen, you don't understand. The whites living here and a number of Mexicans have had enough of Salezar. They are behind you."

"Behind me for what? Ain't really done nothing, I can see."

"What you've done is expose a nerve that's been covered for too long."

Zack looked at Ingram. The man wasn't making any sense.

"Guess I might as well tell you," Ingram said slowly. "That soldier you clipped behind the ear died."

Zack was stunned. "Can't be, didn't hit him that hard."

"And that's what set the kettle to boiling. Everyone suspects Salezar killed his own man, hoping to expose those leading the resistance when they hang you two for the murder." Ingram looked down at the floor, feeling uncomfortable at being the one to bring them the bad news.

"Hang us?" Zack whispered. Both trappers were equally stunned and could only stare at Ingram, who continued to study the planked floor.

Peck literally shook the jail cell with his big hands, his face blood-congested, his single eye flashing fire. He had dropped the empty coffee cup and he stood there now gripping the bars with white knuckles.

"I'll kill the arrogant bastard!" Peck shouted. He turned to Zack and whispered, "We gotta get outa here, boy."

Zack was thinking the same thing. They couldn't wait for some Mexican judge probably bought and paid for by Salezar . . . if Salezar decided to wait that long. Most likely, Armijo was just as involved. Zack felt sure Salezar would take on nothing this important without the governor's blessing.

The jailer hurried into the hallway, his eyes wide, looking scared at Peck's outburst. He stopped ten feet from the cells.

"Time is up. You must leave now," he said to Ingram. His voice sounded worried to Zack, who wondered if the man was afraid he had overstepped his authority by allowing Ingram in here in the first place. Salezar, Zack figured, would not be too pleased.

Ingram looked at the doomed men, "I'll be back later after I see what can be done."

"No, no, señor. It is not permitted. Only Capitán Salezar himself can authorize such requests." Ingram hesitated. "Please, señor, my orders are clear. I took a great risk for you to see your friends."

Ingram nodded his head. "I appreciate that and you do not have to worry, I will tell no one."

The hall door closed behind them and a foreboding silence filled the jail cells. Even the drunken Mexican had stopped snoring.

"The fat's in the fire this time, old coon," Peck said. "What we gonna do about getting outa this place. I feel like a grizzly in a cage." Peck Overstreet was pacing back and forth in his cell.

Before Zack could formulate an answer, the sleeping Mexican got up from his pallet and came over to McClendon, smiling. Peck stopped his pacing and stared through the bars at the Mexican who no longer appeared to be drunk. Zack was just as surprised as Peck at the sudden recovery of the Mexican.

"I am Antonito Montoya, Señor McClendon," the Mexican whispered, "and I can be of service if you will only promise to assist us with the resistance."

Damasio Salezar stood before the washbasin, carefully shaving around his lower lip so as not to cut into his dark mustache. He was proud of the thick growth that flared outward and curled at the ends over his bottom lip. Behind him, a woman stirred in her sleep, rolled over, and came awake at finding the other half of the bed empty.

"Why must you rise so early, *querida*," the woman asked sleepily. Salezar continued to shave as if not hearing the woman. He finished, towelled off the remaining soap, and reached for his uniform shirt. The woman watched as he slipped on the garments.

"It is not even light enough to see. Why don't you come back to bed," the woman said huskily. To tempt her lover, Carmelita Torres sat up, letting the sheet fall to her waist. Salezar appeared not to notice the woman's exposed breasts as he pulled on his boots and reached for his hat. Seeing this, the woman tried pouting instead. "At least give me a goodbye kiss," she said, holding out her arms.

Salezar looked over at the whore for the first time that morning. In the soft glow of the burning lamp, her skin was flawless and silky smooth. In spite of important matters that pressed him, Salezar felt the stirrings of desire once more at the sight of her long black hair falling around her shoulders and caressing each large breast. He walked over and bent down, kissing the woman lightly on her forehead. Immediately Carmelita circled Salezar's neck with her arms and planted a kiss on his lips. With great reluctance, Salezar broke the woman's hold.

"I must be going, there are important matters I have to attend to."

"Maybe you leave so early because you don't want anyone to know you sleep in my bed." The pout was back.

Salezar allowed himself a small smile, just for the woman. "That is not true, for I would kill the man who insulted you. I leave for there is business to conduct with the governor."

"Will you be back tonight?" The woman flashed him a smile. He looked down at her nakedness.

"How can I stay away," he said thickly.

As soon as he was gone, Carmelita's smile faded to a hard expression as she slipped from the bed. She threw on a dress, brushed her long flowing hair quickly and left the room. Her

113

face had lost its softness as she hurried through the narrow back streets of adobe huts clustered together, ignoring the stinking trash and loose animals. In a few minutes she came to a nondescript mud house where a young child was busy feeding chickens. The child looked up at the woman with bright eyes and a smile. Carmelita swooped the child up into her arms.

"Up so early, Pauli." The child giggled and dropped the small pail. The chickens rushed around Carmelita's feet, pecking at the spilled corn.

Still holding the child, Carmelita opened the door and stepped inside. Some distance away a man dressed in peasants clothing and wide sombrero waited a few minutes after the woman entered the house and then slipped quietly away.

"Carmelita, you should not take such chances coming here. You know it is not safe. Salezar has spies everywhere," a fat woman said from her stove. She was making bread and the smell of it filled the tiny room.

"I am not afraid of Salezar!" Carmelita said, her dark eyes flashing. "Someday, I will keel the pig myself." Antonito Montoya came into the kitchen pulling up faded suspenders over his ample belly.

"Hush, child, do not talk so," he chided the woman.

"I am not afraid," she repeated.

Montoya sighed heavily and sat down at the table. His wife hurried over with coffee and a plate of food. The young boy jumped down from Carmelita's arms and went over to sit in Montoya's broad lap. The old man began feeding the child from his plate.

"I know you are not afraid," Montoya said, looking up with tired eyes that held old pain. "Neither was Ignacia, but now my son lies in a cold grave, struck down at twenty, and all I have of his smile and laughing voice is this child."

Carmelita took a seat at the table and the old woman brought her a plate of food and a slice of hot bread which the child reached for, but quickly dropped.

"Wait for it to cool a little, Pauli," the old man admonished.

114

"But I grow tired of this waiting and Salezar's . . ." Carmelita could not finish.

"I know, I know," the old man said, as the child tested the bread once again and found it cool enough to pick up. "It will not be much longer, I promise. The others are with us and just yesterday, two gringos that are to be hanged by Salezar are willing to fight as well."

Carmelita shook her head as she stirred her food with a fork. "What are two men, especially two who would do anything to escape the hangman. Once free, how do you know they will not simply run off?"

The old man smiled. "Because these men *are different*! The big one is accused of killing a soldier two days ago."

Carmelita tossed her head impatiently. "This I know already. Salezar spoke of the gringos he would hang this afternoon in front of all the people so it would be a lesson to anyone that dared attack one of his men. And then he laughed wildly. It was not until . . ." she looked slightly embarrassed but continued, "afterward, he told me of the joke, of how he had personally killed the soldier later with a blow to his head."

The old man's eyes blazed with hate. "That is as we guessed. Salezar will stop at nothing to crush the movement." He placed a wrinkled and calloused hand on her arm. "You must be careful, Carmelita. Don't come back here until it is finished . . . for the child's sake if nothing else. If Salezar knew what you were doing, he would take the boy and kill us all."

Carmelita nodded her head slowly, a tear forming at the corners of her eyes. "I will do as you say . . . to protect Pauli, not myself."

"Pauli will need you after this is over," Montoya said. "We are old and cannot live much longer. Had things been different, Ignacia would have made you a proper wife and a proper father for the boy. For now, it must remain our secret. Salezar is a dangerous killer who will stop at nothing to have his way."

"He will not have his way with me much longer," Carmelita said coldly, taking the boy in her arms once more.

Salezar was sitting straight-backed at his desk, going over routine papers and sipping a brandy before his meeting with Governor Armijo. His face showed a trace of irritation when there was a soft knock at the door. He had left specific instructions with his sergeant that he was not to be disturbed. A little discipline was in order.

"Enter!" he called through the door. The door opened quietly and a slim figure of a man stepped through and closed it behind him. He held a large sombrero in his hand, his face downcast.

"Excuse me, Capitán Salezar, but you said to come when I had news . . ." the soft spoken Mexican peasant said.

"It is okay, Ramon, come closer, take a chair."

Ramon edged over to the huge ornate desk, but did not sit down. He was very uncomfortable in the presence of such a powerful man, and it showed.

"I did as you requested, Capitán. The woman left immediately after . . ." here he paused realizing the personal nature of what he was about to say and changed tactics. "She made her way to an old man's house I know. He was a farmer for a long time, but raises a few goats and chickens now that he is too old for anything else." The Mexican paused to look around at Salezar's office and furnishings, deeply impressed. Salezar waited with more patience than he thought possible for him.

"Are you going to tell me who this man is?" Salezar asked finally. The Mexican's head snapped back around.

"I am sorry, Capitán. It is just I have never seen such an office before . . . The man is Antonito Montoya."

Salezar's eyes narrowed for a minute. Montoya, Montoya. The name was vaguely familiar to him. Why would Carmelita, who had no family, be visiting Montoya so early in the morning?

"There was a small child playing in the yard," the Mexican

116

continued. "She picked the child up as if she knew it. That is all I saw, Capitán."

"You have been exceedingly helpful, Pedro Lamas. You will continue to watch and report to me anything else you learn, understood?" Salezar stood up and handed the Mexican a few pesos.

"Sí, Señor, I will do as you ask," Lamas said, taking the proffered money but avoiding Salezar's eyes. He slipped through the door as quietly as he had entered.

Salezar sat back in his chair, gazing out the window at the parade grounds where Lieutenant Vallejo was putting the troops through their morning drill. Why did the name Montoya disturb him so? More than that, why did Carmelita rush to see Montoya the minute he was gone? He sat aside such thoughts for now, intending to ask Vallejo later. He still had this business of hanging the two gringo trappers this afternoon if Armijo had no objections.

A short time later, when Vallejo had finished with drills, Salezar had the answer concerning Montoya and a light came into his eyes that reminded Lieutenant Vallejo of a man planning someone's death.

CHAPTER 13

Peck looked at the plate of food and felt his nervous stomach churn. It was all he could do to keep coffee down this morning. McClendon looked at Overstreet through the bars.

"Better eat," Zack said washing down a mouthful of food. Peck stopped his infernal pacing and looked at Zack.

"Too worried. Ain't convinced that Mex is coming back with help like he promised."

"Then you might as well eat. Better to be hung on a full stomach," Zack replied with grim humor. "Besides, you act like this is the first time you ever come this close to going under."

Peck Overstreet fixed Zack with his one eye. "Ain't the dying I'm worried over. When I go, I want to make sure it's with a gun in my hand and the mountains at my back, not trussed up like a hog fer market with his gullet fixen to be slit."

"He'll be here," Zack promised.

"Well, he's dang shore taking his sweet time about it. Fer all we know, that crazy Mexican Salezar is just liable to show up early and hang us so's it don't interfere with siesta." They had made attempts to lure the jailer close enough to overpower him when he brought their food, but the wily Mexican used a broom handle to push the plates over to the bars.

The hall door opened suddenly and the jailer came in escorted by three grim-faced men. A fourth man, bringing up the rear, was Lafe Ingram, whose eyes fairly danced in his head. From head to toe, Ingram was dressed in Mexican clothes. McClendon barely recognized him. Ingram smiled broadly at the pair.

"Getting a little worried?" he asked.

Peck glowered at the jailer who looked as if he was going to be sick. One of the men prodded him with a gun and the man unlocked Peck's cell door first. The trapper stepped out and taking the keys from the jailer, Peck shoved him into his own cell.

"Let's see how you like being locked up."

Before Peck could close and relock the door, one of the Mexicans stepped around him and hit the jailer as hard as he could several times in the face. The jailer offered no resistance and he crumpled to the floor. Blood seeped from the corner of his mouth and an eye was fast swelling shut.

"Now you may lock the door, señor," the dark-faced Mexican said. Peck looked at the Mexican with wonder.

"It is the only way we can protect him," Antonito Montoya replied, pushing back his large hat for Overstreet and McClendon to see. He took the keys from Peck and let McClendon out.

"Danged if you didn't come back," Peck said.

The old man smiled. "A Montoya never goes back on his word, even if it means dying." Peck believed the old Mexican.

"Hadn't meant for you to get mixed up in this, Ingram," Zack said as they left the jail hurriedly.

"Part my fault you're here in the first place. Sorry I couldn't talk Delaney into joining me, but he figures to stay with the side holding the most cards."

Zack never figured any different where a man like Delaney was concerned. Somehow his kind would always wind up on the side of money and power. In the outer office, Montoya gave each of them a sombrero and a ragged serape to pull over his head. He looked them over with satisfaction as they shoved their weapons beneath the serapes.

"Where are our rifles?" Zack asked.

"I have them," Ingram said, "and your horses as well."

"We must hurry, gentlemen," Montoya urged. "Salezar will not wait for the appointed hour. I know how the jackal thinks. He will hang you before there is a ground swell of resistance among the white traders. Already you can feel the tenseness in our people on the streets. Everyone is waiting to see whether the traders will come to your rescue."

"What about this Governor . . . Armijo? Can't he control Salezar?" McClendon asked.

Montoya shook his head sadly. "We believe Armijo himself is afraid of Salezar and therefore reluctant to reduce his power. Salezar is a madman who will stop at nothing to achieve his goal."

"And what is that?" McClendon asked as they opened the outer door to the jail.

"*Quien Sabe?* We do not know for sure," the Mexican said. "Maybe governor, and that is why Armijo is so careful with him. Salezar owns many thousands of acres of land and controls all trading into New Mexico. He is very rich and has many spies in his employ."

"Sounds like this Armijo has created a monster and afraid to pull his stinger," McClendon said softly as he stepped from the jail.

Once on the streets, McClendon and Overstreet kept the big sombreros pulled low over their faces as they hurried through the alleyways to Montoya's adobe. Montoya was right.

McClendon could feel the tenseness. Normally busy streets were mostly deserted. A good percentage of the businesses were shuttered and their curtains drawn. People were waiting for the explosion, and their hanging was to have been the lit fuse.

They were at Montoya's only a few minutes before Carmelita Torres arrived, looking worried and nervous. The young boy rushed into her arms. Montoya introduced her to the others. The Mexican woman smiled shyly at McClendon when she was introduced to him. Zack was overwhelmed by her flawless beauty and perfect smile. The child had her features and her lively eyes. Montoya explained his son's death at the hands of Salezar and that Ignacia and Carmelita were to have been married. Now the woman slept with Salezar to gain valuable information, to probe his weaknesses for that day they would rise up and destroy him and his despised men.

"Armijo will suffer the same fate if he does not help the movement when the time comes."

McClendon looked at the woman once again in a new light. In her face there was no shame or sense of embarrassment for what she was doing. McClendon found it remarkable that she could sleep with a man she must passionately hate.

"Appears to me the time has come," McClendon finally said, accepting the coffee and plate of food from Montoya's smiling wife. Peck's eye shined at the sight of food and dug in immediately. "Might even been rushed a little by my meddling," McClendon added as he began to eat.

A thin Mexican slipped into the room, whispered something to Montoya, and was gone again. McClendon ate in silence for a few minutes while Lafe Ingram sat quietly by, sipping coffee with a worried look on his face. McClendon knew he had to do his best and try to get Ingram to leave Santa Fe before trouble started, but he figured it would be a waste of time. The man had backbone. McClendon had come to genuinely care for the trader.

Montoya turned to the waiting men. "You must leave now.

Three of Salezar's men are at the jail. It will only be a matter of minutes before Salezar himself knows of your escape. My men will take you out to Manuel Chaves. There will be others there who are on our side and willing to fight.''

"What about you? Shouldn't you and your wife leave as well?'' McClendon asked.

Montoya shook his head, "I can better serve by remaining here to keep an eye on things. But you must take Carmelita and her child with you.''

Carmelita jumped to her feet with the child clinging to her flowing dress. "I will stay also, Poppacita. Who knows better than I, what Salezar plans.''

"All the more reason you must leave. You will be the first to come under suspicion with a crazy man like Salezar.'' Carmelita opened her mouth to protest, but Montoya held up his hand. "Think of the child. It is too dangerous for him here. If Salezar only knew that the child was Ignacia's, he would kill him without hesitation.'' The woman's expression changed. There was logic in the old man's words.

"Then I go, only to protect Pauli,'' she said resignedly. "To find him a safe place, then I continue to fight.'' Her eyes flashed fire, and McClendon could see where even a man like Salezar could fall under her spell. The woman gathered a small bundle of things for the child while the others made ready to leave.

"Tell Chaves, I will be out later once I learn what Salezar plans to do.'' The old man and woman embraced the child and the woman. Montoya shook hands with the two trappers.

"Won't forget the risks you took, getting us out of jail,'' McClendon said.

"De nada, señors," said the old man, and then he whispered to the tall trapper, "Please look after the woman and child, that is all I ask.''

"You got my word,'' McClendon said before stepping through the doorway and hurrying after the others. The small group was turning the corner when a thunder of hoofs overtook

122

them, and a dozen Mexican soldiers flashed by heading for the Palace of Governors.

"Quickly," one of their guides said, motioning them down a narrow alley filled with rotting trash and broken bottles. At the far end a door opened, and the same slim Mexican that had spoken with Montoya a few minutes before led their horses outside. McClendon checked to see if his rifle was still loaded and primed before mounting. Peck did likewise. There was no horse for the woman, and she held the child up for McClendon. The big trapper hesitated for a second before placing the child in front of him. Before he knew what was happening, the woman leaped behind him and put her strong arms around his waist. He hadn't planned on something like this happening. They continued down the narrow passageway and rode out into a large grassy field. Open country greeted them as they rode along at an easy pace so as not to cause alarm or attract Salezar's men, whom they could see patroling the road leading into Santa Fe from the north. By now his men would be stationed at all escape routes.

McClendon held the boy with one arm while he tried not to think about the woman's body pressing him from behind. He caught Peck's look and could have slugged him the way he was grinning.

Suddenly out of a hidden draw to their left, two soldiers appeared. The soldiers seemed as surprised to see them as they were the Mexicans.

One of the soldiers drew up and shouted for them to halt in Spanish, leveling his rifle at them. McClendon's heart froze. He felt helpless with the boy in front and the woman behind if things developed into gunplay. They came to a stop, with McClendon hoping they looked Mexican enough not to alarm the soldiers. McClendon stiffened in the saddle when the woman whispered in his ear, and what he heard caused him to sweat all over again.

"I know these men. They are as ruthless as Salezar."

Peck caught McClendon's eye and gave him that special

look. McClendon tried to warn Overstreet not to do anything for fear of harming the child and woman.

"Where are you going?" one of the soldiers asked Montoya's guide. The Mexican appeared humble and spoke softly and unhurried.

"We are going to visit my sister who is very ill." The soldier looked the group over carefully before replying. McClendon saw the change in the man's eyes when he came to the child. There would be hell to pay now.

The soldier came closer, while the other remained where he was with his rifle aimed at the group.

"Your sister must be rich to have a hacienda large enough to house all of you." The Mexican approached McClendon and he felt the woman stiffen. Damn! What had he gotten himself into? By now, they could have been half way to St. Louis. As it was, a lot of people were most likely going to die, and so were the child and woman if he wasn't careful.

"Buenos Dias, Señorita." The Mexican soldier smiled at the woman. "Capitán Salezar is most anxious to find you. I think you had better ride back to town with us. The Capitán is mucho upset and I think you could help calm him down, no?" He leered at Carmelita Torres as he came nearer. *Just a little closer!* McClendon thought. The Mexican's horse strayed closer, ignoring McClendon who appeared to be slumped in the saddle with his head on his chest. The boy at least had enough sense not to move or speak. McClendon moved ever so slightly and spit a stream of tobacco on the ground. Under his shirt his muscles were bunched and hard as caprock. It was all the warning Peck needed.

Salezar was having a leisurely breakfast with Señorita Magalena de Vargas Domingo at her father's estate north of town when he was interrupted by an urgent message brought by one of his men on a well-lathered horse. Salezar dismissed the soldier after a few terse words and resumed his breakfast.

"Is there trouble?" Doña Magalena Domingo asked, dabbing at her lip with a silk napkin.

"It is nothing," Salezar said with a flourish as he seated himself once more at the table. A cool breeze caressed the couple as they continued to eat. "Two gringos have escaped the jail. They were scheduled to hang for the murder of one of my men."

"How horrible," Doña Magalena said, her eyes widening.

"I agree, Señorita. I'm afraid not all gringos who come to New Mexico do so with goodwill in their hearts."

"Do you need to leave, Damasio?" Her voice was soft and caressed each word she spoke. Salezar smiled at the beautifully dressed woman. Unlike Carmelita Torres, Magalena was refined, cultured, and well-educated. She was everything he desired in a woman. Marrying her would give him the respectability he had chased after all his life.

"What! And leave such lovely company? My men have their orders. They will see that the two gringos are back in jail before nightfall. They cannot escape." Salezar seemed supremely confident, yet beneath the thin veneer, he seethed with rage.

"If you say," the woman said, "but once we are through with breakfast, I insist you leave and take charge of their capture. We can go for a buggy ride some other time."

"If you insist," Salezar said, poised with his coffee cup at his lips, "but only if we take that buggy ride tomorrow."

"Agreed," Magalena Domingo said, flashing him a beautiful smile.

Don Diego de Vargas Domingo was a wealthy cattleman and owned several businesses in Santa Fe. His sprawling ranch was bisected by the Rio Tesuque and ran deep into the well-watered foothills to the west rising up to meet the Sangre de Cristos. It was rumored Don Diego was even wealthier than Governor Armijo, who also owned a ranch near his and one in Albuquerque. Salezar did not know for sure who had the most money, only that Armijo did not have a beautiful daughter and Don Diego did.

125

Salezar's heavy roweled boots sounded like the clink of Mexican silver as he stepped onto the planked boardwalk and pushed open the door of the jail. He found three of his men standing over the frightened-faced jailer whose eyes widened at the sight of the Mexican Captain.

Salezar ignored the trembling man, and fastened his eyes on the young Lieutenant Vallejo who brought his men to attention.

"What happened here, Lieutenant?"

"The jailer says he was overpowered by the gringos when he brought their breakfast this morning. You can see how badly they beat him."

Salezar came over and looked closely at the jailer, who shrank back in his chair under the captain's scrutiny. One eye was swollen shut and a deep purple. His lips were badly bruised and puffy.

"Did they hit you anywhere else?" Salezar asked kindly.

"No, my capitán," the jailer responded, "only in the face."

Salezar nodded his head and straightened up. "Only in the face," he repeated. He looked at Lt. Vallejo, a slight smile tugging at the corners of his mouth. "Can you not see, Lieutenant?"

Vallejo looked confused and uncertain as to what Salezar was asking him to see. "I do not understand, sir."

Salezar walked around the seated jailer looking at each of his men as he passed by. "You do not understand," he repeated. He stopped in front of the jailer and pinned him with his angry eyes. "You know what I mean, don't you?" he snapped. The jailer swallowed but could not answer. The three soldiers, still at attention, appeared uneasy, as if knowing somehow they were about to catch Salezar's full wrath.

"I am here . . ." he turned back to the Lieutenant, "one minute, maybe two, no?" Vallejo nodded silently. "And already I see the truth as plain as the bruises on this man's face." His voice kicked up an octave. He gripped the front of the jailer by his shirt and jerked him from the chair.

"Please, Capitán," the man pleaded.

"He has no bruises elsewhere because he was beaten in the face to make it look as though the gringos had escaped. That's the truth isn't it!" Salezar screamed in the jailer's face. "Tell me, or I will shoot you myself right now." His face was contorted with rage and he reached down and removed his pistol from its holster. Cocking his weapon, Salezar jammed the muzzle into the man's stomach. The jailer's face lost all color.

"It is true, Capitán," the jailer replied, his voice quivering. "I wanted nothing to do with the scheme, but I was forced. The men had weapons." Salezar dropped the jailer back into his chair and looked around at his men, his face covered by a cold smile.

"Lieutenant Vallejo, you must learn to look beyond the obvious, *no es verde?*"

"That is true, Capitán. I will remember what you have shown me here today," Vallejo promised. Salezar seemed satisfied and turned back to the jailer, who looked like a man facing death.

"Bring me a chair," Salezar said and one of the soldiers broke attention and rushed to get him the jailer's from behind the old desk. When Salezar had seated himself, he reholstered his pistol. The jailer breathed easier.

"Tell me, señor, who were these bad men that held you at gunpoint and released the gringos?" The jailer fixed his stare on the third button of Salezar's uniform, completely cowed by the captain. In a few minutes it was over. Even though the jailer did not know the gringo who came with the Mexicans, Salezar knew of only two men that it could be.

"Bring him outside," Salezar commanded as he stood up and walked over to throw open the door. The two soldiers grabbed the jailer roughly and shoved him through the door behind Salezar. The jailer stood blinking in the bright sunlight, fear etched deeply on his face.

"Lieutenant Vallejo. You will demonstrate to the citizens of Santa Fe what happens to those who cooperate with the rebellion. *Now!*'' A burly soldier quickly bound the jailer's hands behind his back while the other mounted his horse and played out a length of rope.

"*Madre de Dios, por favor,* Capitán,'' the jailer pleaded with Salezar. "Do not hang me. My wife is old and cannot look after herself.''

"Oh, we do not intend to hang you . . . at least not the way you are thinking of.'' A cruel smile settled across Salezar's face as comprehension flooded the jailer's eyes.

"Hang me instead, Capitán, please. That way I will die only once.''

"Precisely why we are not.'' Abruptly, Salezar mounted his horse and rode away, leaving Vallejo to carry out the grim task. The jailer turned his pleading eyes on the lieutenant.

"Please, señor. Do not do this thing. I have done nothing to deserve to die like a mongrel dog.''

Vallejo averted his eyes from the face of the pleading jailer. "I have my orders. I am sorry.'' The soldier with the rope slipped the noose over the doomed man's head and took up the slack when it fell to his ankles. The jailer appeared to be in shock as the soldier took a dally around his saddle horn. The soldier waited for Vallejo to give the order. Vallejo, not wishing to prolong the jailer's suffering, nodded to the soldier, who put the spurs to his horse.

The jailer's feet flew out from under him with such force that his head bounced hard on the boardwalk before plowing up a dusty furrow as the rider put the quirt to his horse. The jailer followed behind, screaming loudly. After riding up and down the main plaza many times, the soldier dropped the rope and left the bloodied and dirt-covered corpse of the jailer in the middle of the street for all to see. It would be nightfall before anyone had the courage to remove the body.

In a way, the jailer's body was a calling card left by Salezar, daring those who resist him to come out of hiding. A lone figure of a man stood looking at the body lying in the street for a few minutes before stubbing out his cigarette and turning

128

down a side street to his waiting horse. A few minutes later, the rider was free of town and riding hard to the southwest. First blood had been drawn.

"Do we have an agreement then, Governor Armijo?" Benjamin Delaney asked, raising his glass of champagne to toast their new-found partnership.

Armijo did not immediately lift his glass. Instead, he folded his arms across the table and stared at Delaney.

"What of the resistance, that Capitán Salezar says must be put down? Can you live with the fact your friends, like Ingram and these two trappers, may be killed as part of the uprising?"

"This is your country, Governor. We are merely interlopers and should not concern ourselves with local politics. If those crazy trappers and Ingram do so, then they must be willing to face the consequences of such decisions. I am here only as a trade merchant, nothing more." Armijo smiled broadly and picked up his glass of cold champagne.

"Then we have an agreement, Mr. Delaney. You will return to St. Louis and bring back as many wagons as you can. Of course, I will personally waive the duties on your return." Both men laughed and tilted back their glasses while the jailer was being dragged to his death.

CHAPTER 14

Zack McClendon was a blur of action before the tobacco juice hit the ground. McClendon drew his pistol from beneath the serape, and, in a wide sweeping arc smashed the soldier in the head as he came within arm's reach. The Mexican tumbled from his horse without a sound. A pistol shot rang out and Zack turned just in time to see the second soldier throw up his hands and pitch over backwards from his horse. Peck sat there holding his smoking gun and grinning at McClendon.

One of Montoya's men rode over, dismounted before the unconscious soldier Zack had struck and drove a long knife blade into the man's heart. He wiped the blade on the dead man's embroidered jacket and remounted his horse. The entire action was completed in less than twenty seconds. His movements had been as matter-of-fact as stopping to kill a snake.

"You should have shot him," Carmelita said at his back.

"Hell, lady, sandwiched in between you and the kid, I figured I had to hit him or take a chance drawing his fire," Zack said. Lafe Ingram looked as though he was going to throw

130

up over the defenseless stabbing, but did a manly job of keeping it down.

Carmelita Torres slid off the back of Zack's horse and jumped up behind the Mexican who had killed the soldier. "Now you will only have to look out after Pauli." She flashed him a beguiling smile. They rode on ahead while one of Montoya's men stayed behind just long enough to dispose of the bodies in the nearby draw.

They rode for another four or five miles until they came to a narrow stream that had eaten its way into the dry country to a depth of several feet, leaving sharp banks on either side. A thin line of green marked its winding course across the broken country. Here they turned back east and rode for several more miles, climbing in altitude. They entered a steep canyon of wooded foothills before coming to a ranch house secluded among the trees. The creek they had been following now rushed madly down the canyon, snaking around wagon-sized rocks and large cottonwoods that edged its banks. The spot was a perfect place to build a home, and Zack liked it immediately. The air was cool here and a refreshing relief from the heat of the open sagebrush country.

They dismounted, taking their rifles with them. Their horses were led away to a shaded corral that Zack had not seen when they first rode up. Next to the corral was a barn and beyond that a small building he figured to be the bunkhouse. There must have been two dozen horses all ready in the pole corral. It was then Zack spotted the guard down by the creek. He was wedged between two boulders and all that was visible was his rifle and part of his hat. Had they not been welcome, Zack figured, somebody would have died without ever having known where the shot came from.

"I apologize for bringing you the long way here," the Mexican who had knifed the soldier was saying, "but from now on we must be extremely careful that Salezar or Armijo does not suspect Chaves as our leader."

"Precautions are always a good idea," Zack said, stepping

through the opened doorway behind the woman and child with Peck and Ingram bringing up the rear. They entered a large room commanded by a huge stone fireplace at one end. Bearskin rugs and hickory furniture were scattered about. There was nothing in the room to indicate the presence of a female touch, and Zack concluded Chaves lived here alone. A group of men, Mexican and white, were conversing in low tones as they entered. They fell silent, scrutinizing Zack and the others with hooded eyes. A pleasant-faced Mexican came over and greeted the woman and boy warmly, all the while looking over her shoulder at McClendon and the others. He came around the woman with his hand outstretched.

"You must be Señor McClendon. I am Manuel Chaves," the Mexican said, smiling. McClendon shook his hand. "I must say, Hank Ledbetter did not do justice when describing you," Chaves said, casting an appreciative eye up and down McClendon's well-muscled frame. "You are one big hombre, no?" McClendon towered over Chaves by more than a foot.

"Old Skin Ledbetter here?" Peck asked incredulous.

"And you must be Peck Overstreet," Chaves said, shaking hands with the one-eyed trapper.

"As I live and breathe," a booming voice rose up from the mists of those seated near the fireplace.

"Skin, that really you?" Peck said, meeting the man halfway in a bear hug. They danced around for a few seconds, pounding one another on the back. Hank Ledbetter had picked up the name after a Gros Venture buck had managed to lift part of Ledbetter's flowing locks before he came to and killed the Indian with his knife. Ledbetter, like McClendon and Overstreet, had trapped the Rockies for the last ten years.

Ledbetter stuck out a big fist for Zack to shake, his face all smiles.

"Skin, we thought you had gone under," Peck said. "Ain't been to the last three er four rendezvous. Jest figgered the worse."

"Ha, this child's still on top and living good . . . at least 'til this Salezar started cramping everybody's style." Ledbetter waved his hand at the seated men. "That's what this meeting is all about." He turned back to face McClendon. "Been up Taos way all week trying to recruit a few old mountain men to join the fracas. Jest got back this morning when I hear from Chaves about your predicament. I'da been down to the jail personally and got you out if'n I had been here."

"Know you would, Skin," Zack replied. "Want you to meet another good man. This is Lafe Ingram. Guided him and his men over Raton after Charlie Marsh died of the fever."

"Old Charlie gone under, huh. Well, expect 'for this shindig is over, a few more of us will do the same." His voice turned serious and a worried look spread across his face.

"How long this Salezar fellar been cuttin' such a wide swath?" Peck asked.

"Ever since the Texas Expedition. When he got back to Santa Fe, he strutted about, bragging how the *Tejanos* were not as tough as they claimed and he had five sets of ears to prove it. It's been hell the last six months for any white man living in Santa Fe. And traders too," he added as an after-thought glancing at Ingram, "unless you manage to cut a deal with Armijo. But not many are willing to trust the bastard. And Chaves here can tell you how much Armijo can be trusted." The Mexican nodded.

"This is true, Señor McClendon, but come meet the others before I speak of such things." Chaves introduced the other men in the room. There was Cap Singleton, a white farmer whose only son had been killed by Salezar's men one day during a drunken spree. They had trampled a cart of vegetables his son had been taking to town to sell. His big calloused hands worked continuously as he recalled the story. His wife was dead and the boy was all he had in the world. Zack wondered how many times the man had ever handled a gun, but he knew he would be here as well if he was in Singleton's shoes.

John Atwell had been a trader before settling down with a Mexican wife and three children. He was scared and told them so, but he looked solid and dependable to Zack and didn't appear to be someone who would fly to pieces under pressure.

June and Tom Banks were brothers who had come West as mule skinners and now owned the gunsmith shop in town. At least they knew how to handle guns, Zack thought as they shook hands. June looked to be the oldest. They each had taken Mexican wives and claimed dual citizenship . . . not that it appeared to matter at this point.

Zack was introduced to a distinguished Mexican whose manner indicated he was used to respect and position. He was Don Diego Domingo. More than anyone else in the room, the ramrod Mexican had more to lose both financially and through his daughter if Salezar forced him to acquiesce and bless their marriage. He had put off such decisions for weeks now, but Salezar was a persistent man.

"How many men can you commit?" Zack asked the Mexican.

"Most of my vaqueros are family men, who know cattle and horses. They are not gunmen. But all thirty-five will stand with us, I have only to ask. That is why I asked Señor Ledbetter to go to Taos and see if we could not find men who were willing to fight. Tough men who know how to use guns. I can afford to pay them well, if they would agree to help."

"Have much luck?" Zack asked Ledbetter.

"Found five or six willing to fight. All ex-trappers like us, just hanging around drinking and doing what odd jobs they could to keep body and soul together. Not a single one wanted any pay. That's how strongly they feel about what Salezar did to the Texans two years ago. But Mr. Domingo insists on paying."

"How many men are garrisoned at Santa Fe with Salezar?"

"More than three hundred dragoons," Chaves spoke up. "But many of them will not stand with Salezar, this I know."

Zack smiled faintly. "Well, unless I miss my counting, we

134

still don't have near enough men to butt heads with Salezar direct.''

"That is why, I sent Cheyenne Jack and Billy Williams north from Taos to look for more men among the trading posts to the north," Skin Ledbetter added. "Since the beaver trade turned sour, ought to be forty to fifty men hanging round doing much of nothing." Zack agreed but whether they would be willing to fight the Mexican Government was something else again. He and Peck had no choice. They were wanted men and subject to be shot on sight because of Salezar, but more importantly they were here because of Bull Stanton.

Carmelita made coffee and she served it now to the men, reserving a warm smile for Zack as she passed by. His thoughts slipped from the present problems and lingered over the woman who returned to the kitchen with the young boy in tow, her dress clinging invitingly to her slender form. He mentally shook himself to clear his head. Now was not the time to be thinking of a woman. Manuel Chaves was speaking.

"What Señor Ledbetter said earlier about not trusting Armijo is true. He is a vain and dangerous man, Señor McClendon. Although he is my uncle, he had my horse poisoned so that he could win a race. My horse, Malcreado, was a great horse and very famous in all New Mexico. He was a big bay with Arab blood. There was not another horse in the country who could beat him . . . not even my uncle's horses were good enough. He challenged me to a horse race, but I didn't want to race against my uncle, for I knew he would never tolerate being beaten. But he insisted and I had no choice. Great Malcreado fell dead fifty yards from the finish line." Chaves's eyes filled with fire just thinking of the horse again. "I planned to kill my uncle after I learned it was he who paid Dr. Philippe Masure three hundred dollars to poison Malcreado. My uncle figured I would try such a thing and orders went out to arrest me and then shoot me for trying to escape. I fled north with American traders to St. Louis.''

"What are you doing back now?" Zack asked.

"My uncle's brother came for me with a special pardon from Armijo." He laughed harshly. "Can you believe it. Armijo has my horse killed and I am the one offered a pardon."

"Why did he do that?"

"He needed help, someone who knew American customs, spoke their language. That was two years ago. I tried to warn Armijo that the Texas Expedition was nothing more than men wanting to establish trade relations with Santa Fe, but he chose to listen to Salezar instead. After that, I have had as little contact with either my uncle or Salezar as possible."

The Mexican who had watched from the shadows as the jailer was being dragged to his death burst into the room with the news.

"What of Montoya?" Chaves asked, concern growing on his face.

"I do not know," the rider responded. "Salezar has many soldiers searching the town for all the whites. It is not safe anymore on the streets even for our own people."

"If Salezar did this to the jailer, it can only mean he told Salezar of Montoya," Chaves replied. He was pacing in front of the huge fireplace. He quickly gave several of his men lounging against the wall orders to mount up. "We must ride back to town and warn Montoya."

"We'll ride with you, Chaves," Zack said.

"No señor, stay here for now. You are wanted by Salezar. We can best serve Montoya if we go without any Americanos. Please."

Carmelita Torres came out of the kitchen as Chaves and several others prepared to leave. She watched as they loaded their rifles and checked their pistols.

"Where are you going, Manuel?" she asked.

Chaves hesitated for a second, knowing how the woman felt about the old Mexican. She would insist on going, and that would only slow them down.

"I have no time to explain now. Señor McClendon will tell you. Let us ride," Chaves said to his grim-faced men. Before

Carmelita could make any further reply, they were through the door. Seconds later they were galloping away in a cloud of dust. The woman turned to McClendon, her eyes wide with certainty that something dreadful was happening.

Zack explained to her about the jailer and the logical conclusion Chaves had reached where Montoya was concerned. Carmelita's hand flew to her mouth, biting back the scream that threatened to rise in her throat. Sensing his mother's fear, the little boy rushed to her, tears forming in his dark eyes.

"Now, now," Zack rushed on ahead. "I'm sure Chaves will get there before Salezar."

"You do not know Damasio Salezar," the woman cried, "Antonito is an old man, Salezar will have him beaten until he dies for he will stop at nothing to learn the names of those plotting against him. Salezar does not even trust his own men. I must go to Antonito," she pleaded.

Don Diego Domingo came over to the distraught woman. He carried himself with the calm assurance that he had life under complete control at all times.

"Señor McClendon is right, señorita. By now, Damasio will have figured out your role in this affair and it would be dangerous for you to be seen in town. I myself still have some influence with the captain and with Governor Armijo as well. I will ride in and see what I can do for Montoya."

Zack's voice stopped the distinguished Mexican at the door.

"Best be careful, Don Domingo," Zack warned, "if Montoya talks, you would be pretty high on Salezar's wanted list, same as us." Domingo nodded then closed the door behind him.

"Antonito will never talk," Carmelita spat at Zack, her dark eyes flashing anger.

"I know," Zack said softly, "but there is his wife . . . what would he do if Salezar threatens her? What if he promises Montoya that your son, Pauli, will not be harmed?"

"Montoya would never take the word of a jackal like Salezar," the woman said in a controlled voice, yet Zack could

137

see that she was thinking once again and not operating on blind emotion. When she spoke again, her voice was filled with great sadness. "Antonito and his wife would both die, gladly, if it means the end for Salezar and that Pauli could grow up free. And die is just what they will do, if Chaves fails to get there in time."

Antonito Montoya was watering the chickens when a young boy came running up with the news about the dead jailer. Montoya took the news calmly and continued with his chore before going back inside where his wife of fifty years was busy at the stove making lunch. Usually he took his seat and waited for the woman to bring his coffee, but today he poured them both a cup, gently took her hand in his, and led her to the table they had shared a lifetime. The woman was surprised but she did not offer any resistance after she saw the look on her husband's face.

Montoya tasted his coffee and acknowledged its strong flavor like an old friend. He looked deeply in the old woman's clouded eyes. He had known for years that his wife was losing her eyesight, yet he had said nothing, for her source of pride was her cooking and their love that had withstood the test of time.

"There is little time left now," Montoya said softly, holding her wrinkled hands in his. "Salezar knows I am the one responsible for releasing the gringos." His wife gasped and clutched his hands tightly. "We have known this day would come. I thank God that Carmelita has taken Pauli away from here. Chaves will see to her needs and so will this big trapper, McClendon. He is a good man, a dangerous man, and it is well that he fights on our side."

"What shall we do?" his wife asked worriedly.

"Do? Why I still want my lunch, old woman, as I have for fifty years. After that, I will go with Salezar, and you will go to your sister's. Stay there until it is over. You must not go near Carmelita and the child. Tell no one, not even your sister where they are hiding." Tears spilled down the woman's hickory face now lined with deep wrinkles. Antonito reached over and wiped them away, then leaned forward and kissed his wife for the last time. Then the door burst inward; several of Salezar's soldiers rushed in, grabbed the old man roughly, and propelled him through the door while the old woman screamed at them. In seconds they were gone, leaving the old woman crying alone in her grief.

Antonito Montoya sat patiently on the provided stool with his hands bound behind his back. He looked around at the bare room, wondering if this was where he would die. A door opened behind him and he twisted on the stool to see Salezar enter with two of his men. One was a great brute, known only as Mateo, whose muscles rippled beneath his dirty shirt. Montoya had seen how cruel this man could be one day when a dog would not stop barking at him. He had crushed the animal to death with his bare hands as if the dog was nothing more than discarded paper. Thinking of it now made his heart heavy against his ribs.

"So, you are the source of my irritation," Salezar said quiet pleasantly. He shook his head and a cruel smile formed on his flat features. "For an old man, Señor Montoya, you are very wise. I give you that. And using the woman to gain information from me. The oldest deception known to man, and I fell for it so easily, did I not?" Salezar walked around the naked room smiling to himself. "Of course the woman did provide some pleasure," Salezar admitted, "and will again as soon as you tell me where she has taken the boy." Salezar saw the surprise in Montoya's eyes before they resumed their blank stare.

"I do not know where she is nor will I give you the names of those men who will one day see you hang. Therefore, you may as well kill me now."

Salezar ignored both the threat and the invitation. "You

didn't think I knew about the boy, did you? That he belonged to your son and to the woman I bedded every night. I know why Ignacia took the woman. Carmelita Torres is very skillful in bed."

"Your days are numbered, Salezar. It started when you chose Zack McClendon as a target. He is not a man that can be intimidated. But you know this all ready. That is why you chose to hang him."

Salezar stopped his walking and stepped close to Montoya, his face revealing his true feeling. It did not matter to him now, for this old man would be dead soon.

"The gringo will pay for what he did, I promise you. And so will all those stupid trappers who venture into New Mexico. I made the *Tejanos* beg for water like little children as we marched them across La Jornada del Muerto, and they are the bravest of all gringos."

Montoya looked Salezar squarely in the face. "But they had no guns and McClendon and the others do. In the end, you will be the one begging for your miserable life." The old man spat at Salezar. Before he could prepare himself, Salezar delivered a stinging blow to the side of his face. The Mexican fell from the stool, but was picked up roughly and sat back down. Blood trickled from his mouth.

"Give me the names of those I seek," Salezar said coldly. The old man clamped his lips together and picked out a smudge on the far wall to concentrate on against the pain he knew was coming.

"Before you die, old man, I want you to know that I will find the woman and the child. I will give the woman to my men for their enjoyment and the child will lose his blood on my saber, this is a promise." If these words were meant to have an impact on Montoya, outwardly it failed. On the inside, Montoya was praying his last to the virgin Mary when a small rope dropped over his head and yanked him backward, shutting off his breathing. The brute, Mateo, who had smashed the dog in a fit of rage, delivered blow after blow

140

to the old man's chest until the bones offered no further resistance to his punches. Montoya was then dumped out in the street beside the bloating body of the jailer as a vivid reminder to those who dared to raise their hands against Damasio Salezar.

CHAPTER 15

Don Diego Domingo rode through the deserted streets of Santa Fe a few minutes after Montoya's body had been dumped beside the jailer. He pressed his lips together to hide his anger and rode straight over to Armijo's office.

Governor Armijo was in a jovial mood. He ushered Domingo into his office and placed a glass of wine in his hands. Considering the fact that the town was under siege, Armijo seemed altogether too calm for Domingo's liking.

"It is always good to have old friends stop by," Armijo said as he took his seat behind the beautifully carved oak desk. "How is your lovely daughter, Magalena?"

"She is fine, Governor Armijo, but I come to you with a grave matter."

Armijo took a sip of wine and settled back in his chair. "What is the problem?"

"What is the problem?" Don Domingo repeated, an incredulous expression spreading across his tanned features. "Governor Armijo, do you not see what is going on around you? Right now, there are two men lying dead in the street. There is no one on the streets and businesses are boarded up. Santa Fe is gripped by fear.''

"Oh, that,'' Armijo said, waving his half-empty glass in the air. "Damasio tells me these men were responsible for freeing two murderers from jail. Gringos. When these men are found, life will be back to normal, you will see. For now, everybody is afraid these two killers will break into their houses. That is why the homes are locked and the curtains pulled. Damasio has his men out searching for them now.''

"But there is strong talk of rebellion. People are wondering if Salezar speaks for the Governor since he has implemented martial law.''

"The people do not understand. Salezar is merely carrying out lawful orders to apprehend these two murderers, nothing more. I have given him full authority and a free hand in this matter. If we are to continue trading with the Americans, we must insure these gringos that if they break Mexican Law, they will pay dearly.'' Don Domingo could see that Salezar had either duped the governor in a grand way or the wily Armijo was putting up a front so the world would think that nothing more was going on other than an attempt to capture two killers.

Don Domingo rose from his chair without ever having tasted the wine. "I must get back to the hacienda then, Governor Armijo.''

"Give my best to your lovely daughter.'' Armijo smiled broadly. "Has a wedding date been set?'' Domingo shook his head, thinking the charade would soon end with Salezar's death. He would kill the man himself before he allowed his daughter to marry that cold-blooded killer.

While Peck Overstreet and Skin Ledbetter talked about old times and the impending trouble with Salezar, Zack wandered down to the rushing stream in the cooling air of late afternoon. Not one to sit around, McClendon wished now he had gone back into town with Chaves. . . . He owed Montoya that much and more. He heard voices and looked upstream to see Pauli near the water's edge, stooping over and picking up rocks. On a nearby rock, Carmelita Torres sat watching the laughing boy. He held up a stone for her to see before tossing it into the foaming waters. McClendon found himself wandering in their direction.

Carmelita looked up at the tall trapper with the gunmetal gray eyes and saw the warmth that lay there waiting to be tapped. She offered him a smile. The boy brought him a rock to examine. McClendon stooped down and picked up the boy, who was nearly wet from head to toe.

"Let's see what you got there boy?" McClendon said. Pauli, with his face beaming, showed him the shiny rock he held tightly in his little fist.

"See," the boy said, pushing the rock close to McClendon's face.

"Why, boy, you going to make a first-rate prospector one day. See those flecks? See how the sun catches the color?" The boy looked closely, his eyes large. "That's gold, boy." Pauli's eyes grew even larger and he wiggled his way out of McClendon's arms and ran to his mother.

"Mommy, Mommy, I found gold. Now we are rich!" The small boy held out the rock for his mother. "For you, Mommy. I'll find us more," and away the child darted back to the water. McClendon squatted down by the woman.

"Is this really gold?" she asked.

"Lot of men would think so," Zack said, smiling. "Except it ain't. It's only fool's gold." He saw the hope fade from her eyes.

"You shouldn't deceive Pauli that way."

"Where's the harm? The boy is having a good time, let him be." The woman's eyes softened once more.

"You like children?"

"Never had much experience either way," McClendon said, "with me and Peck in the mountains mosttimes."

"You have a natural, easy way about you. Pauli senses it. Normally he won't have anything to do with men . . . other than his grandfather." Carmelita choked back tears.

McClendon reached out and touched the woman's shoulders. "You got to be brave for the boy." He felt her shiver beneath his touch and drew his hand quickly away. "I'm sorry, I didn't mean to startle you."

"It is okay. I am just tired of men thinking they can have their way with me, because of Salezar." Then her eyes flashed and her face hardened. "I hated every minute, every time he touched me." She looked at McClendon who saw the pain she had endured with Salezar. "I am not a whore, Señor McClendon."

"Please, call me Zack. And I wasn't thinking of you in such terms. You did more than most women would be willing to do under the circumstances, knowing that Salezar was responsible for Ignacia's death." Her sadness came back.

"Pauli looks just like his father. I thank the Blessed Mary for giving him to me every morning."

"You know, I've been doing a little thinking since Chaves and the others left," Zack said, trying to steer her away from her sadness. The way he saw it, there would be plenty of it to go around later before Salezar was stopped.

"And what is that?"

"How much influence does this Salezar have over Armijo?"

"Ha, Armijo is a vain, egotistical man that cares nothing about his people, only how much money he gets from the American traders. He is afraid of Salezar and can do nothing to stop his madness."

"About what I figured," Zack said, cutting himself off a piece of tobacco. "How long do you think it will take Salezar to figure out that Chaves is part of the rebellion? It's a fact, Chaves has a deep hatred for his uncle. Stands to reason anything he does to undermine the government will hasten Salezar's downfall as well."

"So?"

"Got a strong hunch, we all better drift north to Taos until we can get better organized. Salezar or some of his men will be out here snooping around by morning, less I've forgotten how polecats think."

Carmelita clearly had not thought of this happening and neither had Chaves when they rode in two hours later with the grim news of Montoya's death. Chaves admitted he might have increased Salezar's suspicions by removing Montoya's body from the street.

"That will bring him out here on the run, for sure," McClendon said. "We best pack what things we need, food, blankets and such, and get out of here before it's too late."

"I could not leave the body of Antonito Montoya exposed to the dogs like some common criminal," Chaves said defensively.

"Understand your motivation, Chaves. I would have done the same. But we best get to riding because we ain't got near enough men to meet Salezar head on now."

Chaves understood the logic and reluctantly agreed.

They were five miles away and riding a narrow, pine-studded ridge when McClendon pointed across the valley at the gray-black smoke rising in the distance.

Chaves's eyes narrowed with hate. "Salezar! He has set fire to my home."

"Hell, we'll pitch in and build you another one," Peck said. Lafe Ingram and the others nodded their heads.

"You were right, Señor McClendon. Had we stayed our bodies would be used to add grease to the fire."

McClendon looked at the woman, who seemed to have crawled into a shell since learning of Montoya's death. She had remained silent throughout their packing and leaving. Even Pauli sensed something was gravely wrong with his mother and chose to ride with her rather than McClendon, who first offered him a ride. The woman was carrying around a lot of hate. McClendon only hoped it didn't come out at the wrong time when Salezar was in his sights.

The leaping, yellow flames were reflected in Salezar's cold eyes as he watched the tinder-dry house being consumed by fire. He let his eyes trail to the higher reaches lying behind the ranch as if he could see anyone hiding there in the thick timber. It had been a bitter day for him. First, losing the prisoners, then learning of Carmelita's betrayal and Montoya's involvement. And finally this: Manuel Chaves. The name burned in his brain as brightly as the fire before him now. Who else would betray him? Lieutenant Vallejo? He was ambitious and looking to gain favor with Armijo at every opportunity. Were there others as well? Salezar looked around at his men who stood patiently by waiting for further orders.

Salezar wheeled on his heels and mounted the silver-gray Arabian. By heavens, he would smash anyone who got in his way, including Armijo if need be.

In the soft glow of the overhead moon, the small group trailed silently down out of the foothills and over to Don Diego's hacienda. Chaves wanted to stop by, warn Diego, and tell him of their change in plans.

Don Diego was greatly concerned over the news Chaves carried, and, while he had his cook prepare them a meal, they discussed what the next steps should be.

"We can forget any help from Governor Armijo," Don Diego told them. "In his own way, he is as afraid of what Salezar is doing as any of us."

"My uncle deserves such a man as Damasio Salezar," Manuel Chaves interjected. "He would not listen to me, would not limit Salezar's power, and now he is beyond anyone's control." Chaves was thinking of his burned home and his voice reflected his bitterness towards the man. "If Salezar is not stopped, he will soon take over as governor and there will be no peace for either Mexican or American." They were all seated in Domingo's spacious den having a glass of wine. Pauli had fallen asleep on a nearby couch while Carmelita Torres helped prepare the meal.

"What you say is true, Amigo," Don Diego said with sadness. "As I passed through Santa Fe this afternoon, it was like a ghost town. The people have fled either to Albuquerque or Taos. No one is open for business. Any American traders that have not left town are now being held in the stockade at the Palace of the Governor's. This I learned from one of my vaqueros just a little while ago. Salezar has a stranglehold on Santa Fe, and if we don't release it soon, the town will wither and die."

Doña Magalena Domingo came into the room and immediately everyone was on their feet with hat in hand. She radiated beauty, and her full skirt twirled about her slender frame with an energy of its own. McClendon as well as the others appeared struck by her natural beauty, delicate features, long flowing hair and flashing eyes. Poised and self-confident, she smiled at everyone as the Don introduced her around.

She paused in front of McClendon. "So, I am told they also call you Straight Arrow?" Her voice was soft, yet vibrated with life. McClendon appeared momentarily at a loss for words.

"Go on, boy, tell the lady how you come by that handle," Peck urged, enjoying Zack's discomfort at being singled out. Zack shot Peck a look that could kill.

"Wasn't much," Zack mumbled. "Maybe later."

"I am glad you chose to help my people. We are most grateful."

"Yeah, well, don't go thanking me too soon. It's going to take help from a lot of folks to move against Salezar."

Just then, Carmelita came out of the kitchen to announce dinner. McClendon caught the measured looks between the two women. Chaves made the introductions. Doña Magalena smiled and asked Carmelita about her son, putting them both at ease.

Later over coffee, Don Diego asked McClendon if he had

any ideas how to approach the problem with Salezar and hopefully prevent bloodshed. All eyes focused on the big trapper.

"We're all willing to help as much as we can, but ultimately, it won't do. It will take men like yourself and Manuel Chaves, who command respect from the citizens of New Mexico, to put things right again. If we bring in a group of Americans to fight the battle alone, Salezar will use it as just another example of Yankee aggression and gain even wider support and control over the area."

Don Diego nodded his head in agreement. "You are correct, Señor McClendon. We must stop this madman at all costs and I pledge my help and those of my men to this end."

"I will stay here with Don Diego and help get things organized from this end," Chaves told McClendon.

"I will have the guest rooms prepared. It is best you spend the night here," Don Diego said.

"But what about Salezar?" McClendon said. "I don't want to endanger you or your daughter by staying. Salezar will trust no one now."

"Do not worry about Damasio," Doña Magalena said lightly. "He is in love with me and thinks we will be married soon. I can handle him still." McClendon had his doubts, but kept them to himself.

"If it's all the same to you, Don Diego, we best sleep in the outbuildings. That way there will be less chance of waking up to a surprise."

"I have men posted at several places along the roads approaching the hacienda. If trouble comes, we will be warned in plenty of time," Don Diego said confidently. The men stood up to leave and Doña Magalena turned to Carmelita.

"There is an empty room next to mine at the head of the stairs for you and Pauli. Why don't you tuck him in. It will be a rough ride to Taos tomorrow."

Carmelita thanked the woman and turned to pick up the sleeping boy, but McClendon reached around her with strong arms and scooped him up. "It's the least I can do," he said to the surprised woman. The men left to find their own bunks, except for Peck and Skin Ledbetter who retired to the porch to smoke their pipes.

When McClendon came back down the stairs, he found Doña Magalena pouring brandy. The room was empty except for a large dark-faced Mexican who was cleaning up the room.

"That will be all, Joaquin. You can finish tomorrow," Magalena said to the Mexican. Joaquin Cobo bowed slightly and left the room. Magalena smiled at McClendon.

"Will you have a brandy with me?"

McClendon didn't really want anything to drink. There was much to think about, so much to do, yet he found himself next to the perfumed woman accepting the proffered drink as if it were the most natural thing in the world for him to have a brandy before retiring.

"You know my father wants me to go with you to Taos tomorrow," she said as they sat down in chairs opposite one another.

"I think that would be wise, considering the state of affairs. Salezar won't look too kindly either at you or Don Diego if he learns the truth."

"I didn't lead him on, Mr. McClendon," Magalena said forthrightly. "Mexican men, especially those with power, assume too much in matters of the heart. I think it may be a born weakness." Magalena dazzled him with her smile.

"I simply meant Salezar is a dangerous man who won't let even love stand in his way of getting what he wants. I didn't mean to imply anything else."

"Believe me, *I* know Damasio Salezar better than most people. I even know that his mistress now sleeps upstairs." McClendon looked shocked. She laughed at seeing his face. "It is perfectly okay, don't you see. How can I be jealous of someone I do not love?" McClendon could see the point.

"Will you come with us then?" Zack tasted the brandy for the first time. It went down as smooth as water from a Rocky

150

Mountain stream. Don Diego kept very expensive liquor, he concluded.

"Would it please you?"

McClendon didn't know what to say to the woman, he was caught so completely off guard by the question.

"You do not need to look sick at the prospect," Doña Magalena said, smiling at his obvious discomfort.

"I'm beginning to think, Doña Magalena, that you say things that are meant to shock, to keep your opponent off balance."

"So now I am your opponent?"

"If you are, you are the most beautiful one I ever faced," Zack replied, getting his feet beneath him once more. It was Doña Magalena who was momentarily derailed by his frankness.

She laughed and set aside her glass. "I like you, Zack McClendon. You are so unlike other men I have known. You wear your thoughts and principles close to the surface so people will know who you really are and what it is you stand for."

"Didn't know I was that easy to read," McClendon said, downing his drink before getting to his feet. "Guess that's the reason I was never any good at card playing." The woman stood up and moved closer to Zack. Her eyes were like two dark pools reflected by moonlight, and, without meaning to, McClendon took her hand and kissed it while his heart beat heavily in his chest. He felt foolish for having done such a thing, yet the woman seemed pleased by his manners.

"I hope to see you at breakfast," was all he could say.

Doña Magalena tilted her head slightly. "Perhaps."

McClendon stood on the wide veranda, breathing deeply the night air heavily laced with pipe tobacco. What was he thinking, he wondered. There was no time for such antics, yet it pleased him to have a woman like Doña Magalena showing a little interest. Peck broke in on his thoughts.

"Me and Skin been talking, Zack. Suppose one of us hightail it up the trail to the post at Apache Canyon? We could warn

151

any traders coming along and might pick up a man or two as well." McClendon paused to consider the request. It did make sense. Even if no other Americans were willing to help, it would at least keep them out of the way until the troubles were over.

"Sounds reasonable to me."

"I could drop by the post and cut back along them foothills and meet you in Taos tomorrow afternoon," Skin said.

"Who says I can't do the same?" Peck spoke up.

"I do, old coon. You don't know this country like I do."

"Ha, ain't seed the day I couldn't foller a drainage good as any mountain man ever pulled on a moccasin."

"And I agree with that assumption," Skin Ledbetter said, taking his pipe from between his teeth. "Only thing, them drainage systems run from east to west. Less'n you know where to cut across, you'd be a week gettin' to Taos."

"You two can argue until the sun comes up, but I'm going to bed." McClendon stepped off the veranda and walked back along the hacienda towards the bunkhouse. A figure emerged from the shadows of a shrub near him. McClendon had his pistol out and cocked within the next breath before he realized it was a woman standing there. She moved closer and McClendon recognized the slender form of Carmelita Torres.

"Woman, you could have gotten yourself killed sneaking up on a man that way." He reholstered his gun. She stopped only inches from him and stood there looking up in the soft moonlight.

"I only wanted to thank you for being so kind to Pauli . . . and to me." Her voice was soft and yielding in the night air.

"Least I could do seeing's how the boy just lost his grandpa on account of me." He saw the shiny tears that streaked her face as a sob tore from her. Instinctively, Zack pulled her to him and held her while she cried softly in the hollow of his neck. After a few minutes, she got herself under control, but stayed in his arms.

"Do you want to come back to the room with me? There is

152

a back way into the house." She pulled slightly away from him and looked up at his shaded face. She kissed him lightly at first and then with a deeper urgency.

McClendon came up for air, his breathing ragged. "Lord, gal, but you make a man feel good," he said thickly. She flashed him a smile.

"Come," she said, taking his hand. McClendon hesitated.

"I don't want nothing out of gratitude," he said.

She laughed softly. "You men are all alike." She led him into the shadows where a set of stairs led upwards.

From an unlit window above them, a slim hand allowed the curtains to fall back in place after they had gone.

CHAPTER 16

During the night, drunken soldiers roamed the streets of Santa Fe, shooting their pistols at imaginary shadows, breaking into stores, stealing whatever they wanted, and generally terrorizing those few souls who ventured out of hiding. The cantinas had no patrons other than the rowdy soldiers. The frightened owners dared not ask for money, and most just prayed they would soon run out of liquor so Salezar's men would leave.

Around the plaza, activity was intense. Frequent shots rang out, mixing with the laughter and cries of the low-lifes of Santa Fe who congregated with the soldiers and beckoning whores who were as drunk as the patrons. Men were knifed in alleyways for the few pesos they carried. Others were simply hit over the head with the butts of pistols. When light spread over the city the next morning, drunken soldiers lay asleep beside the bodies of those killed during the night.

Benjamin Delaney was up early, filled with the eagerness to get under way now that he had worked out an agreement with

Armijo. Why make this his last trip, now that he could become wealthy and with the governor's blessing?

Pete Hamilton knocked at his door and Delaney let him in, taking note of Hamilton's tired expression and bloodshot eyes. The man was plainly worried.

"You look as though you've not slept," Delaney said, wiping away the remnants of lather from his face.

"Couldn't, not with all the shootings and horses thundering past my window. Haven't you looked outside?"

"Why no, what is wrong?" Delaney splashed on a sweet aftershave, pulled back the curtains over his window and looked down into the street. The plaza was a shambles, littered with the bodies of dead Mexicans. Goods from looted stores lay scattered among the dead and the pigs and goats rummaging for food.

"Was there a riot?" Delaney asked incredulously, turning back to his wagon driver.

"It's got something to do with McClendon. He was sprung from the poky by friendly Mexicans, and this Salezar fellow's mad as hell. Been shooting his people left and right." Hamilton's voice betrayed the fear he felt about the rising tensions.

Delaney pulled on his silk coat and set his panama on his head at a rakish angle. He looked at himself in the mirror, turning his head from side to side to study his profile. The roughly dressed Hamilton stood by, clearly distressed at this display of vanity.

"If you ask me, this brute McClendon should get his just deserts. Men like him don't know how to act civilized. That's what spending years in those godforsaken mountains will do to a man. I, on the other hand, had a long chat with Governor Armijo yesterday and, as only gentlemen can do, we have formed a pact. Together, we will bring in goods from St. Louis in as many wagons as we can put together." Delaney smiled smugly. "And of course duty free. One of the benefits of having the governor as your partner." Delaney laughed and slapped Hamilton on the shoulder. "Come, I'll buy us breakfast and we'll be off."

Hamilton picked up Delaney's bags, feeling a certain amount of relief to be getting out of Santa Fe. He wished now that he had left with the others yesterday, but he couldn't force himself to abandon "Dandy Delaney," as his men had come to call him behind his back.

Downstairs, Hamilton tied their bags to a pack mule Delaney had bought off Lafe Ingram. Hamilton wondered where the mule skinner was. His men had scurried out of town the next morning after McClendon and Overstreet were thrown in jail. Hamilton realized how dumb he was for staying behind. He looked up the quiet street, feeling the tension behind every closed and locked door.

Delaney came out of the shabby hotel, looking surprised. "I can't find anyone to pay for the rooms. I checked the kitchen and the stove is cold. We'll have no breakfast after all."

"We can grab a bite at the post in Apache Canyon," Peter Hamilton said, eager to leave this place behind. Delaney stood on the boardwalk with his thumbs hooked in his fancy vest as a group of Mexican dragoons swept into the plaza, their brightly colored uniforms and flashing sabers a reminder that Santa Fe under martial law could be a dangerous place for Americans.

"We best get going, Mr. Delaney," Hamilton said, mounting his horse. He didn't like the looks of the hard-eyed soldiers.

"Oh, very well, Peter. But do try to calm down. Remember I have the Governor in my hip pocket. Nothing can possibly go wrong."

"That might be, Mr. Delaney, but if it's all the same to you, I'll feel a lot better when we put a good days ride between us and Salezar. The man is pure poison."

They shared a late breakfast of beans and tortillas at Canoncito along with fifteen white traders who had just completed the last leg of their journey before reaching Santa Fe. None were happy over the state of affairs in town. They had sweated, starved and nearly died of thirst crossing the Cimarron cutoff only to be told traders were no longer welcomed. What were they supposed to do with the eight heavily loaded wagons, they asked the Mexican who owned the post. The fat Mexican offered to buy what they had for less than what they themselves had paid. The post owner shrugged and turned away, leaving the Americans no better off than before.

Hamilton tightened the cinch on his red sorrel and climbed aboard. He led the pack mule over to where the confused traders stood talking the situation over.

"Any more traders you know coming down the trail?" Hamilton asked.

"Suppose to be a wagon train behind us. They were looking to leave St. Louis about ten days after we pulled out. Don't know if they did or not. Why you ask mister?" the weary-faced leader of the group asked.

"Just curious is all."

"You just come from Santa Fe. Hell, we can practically see it from here. Is it as bad as this old Mexican tells us?"

Hamilton nodded. "Worse. I saw over a dozen dead men in the streets this morning. Soldiers are everywhere, drunk and hard-assed mean. Ain't no trading being done at all. If I was you, I'd trail them wagons south to Albuquerque."

The man's shoulder visibly slumped. "Mister, we about played out. Don't know if any of us is up to much more of this."

"It's either that or sit tight here and hope the trouble passes in a week or two." Delaney came out of the outhouse, pulling on his fancy coat.

"Week or two," a man spoke up. "Latham, I for one ain't hanging around here for that long. I say we push on to Albuquerque like this man says."

"Don't bust a gut, Donaldson," the man called Latham said.

Delaney looked the small group of traders over carefully. Hamilton didn't like the look in Delaney's eyes. It usually meant Delaney was about to make a snap decision Hamilton was sure he would not like.

157

"Gentlemen, while I was enjoying a moment of solitude, it occurred to me that I might be of some help to you in your predicament." The trail-weary men studied Delaney as if looking at a new species.

Finally, the one called Latham spoke. "How's that?"

"Well, I am prepared to buy your goods at a reduced rate of, oh, . . . let's say, two hundred per wagon above your cost."

"Hell, that ain't much better than the Mex offered," Donaldson interjected. "Them trade goods are worth more than five times that amount."

Delaney smiled. "True, but don't forget, I'm willing to absorb the five hundred dollars in duties you'll be facing. Had to pay it myself."

"Why should you take on our goods?" Latham asked. "Thought you was headed back to St. Louis as fast as them horses could take you?"

"I am, gentlemen, but if it means delaying my trip for a day or so, it's not a problem."

"How can you sell goods in Santa Fe after this man here," Donaldson indicated Hamilton sitting quietly by on his horse, "tells us it ain't even safe to ride down there, much less try to do business?"

"That is the risk I am willing to take," Delaney said. "What you have to decide is whether you want to make a small profit now or take a chance on reaching Albuquerque safely."

Peter Hamilton looked at Delaney as if the man had lost his mind. If he was crazy enough to buy these traders' goods, Delaney could just leave him out of the deal. He was heading east, with or without Delaney.

The traders walked back to their wagons to discuss Delaney's offer. Angry words drifted back to them as things heated up.

"Ain't staying another day, Mr. Delaney," Hamilton said softly.

Benjamin Delaney looked up at Hamilton. "Come now, Ben. I told you Governor Armijo and I have an agreement.

Both of us stand to make a huge profit from this and without much effort on our part.''

''What you don't have is an agreement with Captain Salezar, and he's the one running the show back there, case you ain't noticed.''

''I'm sure Governor Armijo can handle a captain in his army without any problems. Tell you what, Pete, what do you say to two hundred extra dollars for staying one more day?''

Peter Hamilton shook his head. ''Dead men don't need money, Mr. Delaney, not even two hundred extra. You got a pack mule loaded with Mexican silver and gold. That ought to be enough for any man.'' Hamilton stepped down from his saddle and stood by the pack mule to remove his belongings if the traders agreed to Delaney's offer. ''Them traders sell to you, I'm riding on alone.''

''It isn't safe, man.''

''Rather take my chances with what's out there then trust a drunken Mexican soldier with my life.''

Delaney could see Hamilton had made up his mind. ''Very well, but you owe me for the horse,'' Delaney said.

Hamilton looked at Delaney with disbelief. ''You said the horse belonged to me for staying behind with you.''

Delaney smiled coldly. ''Staying with me means just that. Now you're talking about pulling out, leaving me behind. That wasn't the deal.''

Peter Hamilton slowly realized just how greedy a man Benjamin Delaney was. Money and the power over other people were all he lived for. Hamilton handed over the seventy-five dollars to Delaney, who counted the money.

''Don't forget the saddle was twenty-five.'' Hamilton fished out the extra money and shoved it into the man's hand. He removed his warbag from the pack animal and tied it behind the sorrel. ''You didn't have to pay me just yet. They might not agree to sell to me,'' Delaney said, glancing at the traders who still seemed to be in deep conversation.

Peter Hamilton looked at Delaney across the back of his

saddle as he checked to be sure his bedroll was securely tied. "Don't need to. Through riding for a man like you." Hamilton threw a leg over his horse and loped off without looking back.

Delaney watched the man ride off. "What the devil's got into him?" he wondered. The traders came over. "Well, gentlemen, what's it going to be?" If they weren't interested in his deal, Delaney figured to catch up with Hamilton and smooth things over between them.

"We accept your offer, Mr. Delaney, but with some reluctance."

"Good! Let's get started for Santa Fe then. The sooner we get there the sooner you can have your money."

The traders looked at one another. "That ain't the deal," Latham spoke up. "We want our money now. We figure to turn back."

"But gentlemen, surely you can see I can't drive eight wagons to Santa Fe by myself?"

"It's either pay us or we take our chances in Albuquerque."

Delaney held up his hand. "Okay, okay. You have me over a barrel." Delaney walked back to the pack mule to get the money.

"It's us you have over a barrel, Delaney," the outspoken Donaldson said. Several traders shook their heads in agreement.

"Tell you what," Delaney said, unperturbed by the man's comment, "I got an extra hundred for any man that'll drive a wagon down to Santa Fe. Now that's a lot for such a short distance, but I need to get these wagons to town today. The rest of you can even stay here at the post until the others get back this afternoon. What do you say?"

"I'll drive a wagon," Latham spoke up, thinking he and his family could use the extra money, since they were selling out so cheap.

"Hell, if we going to drive these wagons to Santa Fe, we may as well sell the goods ourselves," Donaldson said.

"You can," Delaney said, "but don't forget, the risk is

160

yours then, not mine." In the end, the traders sold to Delaney. Latham and Donaldson along with six others finally agreed to drive the wagons into Santa Fe.

As the slow procession crossed Arrayo Hondo, three miles out of town, a group of soldiers under the command of a slovenly sergeant by the name of Ramon Garcia intercepted them. It was obvious the Mexicans had been drinking heavily as they rode up shouting and waving their pistols about. The hot dust rose up around the wagons like a yellow curtain.

Sergeant Garcia drew up in front of Delaney, who was leading the way on his white mule, and said something in Spanish. Delaney looked pained at having dirtied his suit in such manner.

Garcia switched to broken English. "Where are you going, señor fancy pants?" he asked Delaney. Garcia's men hooted and laughed at the name-calling. Garcia swayed in the saddle, and the smell of his dirty, sweat-stained uniform assaulted Delaney's nostrils.

"We have trade goods and I should remind you sergeant that I am a personal friend of Governor Manuel Armijo," Delaney said, not intimidated in the least.

"Oh ho," Garcia said, looking around at his men and rolling his eyes. "The gringo is mucho dangerous, no?" His men howled with laughter. Several rode close, lifting the corners of blankets to see what goods were underneath.

"See here, you men leave those wagons alone. Part of these goods belong to Governor Armijo," Delaney said, hotly. Latham and the others never moved or opened their mouths, all thinking how smart they had been to sell to the pretentious Delaney.

"You say half of thees things belongs to Armijo?" the drunken sergeant asked.

"That is correct, now get out of our way, we have business to conduct."

"I don't thin so, señor fancy pants," Garcia said, tilting a bottle to his bearded lips.

Delaney looked at the Mexican blankly, "why, whatever do you mean? I told you I am a personal friend of Governor Armijo. I demand safe passage for my men and wagons."

Garcia's eyes turned cruel, "you demand nothing, gringo." A pistol fired and Delaney's panama flew from his head. A Mexican soldier waved his smoking gun, laughing insanely.

"You are all under arrest by orders of Capitán Damasio Salezar." Garcia spoke rapidly to his men in Spanish and several soldiers rode over and took the white men's guns. "You will follow me," the sergeant ordered Delaney.

The bareheaded Delaney looked back at the white-faced Latham. "Don't worry, I'll straighten everything out with Armijo," he said confidently. "I'm sure he will have this pig of a sergeant shot immediately."

But Delaney was given no chance to see Armijo. He and the others were thrown into a crowded room where eight others like them were being confined. The sweltering air in the room reeked of sweat and body wastes. Delaney immediately became sick and threw up on the suit he was so fond of. It had been a long fall since early morning for the proud Delaney.

CHAPTER 17

McClendon crept down the backstairs an hour before sunrise, the feel and taste of the woman still strong in his mind. Peck was already up and smoking his pipe when he passed the corral.

"Don't need to ask which one you spent the night with. Know soon enough when they come down fer breakfast."

"You spying on me, old man," Zack said, trying to sound tough, but failing. He was feeling too good about himself right now. He wanted it to last a little longer before the day's problems crept back in and pushed aside the nice things.

"Ain't me sneaking down backstairs in the dead of night," Peck chuckled.

"Only reason you ain't, is because nobody invited you up."

"You got a pint, boy."

"Others up?" Zack asked.

"Only Skin and me and he's roostin'. What time you reckon they put on the coffee around here?" McClendon had turned to the corral, where he found his big buckskin nuzzling his arm. He stroked the horse's ears and neck, the weight of the day settling over him like a black cloud.

"When we see how many trappers we got to help us, I figure we'll sneak back here to Don Diego's and formulate our battle plans with the women out of the way."

"Reckon that Houseman fellar made it over to Taos?" Peck asked as Skin Ledbetter came up grinning at McClendon, who ignored the insinuation.

"What I wonder more than that, is the fact he was hiding something from us. Why he decided to head to Taos is anybody's guess."

As the sun bled over Thompson Peak in the Sangre de Cristo Mountains to the east, the small group was cinching their saddles for the sixty-odd-mile ride to Taos. Doña Magalena had been rather cool to McClendon after their conversation of the night before, but Zack merely thought it was because the old Don was forcing her to go with them to Taos that had her upset.

"You sure you know where to go now?" Manuel Chaves asked as they climbed into their saddles. They even had a small paint for Pauli to ride.

"Done told you," Skin Ledbetter said, "I know every rock around that country, especially where the Rio Chiquito and Grande del Rancho meet. Trapped beaver between them drainage systems of the Fernando Mountains." Don Diego insisted on sending one of his men to Apache Canyon to warn other traders, thus settling the matter between Peck and Skin over who was going.

"You be careful, Chaves," McClendon warned. "Now that Salezar knows which side of the river you're riding, he'll be after your hide as much as he's after mine or Peck's. Same goes for you, Don Diego, as soon as the truth gets out how you helped us."

"We will be careful, señor," Don Diego answered for both of them. "As soon as you get enough of your friends together,

164

hurry back. Manuel and I will be organizing as many as we can here."

They pulled away from the ranch in a thin cloud of dust with Skin Ledbetter leading the procession followed by the two women and then the rest of the men. By mid-morning they had picked up the Rio Grande and followed the winding river for twenty-five miles as it ate its way through mesa country. At noon they stopped to rest the horses and eat a bite beneath Black Mesa, which jutted above the river a thousand feet.

While Peck built a fire to make coffee, McClendon took Pauli on a short walk along the crumbling, weathered country. The boy was delighted and skipped ahead of the towering trapper, picking up colored rocks along the water's edge.

Carmelita smiled at the tall man and little boy running along beside him, while Peck was just plain dumbfounded. Zack had never shown an interest in children. Doña Magalena sat on a rock nearby, watching the proceedings with cool appraisal.

Peck shook his head and added coffee to the pot of boiling water. Zack couldn't see it building, but he could. Before this party was over, old Zack was gonna have to choose between two women, that is, if they didn't settle it sooner. Peck had observed the measured looks this morning, the flashing eyes of Carmelita Torres as if saying she had already put her mark on McClendon by virtue of last night. Peck knew better. A woman roped Zack would need more than that to hold him. . . . Course there was the kid.

"Strangely beautiful country, almost haunting." Lafe Ingram cut in on his thoughts. "Rather cool here in the shade of that big flat-looking rock."

"That rock is Black Mesa. About a hundred years ago, a party of Spaniards ventured into this country and was pinned down close to this spot by hostile Tewas from atop that mesa. Before the day was done, the Rio Grande flowed red with Spanish blood. Story goes, not a single man escaped."

"What Peck says is true," Skin Ledbetter said from where

he was lounging. "Back a ways in that little canyon," Skin pointed to his shoulder, "found a rusted breastplate all battered to hell. Nearby was a few scattered bones and a skull coyotes been gnawing on. You can't get an Injun to spend the night within ten miles of these parts. Says it's haunted by ghosts of the Spaniards that walk around late in the evening. A few Injuns swear they seen the sun reflected on their armor."

Fifteen miles further, found them at the entrance to a deep gorge where the Rio Grande had cut through the desert bed centuries before. It was here Skin Ledbetter held to the right of the gorge and skirted a mesa that formed one side of the gorge. They climbed steadily upward and across Hondo Canyon that gave them a commanding view of the valley floor to the west and north. Through the shimmering heat, flanked by the rising mountains to the east, lay the dark mud-colored town of Taos some ten miles distant. Beyond was the snow-capped peak of Taos Mountain, a sacred place to the Pueblo Indians who had lived at its base for some eight hundred years.

Skin Ledbetter followed the Rio Chiquito east into a steep canyon filled with thick timber and large boulders. Where the river cut away from the side of the mountain there was a cabin built among the pines. Deeply shaded, the cabin was nearly invisible from the rushing river.

They rode up to the dark cabin and stepped down. Carmelita gave Zack's arm a gentle squeeze as he helped her down from her horse. He turned to help Magalena but Lafe Ingram was already offering her his hand.

"Been a number of horses here recently," Peck said, studying the ground. Skin banged on the door, but there was no response. McClendon turned his attentions to the surrounding woods. Something didn't seem right all of a sudden. Things were too quiet to suit him.

"Check the back, Peck," Zack said softly. Peck knew the look McClendon gave him and he eased way with his rifle. Skin pushed on the door and found it open. Lafe Ingram and the two Mexicans accompanying them took the saddle horses over to the pole corral, where a skinny pinto watched the proceedings with cautious eyes.

"Guess he won't mind if the ladies wait inside," Skin said, and pushed the door open wide. Ledbetter took one step backward, having caught the smell of fresh blood.

"What is it?" McClendon asked, seeing the old trapper tense. There was a flutter of wings in a nearby clump of willows and McClendon sprang into action with Ledbetter right behind him.

"Everybody inside!" he shouted, shoving the two women and the boy ahead of them. Skin Ledbetter covered the group with his back to the cabin wall when a shot rang out, and he gasped as a bullet caught him high in the leg. A big rifle answered the shot from the corner of the cabin where Peck was located. There was a wild burst of fire from the screen of trees as Peck, Ingram and the two Mexicans raced for the doorway. McClendon cut loose with his big rifle and heard a scream from the woods as he reached out and helped Ledbetter into the cabin. Peck slammed the door shut behind him as bullets tore splinters from the door frame.

"Carmelita, take a look and see how bad Skin is hit," McClendon ordered and stopped in mid-sentence when he saw the look of horror on the woman's ashen face. Doña Magalena was just as frightened, and it took a minute for McClendon to realize there was someone lying in the bed with the covers drawn up to his neck. Blood had seeped through the covers and puddled beneath the dead man on the floor.

"Chaves's cousin?" McClendon asked Carmelita, who nodded her head silently. Peck and the others were returning fire from the two windows. Skin Ledbetter had crammed his handkerchief into the bloody wound and limped over to the window Peck was shooting from. A bullet found its way through the chinking and struck the stove with a loud ring.

"Get down on the floor!" Zack commanded the women, going over to cover the face of the dead Mexican. The women retreated to the far wall and crouched down.

"Danged if we didn't ride into this ambush like a couple of pikers," Peck grumbled to Skin.

"Knowed I was getting old," he returned, "but this . . . ." He shook his head. McClendon eased over to them, reloading his rifle all the while.

"How many do you figure's out there?" Ingram asked, plainly worried.

"No more'n a division, I figger," Peck returned, taking aim at a shaking bush and pulling the trigger. A figure stood up and quickly flopped back down. It was enough to see the uniform.

"Damn! Them's Salezar's men," Peck said. "How the devil did they get here so fast?"

"More important, how did they know we were coming here?" McClendon said.

"Seems we got ourselves a spy back at Don Diego's," Peck said, reloading his rifle. Doña Magalena heard the remark.

"My father's men are all loyal. Many have been with him for thirty years."

"Somebody got the word out," Zack replied. "Your father hired a new man lately?" While the woman considered his question, the firing stopped and a voice called to the cabin.

"Send out the women, Chaves, you have my word they will come to no harm."

"Manuel Chaves is not here," McClendon shouted back, "who am I talking to?"

"We will take our chances here with you," Carmelita said to Zack, clutching the frightened child to her.

"I am Lieutenant Vallejo," came the reply, "and you?" Vallejo and his men had been on routine patrol to the north of town, when their man at Don Diego's brought them the news that Chaves and the others were planning to travel north to Taos. With only himself and six men, Vallejo dared not attack them while at the ranch. Instead, he determined to trap them at the cabin. He and his men had ridden most of the night and struck the undefended cabin the next morning, killing Rafa

Tafoya, Chaves's cousin, before he could even get out of bed. His only regret was that he hadn't taken the time to send one of his men back to Salezar with the news.

"Zack McClendon." They waited as the silence between the two groups increased.

"McClendon, you and the others are also under arrest. I give you three minutes to come out without your weapons. You must send the women out now!" Vallejo shouted.

"You see anything?" Zack asked the others. "Don't believe this Vallejo would be talking surrender if he had many men with him."

"Counting the two we know were hit," Peck said, "cain't be over six er eight of them."

"And that ain't enough muscle to hold the likes of us fer long," Skin grinned from the other window.

McClendon turned to Magalena who coolly held his stare. "You heard this Vallejo. You want to take your chances with the Lieutenant? Salezar would skin him alive if he let anything happen to you."

The woman came over to the window where McClendon was standing. He pulled her away from the opening. "I would rather be shot here than to accept Vallejo's protection. By now, Damasio Salezar will have learned the truth. He will feel scorned for the second time, once by his mistress and now by the woman he loved." She looked deeply into McClendon's eyes. "Damasio would only turn me over to his men until they grew tired of the pleasure. Afterward death would be a welcomed prospect."

"You don't have to worry," Zack promised. "Ain't noway we surrendering to Vallejo or to Salezar. Have no doubt we would all be shot within minutes of surrendering." Magalena touched his arm, her eyes telling him there was a chance between them yet, if only he acted.

"You best get back over to the corner with Carmelita and the boy," Zack said softly. "Expect there's going to be a little shooting before it's finished."

Doña Magalena turned as if to leave, but shouted through the open window at Vallejo. "This is Doña Magalena Domingo, Lieutenant. Do you know who I am?"

"What you up to woman?" McClendon asked, yanking her back from the window. He continued to hold her.

"Trying to give us an edge," she replied.

"Sí Señorita," Vallejo finally called back.

"Then you must know, Damasio and I are very good friends," she continued, yet remaining close to Zack. A long silence ensued.

Zack used the time to ask Peck about the rear of the cabin. He could feel Carmelita's eyes on him, but all he could see at the moment was Doña Magalena. It left him slightly embarrassed under the present circumstances.

"Ain't nothing back there but an outhouse and a big stack of firewood." McClendon had checked for a rear door the moment he had stepped into the cabin, so he knew he didn't have to worry about trouble coming from that direction. He hoped the Mexicans wouldn't think about using the firewood. Under the present circumstances, they couldn't even reach the horses without suffering casualties.

"Señorita Doña Magalena," Vallejo called, "Capitán Salezar would want you leave there immediately."

"I will not leave my friends, Lieutenant Vallejo. You leave."

The young Lieutenant looked around at his men, all wondering the same thing he was; should they simply do as Doña Magalena suggested or keep fighting? Vallejo was sure to incur the wrath of Salezar no matter what position he chose. As things stood now, he had one man dead and two wounded, one severely. That left him with a fighting force of four, counting himself. Those were not good odds even though he had the men pinned in the cabin with nowhere to go but straight out the front, directly in his line of fire. The men inside the cabin were deadly shots and did not rattle easily. By rights they should have killed them all in the yard, but for the big trapper, who pulled them together.

On the other hand, if he, Vallejo, managed to take them prisoners without harming the woman, Salezar would be duly impressed by his actions and so would Governor Armijo. It was something to consider. In the end he chose the only course open to a true soldier. Vallejo motioned for his remaining men to fan out and wait for his signal.

"Señorita Doña Magalena, you must come out now," Vallejo shouted. "Those men are wanted for murder and I, as an officer in the Mexican Government, am honor bound to bring them to justice."

"Then you will die here, Lieutenant," the woman spoke for the last time. She gave McClendon a little smile as if to say she had tried and went back to her place beside Carmelita. Neither spoke or acknowledged the presence of the other. Zack could see there was trouble brewing there in a different kind of way and he had the distinct feeling he was at the center.

A rifle sounded from the woods by the river, and one of the Mexicans standing with Lafe Ingram fell backwards with blood pouring from a head wound. The man was dead before he lost his grip on his rifle. It was a signal for the others and lead flew about the room for a few tense minutes while those in the cabin answered it in kind. Easing his big rifle across the window frame, McClendon waited for the puff of smoke to appear above a jumble of rock and cottonwoods. When it did, Zack squeezed the trigger gently on the big gun. There was no further shooting from that direction. Peck had watched the proceedings with a tight smile.

"You doing all right, boy, but whatcha gonna do 'bout that Mex slipping around back," Peck said. "Don't take a genius to figger out what he's up to."

McClendon looked up at the ceiling of peeled poles and cedar shingles. "If they ever get a fire started on the roof, they will pick us off like rats from a sinking ship." There were fewer shots from the river now, but well placed. A bullet ricocheted off an iron skillet hanging on the wall and plowed a furrow across Cap Singleton's ribs. The farmer never flinched, just stuck his rifle through the window and fired away.

"You boys give me cover. I'm going out," McClendon said, laying aside his rifle and checking the loads in his pistol.

"Just you be careful," Peck warned. "I'm too old to go huntin' fer another partner this late in life." Zack grinned crookedly at the old trapper, but said nothing.

McClendon was through the door and around the side of the cabin before any of the soldiers could react. He heard Magalena call his name but he didn't know what she was saying. Someone called from the brush at the river and McClendon went driving around the side of the cabin as fast as he could go, knowing Vallejo was probably trying to warn his man.

The Mexican soldier had an armload of wood he was piling at the back of the cabin when McClendon skidded around the corner. The surprised soldier dropped the wood as a bullet from McClendon's pistol tore through his right eye. Zack was off and running for the distant brush before the Mexican crumpled to the ground. From the safety of the rocks he called to Vallejo.

"You down to one or two men, Lieutenant. Give it up or I'm gonna be forced to kill you." From inside the cabin, Peck grinned at Skin Ledbetter.

"Kinda like old times, ain't it Skin?"

Skin Ledbetter was hurting some from the wound, but he didn't allow the pain to dampen his spirits any.

"Ain't nuthin' like old times, coon. This here is more like a cakewalk compared to the tights we been through."

"Anything worse, and you can count me out," Ingram said, wiping away the blood on the side of his face where a bullet had sent splinters of wood into the skin after striking the window jamb.

"Lafe, you got grit," Peck said. "Expect 'nother time, you woulda made a hell'va trapper." Lafe Ingram looked at Peck Overstreet, seeing the newfound respect in the grizzled man's

172

one eye. Ingram didn't know what to say and ended up looking back at the river.

Outside, McClendon worked his way quietly towards the river, his steps measured and feeling for uneven ground by instinct while his eyes probed the screen of green in front of him for danger.

For all practical purposes the shooting had stopped. Vallejo was now the hunted and he was hesitant to give away his position to the big man he knew was stalking him. The young Lieutenant worked his way carefully back to where his wounded men lay and found one had died. The other, with a bad stomach wound, would never ride his horse again. The man was dying hard and Vallejo offered him a drink of water. The man refused. He managed to raise himself a little and look at Vallejo through eyes that showed a mixture of pain and hate. He gripped Vallejo's arm with one hand.

"Keel the gringo for me, Vallejo, that is all I ask." The man slumped backward again while bright blood pumped out of the wound.

"You have my word," Vallejo promised, his face hardening to the task. To the north of his position he heard a horse being ridden hard over rocky ground and knew his only other man, had taken flight. He looked through the dense brush as men appeared cautiously at the cabin door, stepped outside and swiftly disappeared around the corner. Vallejo removed his huge spurs and stripped away the sword and his bright red sash. He wanted to be neither heard nor seen while he pursued the big gringo.

McClendon worked his way carefully through the jumble of boulders. He had heard the horse as well and knew it had come down to just him and the lieutenant. The trapper was in his element now and moved across the ground with the easy grace of a cougar and as quietly as a fish in water. He came on the soldier working his way along the water and rather than shoot him down, McClendon stepped from the forest of green into Vallejo's path.

"Give it up, man," Zack warned. The Mexican officer froze as if not believing he had been tracked down so easily. For a moment, McClendon felt sure Vallejo was going to concede defeat, but suddenly the Mexican brought his pistol to bear and two shots rang out. Vallejo stumbled backward a step and crumpled to the ground with McClendon's bullet through his heart.

Peck came running over, his pistol at the ready. He looked over at the Mexican officer and back to Zack, who was putting away his weapon.

"Guess that's that."

"All except the one who got away," Zack said quietly. "Expect he'll take the bad news back to Salezar."

"Means we cain't stay here, fer shore," Peck said. "What we gonna do now?"

"Gather up the dead and bury them for now. We'll move out around dusk."

"Where to?"

"To see an old friend of ours," was all Zack said, leaving Overstreet scratching his head. He couldn't recall either one of them ever having any friends in these parts.

CHAPTER 18

Benjamin Delaney's big nose seemed to glow in the dark as he paced back and forth in the cramped quarters. He was sick to the bone. Not only had everyone refused his request to see Governor Armijo, but stories were filtering in of an all out assault by Salezar and his drunken soldiers on innocent Mexicans and whites who still remained in Santa Fe. The crackle of gunfire was almost constant and Delaney learned to ignore it. What concerned him most were the bags of Mexican silver and gold taken from him. He was sure Salezar was in possession of the money and quite possibly shared it with Armijo as well. Maybe that was the reason Armijo had not been to see him? Anger welled up deep inside Delaney and threatened to destroy what little sanity he had left. He should have listened to Hamilton and McClendon as well, much as he hated admitting it.

"Christ, man, why don't you sit down?" Latham said from his place on the bare floor. He and the other drivers in his group had turned sullen and fixed their eyes on the very reason they were here in the first place.

Delaney stopped to look at the dejected traders. "You weren't the ones robbed of over two hundred thousand dollars! I had a deal with Armijo."

"Yeah, well we done heard enough of your deal with that greaser of a governor," Donaldson said sharply. "You ain't the only loser in this deal, Delaney. Most of us sweated blood putting together enough wagons to turn a profit and we just let you waltz up and take it away."

"I didn't force you to sell to me!" Delaney yelled shrilly. His fleshy nose seemed on fire. The well-muscled Donaldson sprang from the floor as if a powder charge had been placed beneath him. He grabbed the fancy Delaney by his soiled coat.

"One more word outta you and I'm going to break your fat neck! Understood?" Delaney nodded meekly, too surprised by Donaldson's actions to even speak. In his entire life no one had ever dared speak to him in such a manner. Donaldson shoved Delaney backward. "Now sit down." Delaney backed against the wall and slid down to a half-sitting position, his face showing the strain of the encounter.

A door opened down the hall, and a man with a key stopped in front of the imprisoned men. He wore a filthy uniform and appeared drunk as he tried inserting the key into the cell door. It took him three tries. He leered at the men inside as if enjoying a private joke they were not privy to. He pushed the cell door open and stepped back, drawing his pistol.

"Wheech one of you ees Delaney?" the Mexican asked, swaying on his feet. Delaney jumped to his feet. The guard stepped back, pointing the pistol at the trader.

"I'm Delaney." Hope glowed deep in his dark eyes once more. Finally, Armijo had arranged for his release.

"You weel come with me." The soldier waved his pistol at Delaney, who stepped quickly through the door. The Mexican relocked the door with some difficulty.

"Governor Armijo wants to see me, right? I knew he

wouldn't leave me in such a filthy place once he heard." He gave the men on the other side of the bars a smug look as he tried to straighten his grimy clothes. "Hope you all rot in here."

"Shut your mouth," the soldier said, jamming his pistol into Delaney's side. "Walk carefully, gringo. I might shoot you." The Mexican grinned at the men left behind.

Delaney walked to the end of the hallway. "I intend to speak with Governor Armijo of your insolent manner. He will have you horsewhipped." Delaney clamped his mouth shut when he heard the Mexican cocking his pistol.

McClendon was cinching the saddle on Carmelita's horse while the others tended to the burying. Skin Ledbetter watched the proceedings from a chair brought out into the yard for him. Carmelita had cleaned his wound and bound it tight with strips of sheeting found in the cabin. Ledbetter was a tough old bird, like Overstreet, and had suffered more serious wounds alone in the mountains without a pretty woman to fix him up. Even as Carmelita cleaned the gunshot, Ledbetter had insisted on pouring a little Taos Lightning in the hole and chinking it with a wad of tobacco.

"When do you expect Cheyenne Jack and Billy Williams back?" McClendon asked Ledbetter.

"Any time now. Where you plan on leavin' the women 'til the fracas is over?"

"At the mission with Father Fray Escalante. They should be safe there."

Ledbetter nodded in agreement. "Didn't know you knew the padre, you being heathen and all," he said with a grin.

Before McClendon could make a reply, Carmelita Torres and the boy emerged from the cabin. She wore a short yet simple full skirt and a loose low-cut blouse the color of sandstone that exposed enough cleavage to arouse a dead man. Against the evening chill, she wore a brightly colored *rebozo*,

177

or scarf, on her head. Ledbetter simply rolled his eyes as the woman came up to McClendon. Pauli broke away and ran down to the bubbling river.

"Do not go in the water," she called after the child who seemed not to have heard her.

McClendon, finished with the saddle, handed the reins to the woman. Carmelita almost seemed innocent of the effect her appearance had on men.

"I best saddle the others," McClendon mumbled. She caught his arm as he turned back to the corral.

"Are you not pleased with me, Zack?"

The question startled McClendon and he stopped to look at the woman closely. "Whatever gave you that idea? Any man would be proud to have you for his own."

"I only want you to be happy," Carmelita said. "I do not seek to own you or force you into anything against your will. What happened last night was natural and right. I make no claims against you or you to me."

"It's just not good timing for me," McClendon stumbled around for proper words. "We have a lot facing us right now just dealing with Salezar. I need to be free to think of nothing else."

Carmelita nodded, but said what was in her heart. "Doña Magalena is very beautiful, don't you agree?"

"Yeah, guess so," McClendon said uneasily.

Carmelita reached out a hand and touched him on the shoulder. "I am from a poor family. My father, now dead, had little to offer even an only child except a one room *jacale* and all the love in the world. Most of our people are peons, McClendon, and will die peons. That is the way of life here, but as Salezar's whore, I can expect little from my own people," she said sadly.

"But you did it out of love for your people so they could at some point be free of such men."

"What you say is true, but they will soon forget the reason and remember the act." She turned away with tears in her

178

eyes. "But I have Pauli, and nothing can change that. He is the most precious thing in my life." McClendon didn't know what to say, and Carmelita headed down to the river where Pauli was throwing stones, leading the horse behind her.

McClendon watched her go, feeling a little ashamed at himself for having taken advantage of the woman. But the need had been powerful and beyond his control at the time. And then it occurred to him what she was saying. She was giving him free rein where Doña Magalena was concerned without having to worry about her own feelings. McClendon concluded as he finished saddling the other horses that the slender Mexican girl had a lot more wisdom than he had at first given her credit for.

They paused in the shadows at the rear of the mission church where Father Fray Escalante had been serving the needs of the small community of Mexicans, Indians, and trappers for ten years. Twice a week he visited Taos Pueblo to hold outdoor mass for those unwilling to come to the mission.

Escalante was happy to see McClendon and Overstreet once again, and the portly man welcomed the two women, no questions asked. While McClendon helped them get situated at the mission, the others drifted across the plaza to a cantina where trappers and mountain men usually hung out when in town. McClendon promised to be along directly. Due to a shortage of rooms, the women were forced to share one. Doña Magalena smiled wanly at the spartan room with its single washstand and cracked mirror. A coarse wool rug covered the floor. In the corner was one small bed.

"I will have another bed brought in for you Señorita Magalena. I am truly sorry the accommodations are so sparse," the padre said as a way of apology. He had visited with Don Diego many times in the past and knew of the opulence the woman was used to.

"Carmelita and I will make do quite nicely, Father," she said, giving him her best smile.

"And how is your father, Don Diego?"

179

"Worried and concerned about the future as is everyone else for as long as Salezar lives." The priest nodded.

"Damasio Salezar is an evil man, even though I should not say this. You must be hungry, I will have something prepared." The priest scurried off after warning McClendon to be careful—even in Taos, Salezar had his spies.

McClendon stood in the doorway with his hat in his hand, not really knowing what to say to the two women. Pauli was already fast asleep on the bed after the short ride.

"You heard what the padre said. Keep close to the mission and don't go out at night," McClendon said and then smiled ruefully. "Whether you like it or not, you both have something in common—Salezar, and he's not going to like being duped by either of you." McClendon knew he was probably wasting his breath. Both headstrong women were going to do as they pleased, no matter what he said. Carmelita picked up the pitcher from the washstand.

"I will get us some water." As she slipped past McClendon, Carmelita gave him her private smile.

Doña Magalena stood there coolly appraising McClendon. "Do not worry about your woman, Mr. McClendon. I will see no harm comes to her."

McClendon looked surprised. "*My* woman! Whatever gave you that idea?" Magalena smiled, exposing even white teeth.

"I am a woman, señor," she laughed. "Besides, I saw you slip up the backstairs last night." McClendon colored deeply, not knowing quite how to respond to the statement of truth.

"She's *still* not my woman," he managed to mumble. Magalena moved closer, her eyes dancing.

"Oh, then perhaps you should tell her."

"Don't see the need to tell anybody anything," McClendon said, feeling he better leave while he had the chance. The woman moved closer and all McClendon could see were dark teasing eyes, a fragile nose and full crimson lips. Magalena slipped her arms around Zack's neck and kissed him hungrily.

He resisted for a moment then crushed the woman to him, tasting the sweetness of her.

When they broke the embrace, they found Carmelita Torres standing there with the pitcher of water. She brushed past them as if nothing had happened while McClendon turned crimson. Doña Magalena merely smiled at his discomfort.

"Gotta go," McClendon mumbled and backed out of the doorway. Outside, he leaned for a moment against the neck of his horse to steady himself. Why had he allowed that to happen? He was still turning over the strange events with the two women when he entered the smoky interior of the cantina and located his group at a far table.

"Having female troubles?" Peck asked as McClendon drew near.

"Now don't you start on me," Zack warned the old trapper. Peck and the others around the table laughed at the touchy McClendon.

"Jest wondered if you wuz goin' to look up Rosita, now we back in Taos." Peck's one eye fairly danced in his head. Zack gave him a look that would kill a rattlesnake.

"Have a shot of Taos Lightning, Zack," Lafe Ingram said, pushing an amber bottle in front of him. McClendon sat down in a vacant chair, uncorked the bottle and took a long drink. Peck looked on, amazed. McClendon wasn't much of a drinking man, and, when he was, he usually steered clear of the potent brew. Skin Ledbetter took the bottle from McClendon and finished off the contents.

"Danged if I don't believe this stuff's been cut with water and plug tobacco. Peck, suppose you fetch us another bottle and tell that bartender he best give us the real McCoy." Peck went off to the bar while McClendon looked around at the rough-dressed crowd of trappers, mixed breeds and Mexicans, drinking at nearby tables or at the planked bar. The liquor caused a mild explosion in the pit of his stomach and he belched, a sour taste rising in his mouth. He remembered now why he didn't drink Taos Lightning. It soured him every time. When Peck came back he brought along a beer for McClendon.

"Knowed you was out of yore head to be drinking anything stronger than a beer."

McClendon smiled weakly and took a sip to settle his stomach. "Find out anything?" he asked Ledbetter, wanting to put aside thoughts of the two women.

"Ezekiel Smith and five others are bedded down in the brush by the Rio Lucero. They were over to the Moreno Valley when they run into Cheyenne Jack and Billy 'a headin' fer Bent's place."

"Thought old Ezekiel was killed by Blackfeet some years ago," McClendon said.

"Done asked that question myself," Peck said, pouring the others drinks. "Zeke's been over to the San Juan trapping beaver 'til the Utes and Jicarilla Apache killed his partner and sent him packing with nothing more'n bad luck fer clothing."

"He's been across the Sangre de Cristo doing a little trapping and such for the last three, four years," Ledbetter cut in, glaring at Overstreet for butting in.

"Suppose we camp with them," McClendon asked Ledbetter. "May as well make it hard as we can for Salezar's snooping spies to keep an eye on us."

"Sounds good. We stay in town, it won't take long fer trouble to find us," Ledbetter said.

"Well, would you look at that?" Peck said, staring at the door. McClendon glanced over his shoulder and was surprised to see Sylvester Houseman standing there. The look on Houseman's face indicated he was just as surprised at seeing them. The man glanced away, anger replacing the startled look on his face. He moved off to the far corner of the bar and ordered a beer.

"That is one strange man," Zack said, shaking his head. "Reminds me of someone who's hiding something."

"I've thought that all along," Peck confided.

"You think he killed his partner?" Ingram asked.

"Don't honestly know. Might go even deeper than that, just can't put my finger on it," Zack said, picking up his beer. He turned to Ledbetter. "You ever seen him around here before?"

Skin had gotten a good look at the man as he stood there in the doorway. "Don't recollect it if I have," Ledbetter said.

"Suppose I go have a talk with this unfriendly jasper," Peck said, feeling the Taos Lightning taking effect.

"Best leave him alone," McClendon said, putting a hand on Overstreet who was beginning to rise from his chair. "Less ruckus we make, the better off we'll be." Overstreet settled back down, but continued to glower at the odd man.

They finished their drinks and left the cantina. Climbing into their saddles, Ledbetter led the way out of town. The night air was laced with a cold wind that whipped circles of dust around them as they rode northwest. The moon hung in the clear sky like a giant yellow light. A few minutes later, Houseman paused at the door of the cantina and then slipped away in the night.

A cool breeze blew across the parade ground as Delaney and the Mexican guard stepped from the building. It felt good to be breathing fresh, clean air once more, and Delaney drew in a deep lung full. Never had he smelled anything sweeter. The guard prodded him with the weapon and Delaney started across the grounds, the night air lifting his spirits somewhat. The guard pointed him to a wooden door and Delaney opened it slowly. This was not Governor Armijo's office. The first shivers of dread entered his body.

The guard pushed him down a long hallway and to a polished walnut door that opened quietly on well-greased hinges. Delaney stepped in, blinking his eyes at the sumptuousness of it. In the center of the room stood a large, ornate wood desk, plush chairs, a side cabinet that held several different types of whiskey, and a settee of French design. But what impressed Delaney the most was the cold-eyed man that sat behind the desk. It struck a deep fear in Delaney's heart. What was he doing here? He was supposed to see Armijo.

"Sit!" Salezar said. Delaney moved quickly to obey, taking the chair directly across from Salezar's desk. The Mexican guard, who didn't look or act so drunk now, simply backed up against the wall. Delaney wondered if the ruse was to try and get him to make a break for it so the guard could shoot him. They obviously did not understand his connections to Armijo. He couldn't wait to see the governor so he could tell him how badly he had been mistreated.

"Why am I here?" Delaney asked. Salezar had been busy writing and now he sat back in the plush chair and stared intently at Delaney.

"You don't look like you feel well, haven't they been treating you okay?"

Delaney's face and nose reddened deeply as the anger and resentment of his confinement sought an outlet. But even in his self-righteous indignation, Delaney was smart enough to realize Salezar was not a man to tolerate verbal abuse. The man was more dangerous than a stepped-on rattlesnake, and Delaney got a grip on his emotions before he spoke.

"I'm willing to forget the imprisonment as an unfortunate mistake, if I can just see Governor Armijo at this time."

Salezar studied the man before him. He hated all gringos, and for some strange reason he disliked Delaney even more than McClendon. At least with McClendon, Salezar knew what to expect, but Delaney was more like him, ready to roll any direction that benefited him the most.

"Tell me, where might I find Zack McClendon and the rest of those trappers?"

Delaney looked genuinely surprised. "Why, I have no earthly idea. I have not seen the ruffian since the first day we arrived."

Salezar smiled as if toying with a child. "But you and this other man . . . Ingram, I believe it was, traveled together."

"Only met them on the trail. Believe me, it was not my idea

184

to team up with them, but we came under Comanche attack and afterwards, McClendon found this man who had been lost in the desert for days.'' It was Salezar's turn to be surprised and for a moment his eyes brightened and then narrowed down again.

"What man was that?"

Delaney hesitated, realizing Salezar was the very one who had contributed to the man and his companion's death. He best proceed with caution.

"Called himself Bull Stanton.'' Delaney saw the change in Salezar, the subtle way he sat upright in his chair.

"Where is this Stanton now?"

"Dead. Died sometime during the night according to Ingram. I don't know much more than that. We camped separately from McClendon and the others.''

"What of the other two men?'' Salezar asked. It didn't slip by Delaney that Salezar knew the number of men who were with Stanton.

"One of the Indians killed during the attack had on a hat Stanton recognized. McClendon had given the hat to Ingram since he had lost his own. Everybody figured the Indians must have killed them.'' Salezar slowly relaxed once more.

"Surely Stanton must have told McClendon how they come to be there in the first place?'' Delaney shrugged his shoulders with an unconcerned air. He knew who was responsible, but damned if he was going to let this snake-eyed killer know that. It was something he could mention to Armijo later.

"You must understand, McClendon and I had a few words and from then on we stayed away from each other.'' Salezar seemed satisfied for the moment. Delaney pressed forward with the uppermost thing on his mind.

"Do you know what happened to my pack mule and wagons your sergeant took from me yesterday? I have a considerable amount of goods and money I want returned.''

Salezar's eyes seemed hooded and dangerous of a sudden and Delaney almost wished he had waited to ask Armijo about them. Salezar got up and went over and poured them each a drink. He came back and handed one to Delaney. Delaney accepted it gratefully and swallowed half of it with his eyes closed. Nothing ever tasted so good in his life.

"Your wagons have all been confiscated by the Mexican Government. That includes your white mule and all the money."

Delaney turned white then red. "That's out and out thievery!" he shouted, forgetting momentarily who he was speaking to.

"You call me a thief. Are you and Armijo not planning to import trade goods and split the proceeds without paying duties?" Salezar returned to his desk and sat down again. Anger filled his eyes.

"I naturally assumed Armijo would take care of his officers, men like yourself."

"You lie, gringo, and not very well, I think."

"I demand to see Armijo."

Salezar's laugh was harsh and without feeling. "You are in no position to demand anything, heh, gringo?"

"But Armijo can straighten this whole affair out," Delaney pleaded.

"Armijo ees not here right now." Salezar smiled again. "He ees with his mistress, Doña Barcelo. Perhaps you have heard of her? She is the best monte dealer in all of New Mexico." Then he leaned forward in his chair. "But you see, gringo, eet is not cards they are playing tonight." Delaney could feel his fortune slipping away and he slumped down in the chair, feeling suddenly old.

A dishevelled soldier burst through the door with a frightened look on his face. His clothes were dusty and sweat-stained.

"Pardon me, Capitán. It is urgent I speak with you." He looked at Delaney with open hostility.

"Where is Vallejo?"

"Did you not get the message?" the soldier asked, dumbfounded.

The skin around Salezar's eyes tightened into fine lines. "Do you think I would be asking if I knew?"

Delaney didn't know what to make of this new development and he sat there quietly.

The soldier stammered and looked down at his grimy boots. "Lieutenant Vallejo is dead, Capitán," the soldier said softly.

Salezar looked at him for a full minute before he said anything. "Dead!" he finally screamed. "What are you saying, out with it man?"

The soldier spoke rapidly for a few minutes, while Salezar listened to the grim details. Only the muscles jumping along his jawbone gave away his true feelings. When the soldier spoke of the two women, Salezar came halfway out of his seat.

"Are you sure it was Doña Magalena with McClendon and the others?" Salezar spoke as if it was the hardest thing in the world for him to ask.

"Sí, Capitán. I am sure." The soldier kept his eyes on the floor. Salezar sat back down while the enormity of the soldier was saying hit him. The whore he figured would be part of the rebellion . . . but Doña Magalena? He had been played the fool by both women. They probably even knew one another. It made him feel like smashing something . . . anything. A cold fury shook his lean frame. It followed too that Don Diego was part of it as well. And he had played right into their hands like a green recruit. Salezar looked up at the humble soldier.

"How come you are not dead as well?" he said angrily.

"I . . . someone had to escape, to warn you."

"You left your commanding officer behind in the field, alone and outnumbered. You chose to run while Vallejo, being a gallant officer, resisted to the end. You were not worried about bringing me messages, only saving your worthless skin." Salezar voice was full of contempt. He stood up and held out his hand.

"Give me your pistol." The soldier looked up from the floor and realized what was being asked of him and he backed up a step. Delaney froze in his chair scarcely breathing.

"You are wrong, Capitán. I came to warn you. I am not afraid of death."

"Then give me your pistol," Salezar demanded once more.

The soldier shook his head and began backing towards the door. "No, I will not, Capitán."

"Tomas!" Salezar shouted. The Mexican guard lounging against the wall sprang into action, drew his revolver and shot the retreating soldier through the head, covering the nearby door and wall with blood and bits of his brain. Delaney looked on, horrified by the sight of a man being shot at point-blank range. He felt he was going to be sick from the smell of black powder and fresh blood.

"You look sick, gringo. Finish your drink, it will settle your stomach," Salezar said, perfectly calm once more. Delaney stared at the man. *How could anyone order a man murdered so calmly?* What about him? Would Salezar have the same thing done to him? He swallowed the rest of his drink to steady his nerves as well as his stomach.

A number of soldiers appeared at the door as if by magic and carried away the dead soldier. The guard went back to his place by the wall as if nothing at all had happened.

"I do not like cowards," he explained to the pale-faced Delaney. "Now that I know where to find McClendon, what am I going to do with you?"

"Let me talk with Armijo . . . please. I don't care what you do with McClendon and the others. It's none of my affair."

Salezar downed his drink and stood up. "Tomas, put Delaney back with the others." An evil grin spread across his features.

They were halfway across the parade grounds, with Delaney stumbling along, not willing to believe he was going back to that filthy hellhole. But worse would be the ridicule he would be forced to endure from Latham and Donaldson, especially after what he had said to them. God, he just couldn't do it. Without really realizing it, he found himself running as hard as his big stomach would let him, towards the protective shadows of the stables. He heard the guard shout for him to stop. Just a few more feet and he would be lost from view. Something slammed him hard between the shoulder blades and he pitched forward on his face as the report of the pistol shot echoed across the flat ground.

Tomas ran over still clutching the smoking gun. "You crazy gringo, why did you make me shoot you?" But Delaney was beyond talking. His body twitched once and slowly relaxed. He had no time for last thoughts.

CHAPTER 19

"We come a long way since that winter on the Popo Agie," Zeke Smith said to McClendon over coffee the next morning. Ezekiel Smith was as wild a looking man as ever set a foot on a mountain trail. His hair and flowing beard, the color of snow, stuck out from the side of his head as if he was constantly in a wind storm. Zeke wore a suit of leathers fringed with multicolored quills and beaded moccasins and leather hat, products of Smith's Flathead squaw. He smelled of bear grease and sage. Skin Ledbetter came limping up to the fire and helped himself to coffee.

Zack rolled his empty cup around in his big hands, while he considered Zeke's comment and finally decided they hadn't come very far at all. None of the men here had much to show for a lifetime of trapping and high mountain living . . . except maybe a free life, a good life at times, but McClendon thought this only because he was still on top and not gone under like the hundred-odd men he had known back in '28.

Squatting on his heels, Ledbetter eyed the beautiful leatherwork of Smith's clothes. "Wish I had me a big-tittied squaw to make me a fine set of leathers like that." Zeke looked down at himself as if surprised anyone would notice his appearance, even though his clothes were a source of pride to him.

"Why hell, Skin, never knowed you to care much about clothes one way er the other."

Skin Ledbetter smiled, a gleam in his eyes. "Don't, it's your squaw I'm after." He laughed, rocking back and forth on his heels. It was a well known fact, Ledbetter had been a real ladies man in his prime, and many a time, Skin had left some Indian village with an irate buck hot on his trail.

"Well, you kin shore have her," Zeke said, sadly. "She's the size of a half-growed griz now and don't do nuthin' but complain how I ain't providin' a decent livin'. Why you think I'm down here? A man's takes his rest where he can find it . . . even if it is shootin' greasers."

Peck Overstreet came riding up through the screen of willows and stepped slowly from the saddle. The three men at the fire eyed Overstreet critically. He had elected to remain in town and renew old acquaintances at Ortega's cantina. He hadn't found the woman from his past and, in truth, never expected to. But he had found companionship in one of old Juan Ortega's three daughters. The night had been long and sweet and now he was paying the price.

Peck ignored their looks and went straight for the pot of coffee.

"Looks like you shouda hung with Peck last night, Skin if you was in need," Zeke said.

"Cain't stand the pain no more," Skin said, grinning.

"Get a way!" Zeke said, "why you ain't a day older'n old Peck here and you can see he pulled through jest fine." Peck sipped the hot coffee, trying to ignore their digs.

Zack stood up and looked around the camp. They were a far cry from giving Salezar trouble. He only hoped Cheyenne Jack managed to do better at Bent's recruiting men.

"Guess I'll ride into town and see how the ladies are making out," Zack said lamely.

"What you want us to do?" Peck asked, hoping to draw the other two away off his case.

"You can break out your bullet molds and make as many balls you think you can shoot in a week. Expect as soon as Cheyenne Jack gets back, we'll need to be ready to ride immediately."

McClendon caught up his big buckskin and loped into town, his mind busy with details of the impending fight with Salezar.

Sergeant Santiago Sagasta lifted the field glasses to his eyes and studied the approaching dust cloud through the shimmering heat. The group of riders jumped into focus.

"*Quantos?*" a lean-faced Mexican officer asked Sagasta. His voice betrayed his impatience in the stifling heat.

"I count eighteen, maybe twenty," Sagasta said. "It is difficult with the dust."

"Demelo," the Mexican officer said, holding out his hand. Sagasta handed the field glasses to Lieutenant Luis Gomez. Gomez put the glasses to his eyes and counted slowly out loud. He stopped at fifteen. Santiago Sagasta felt some satisfaction in having bested the snappy dressed officer in such a small way.

For weeks now they, and sixty other soldiers, had been encamped on the Mora River. The waiting had been worse for Gomez, who complained daily of the dust, the heat, or anything else that intruded upon his gentleman sensibilities. The troopers had suffered his constant berations in silence.

The officer and sergeant stood on a low hill that gave them a sweeping view of the Mora River as it curled eastward between two ridges, rimmed with rock and scrub pine.

"Shall I alert the men, Lieutenant Gomez?" Sagasta asked quietly after a few minutes of silence.

Gomez lowered the glasses and looked at Sagasta. "Those

192

men are not traders. They have no pack mules or wagons and they stray from the trail. Capitán Salezar was correct.''

"These are the mountain men we were warned of?'' Sagasta asked, his interest quickening.

"Of course they are!'' Gomez said with growing impatience. "They are headed for Taos to join the others. Why else would such a large group of well-armed men travel this way?'' Sagasta said no more, thinking that many men would soon die and not all of them would be these mountain men, who could shoot with deadly accuracy. The two soldiers mounted their horses and rode quickly back to the waiting soldiers. Gomez gave a few quick orders, and the soldiers moved out and formed a line of defense in the thick brush that bordered the Mora River where the trail passed between two steep foothills. Once inside the narrow opening, there was little room to maneuver. Gomez was supremely confident of his success and doubted he would even lose a single man.

They waited in silence, listening for the shot Gomez himself would fire as a signal to begin. Sagasta stood next to Lieutenant Gomez, listening to the approaching horsemen, his pulse beating heavily in his ears. He gripped his rifle tightly, seeing Gomez stiffen and then raise his own rifle to his shoulder.

Through a haze of green foliage, Sagasta watched as the first of the riders came into view. All were heavily armed and wary as they entered the narrow part of the trail. They looked inhuman to Sagasta, with their full beards, leather clothes, all dust-covered and grimed by a week of hard riding. He was awed by their appearance and a little frightened as the leader's eyes swept the area ahead of him like a lobo wolf, scenting the trail.

For a moment Sagasta held his breath, afraid Gomez would fire before all the riders entered the trap, but the last rider came into view at the same time Gomez fired. The lead rider rolled in the saddle and slowly tumbled to the ground. The air was filled instantly with the cracking of Mexican rifles followed quickly by the deep-throated long guns of the mountain men who held their ground coolly in spite of being caught off guard. A large, black-hatted trapper appeared in Sagasta's rifle sight and he squeezed the trigger not knowing if he hit the man or not, what with the dust, the lunging horses, and the yelling of the mountain men. The whole scene unnerved him, especially the screams of the dying on both sides. Sagasta knelt back down to reload his rifle as the carnage continued around him. The narrow passage reverberated like thunder from the fusillade of shots. Suddenly, it was over as quickly as it had begun.

Mexican soldiers poured out of the thickets with fixed bayonets and raced among the fallen mountain men. Whenever one groaned in pain, there would instantly be a half dozen bayonets thrust into the victim. Gomez and Sagasta came down from their hiding place and walked among the dead men and dying horses.

Near the edge of the river they watched as a wounded trapper rose up out of the rocks and pointed his pistol at a nearby soldier. Several rifles fired at the standing trapper who jerked his weapon around, his already dead fingers pulling the trigger. A soldier laughed at the trapper's feeble attempts of shooting one of them. Sagasta heard the air rush from Lieutenant Gomez's lungs and he looked around to see bright blood staining the officer's clean uniform. There was a look of disbelief on Gomez's face as he tried to speak. Sagasta caught him in his arms and eased the officer down into the blood and dust.

"Water!" Sagasta screamed at the shocked soldiers. One of them ran over, stripping off his field canteen and giving it to the sergeant. Sagasta tilted the officer's head and put the canteen to Gomez's lips before realizing that he was dead. He sat there for a few minutes cradling the dead officer's head, waiting for the shock to pass. Slowly he eased the dead man's head to the ground and stood up to look around.

"Lieutenant Gomez is dead," he said quietly. "Strip the dead of their weapons and somebody bring me the lieutenant's horse."

A few minutes later Private Carlos Jurado came up leading

the horse and helped the sergeant tie the dead lieutenant across the silver-trimmed saddle he had been so fond of.

Sagasta gathered his thoughts and asked for a status report now that he was in command.

"We killed eighteen of the enemy, Sergeant," Private Jurado said proudly.

"And how many men did we lose, besides the lieutenant?"

"We do not yet know, Sergeant. We are still pulling dead soldiers from the bushes."

"Well, how many so far?" Sagasta asked testily.

"Twenty-two." Sagasta looked at the young private, thinking about what could have happened had they met the mountain men on equal terms. He felt sure the gringos would be the ones taking a head count right now.

The Mexican soldiers pulled out an hour later and headed back east to the little town of Mora to tend to the wounded. Twenty-nine dead men lay strapped across their horses, yet Sagasta was satisfied. They had killed all the gringos and even with Gomez dying, Capitán Salezar would be pleased with their performance.

From a rocky crevice, a leather-shirted man eased to a standing position, holding a bloodied arm. He stood looking at his dead friends while dusk settled over the narrow passage, the pain in his heart, for the moment, greater than the pain in his shattered arm. He made his way over to where Cheyenne Jack lay face up in the trail. Jack had been the first casualty. Billy Williams reached down and pulled the powder horn from the dead man the Mexican soldiers had overlooked. Next, he washed his arm in the cold waters of the Mora and picked up his rifle. He turned west towards the Sangre de Cristos and had taken no more than a dozen steps when something in front of him moved. He managed to cock his rifle, steadying it across his injured arm. A riderless horse came trotting up out of the gloom. Billy quickly grabbed the reins and steadied the nervous animal, speaking in soothing tones. It was Cheyenne Jack's black, and Billy rubbed the animal's neck for a few minutes, remembering how much Jack had cared for the horse, before he swung into the saddle and headed up the trail, his heart black with anger. Out of nineteen experienced mountain men that left Bent's Fort, only Billy Williams was left to spread the news of the horror of what happened here in this narrow valley of death.

Before the day was over, eight more idle trappers drifted into camp, having come by way of the Rio Grande skirting the western slopes of the Sangre de Cristos into Taos. That made a total of twenty experienced men whose mettle had been tested on many occasions. None were impressed by wounds, gunshot or knife. They had all tasted their own blood before.

"If Cheyenne Jack comes back with fifteen or twenty more men, expect with what Don Diego and Chaves can muster, we ought to be ready to try Salezar on for size," McClendon said to the group of silent men.

"Cheyenne Jack and Billy ought to be ridin' in jest any day," Skin Ledbetter said, nursing his pipe and honing the big knife he carried at his belt.

"That's what I was thinking," McClendon continued, "though it might be a good idea for all of you to slip down to Don Diego's and help out with the defense while I wait here for Cheyenne Jack."

Peck's eye twinkled. "Shore you ain't hangin' 'round fer other reasons?" McClendon looked at his one-eyed partner. It was times like these he could shoot his other eye out, yet what Peck implied was true. He wanted to see both women were made safe, although his reasons ran deeper than that, and he freely admitted it to himself. At the same time, he wasn't about to underestimate Salezar's drive for revenge against both women now. If he did ride north with his men, it would be a lot easier for him and the two women to slip into the mountains and escape than a large group of riders.

"Just you see to it that the men Don Diego has are whipped into fighting shape before I get there, old man," McClendon replied gruffly.

CHAPTER 20

As the gathering light to the east broke over Thompson Mountain an unbroken line of splendidly dressed soldiers, numbering over a hundred, sat their horses less than a mile from Don Diego Domingo's hacienda. In the fading cool of morning sunlight glinted off sabers and silver-studded saddles as the battle-hardened men waited for their leader to give the signal.

Captain Damasio Salezar, looking every bit the Mexican officer, sat proudly in his saddle, waiting for full light to descend across the valley. His eyes were puffy, and he had gotten little sleep since receiving the news late last night from Sergeant Santiago Sagasta of their success against the mountain men and of Lieutenant Gomez's unfortunate death. And now he was about to put the second phase of his plans into action before the gringo, McClendon, and Don Diego grew any stronger.

Salezar drew his saber and raised it high over his head. He looked up and down both lines at the hearts and souls of men completely loyal to him, and he swelled with pride at the sight of their brightly colored sashes and plumed hats. One day, very soon, with these same men, he would depose the stupidly vain Armijo from his seat as governor and appoint himself to that position. But first, he intended to crush the "Liberation Fighters," as they called themselves, find this McClendon, and hang him in the town square so that all the people could see how strong Damasio Salezar really was.

"Take no prisoners," he shouted to his men, cutting the air with his saber and putting the spurs to his big white horse.

Don Diego was still in bed when he was awakened by the thunder of hooves and the rattle of metal—the sounds of soldiers galloping across the open ground. Diego rushed downstairs after throwing on a housecoat. He yelled into the kitchen for the cook, who came out clutching a large knife. He had heard the approaching soldiers as well.

"Run, warn the others," Don Diego said, lifting his rifle and throwing open the front door. The cook disappeared into the kitchen and out the back door. Don Diego could hear his men calling to one another as he leveled the gun at the line of rushing soldiers and squeezed the trigger. Through the smoke he saw a horse stumble and fall, spilling its rider. Puffs of smoke appeared along the line of horsemen, and Don Diego heard the tinkling of breaking glass as bullets thudded into the house.

Don Diego slammed the door shut and bolted it. He ran to the corner of the fireplace where he kept his powder and lead and began reloading the rifle with nervous fingers. The kitchen door banged open and a big Mexican entered. Don Diego looked over his shoulder as the man stepped into the room.

"Oh, it's you. Thank God, I thought it might be the soldiers. Can we hold out?" Don Diego asked the Mexican.

"There are too many this time, Don Diego. There is no hope of escaping." Don Diego looked sharply at the Mexican. "Don't talk like that, get over there and cover a window," he ordered. In the background, they could hear the screams as men were being shot in their tracks, the noise of the soldiers' guns sounding like so many fireworks at festival time. The Mexican did not move.

"It is over for you, Don Diego," the Mexican said quietly. It was the tone of voice that caused Don Diego to look around at the Mexican who was now pointing a pistol at him.

"Why?" Don Diego whispered, forgetting the useless rifle in his hands.

"For money, what else," the Mexican said, firing. Don Diego was slammed hard against the stone fireplace where he hung for an instant, a spreading stain of crimson appeared on his chest. The Mexican came closer and pointed the gun at him just as the door flew open and Damasio Salezar strode in still clutching his saber. His eyes met Don Diego's.

"Wait!" Salezar commanded the Mexican who lowered the pistol. Don Diego slowly slid to a sitting position on the hearth. Salezar strode over to the fallen Diego and knelt down in front of the dying man.

"I now ask for your daughter's hand in marriage," Salezar said with an evil grin. Don Diego coughed up frothy blood.

"Go to hell, Salezar. Magalena will never marry you. She's never loved you. Our people will yet succeed against you," Don Diego said weakly, his breathing coming in gasps.

Salezar laughed harshly, "It is you who have failed, Don Diego. All your men are dead. I now claim your hacienda as my own and when I tire of your daughter, I will sell her to slave traders or give her to the Indians."

"Where I have failed, Zack McClendon and his men will not," Don Diego managed to say.

Salezar laughed even more and told Diego how his soldiers had crushed the mountain men in Mora. "So you see, nothing stands in my way of becoming governor." Don Diego looked defeated as his life ebbed from him.

"You still have not taken McClendon, and you will die when you try."

"This McClendon is not a god, Don Diego. He is flesh and blood, and we will kill him this day and the others who ride with him.'' Don Diego smiled weakly and looked up into the cruel face of the officer.

"Not this time. McClendon will see that you die.''

Salezar stood up, tired of the game with the dying rancher. In a sudden burst of anger he thrust the blade of his saber through the fallen man. Don Diego barely acknowledged the blow, dying quietly. Salezar wiped Don Diego's blood from his saber using a corner of his housecoat. He turned to the waiting Mexican.

"You have been most valuable to me, Joaquin, and you will be amply rewarded. Now, gather the men outside and make sure that no one escapes north to warn McClendon.'' Joaquin Cobo, trusted friend and confidant of Don Diego, turned to the door, but was halted by Salezar's voice.

"Bring me the body of Manuel Chaves, I want to see it for myself.'' Cobo shook his head.

"Chaves is not here, Capitán. He left during the night, riding south. I did not think it wise to try and stop him and alarm the others, so I let him go.''

Salezar was keenly disappointed but he did not let it dampen his spirits. "There is still time. Besides, where can he go? Send in two men and throw Don Diego into the hog pen where he belongs.'' Cobo left Salezar alone with the dead rancher. Salezar wandered into the kitchen and reappeared a few minutes later with a plate of food obviously being prepared for Don Diego.

"You don't mind if I eat your food. You see, we were forced to leave so early this morning, I missed breakfast,'' he said to the dead rancher. Salezar threw back his head and laughed loudly at his own attempt at black humor.

Thirty-three vaqueros lay dead, some still in their night-clothes, three in their beds. Only a large black dog escaped the carnage. The fat cook was shot full of holes while hiding in the outhouse. Only five soldiers died in the feeble resistance. Salezar was proud of the success and of his men and told them so.

"Rest yourselves, eat, muchachos," Salezar said, from the shaded veranda. "In two hours, we ride to Taos."

Less than an hour later, a picket came galloping up from the north where he had been watching the road. Salezar was resting on the veranda, enjoying a bottle of Don Diego's fine wines.

"What is it, hombre?" Salezar asked as the rider pulled to a dusty stop in front of him.

"Excuse me, Capitán. A large group of men ride this way. Americanos." Salezar stood up, the glass of wine he was holding forgotten for now.

"Find Cobo, quickly," Salezar commanded. The soldier sprinted around the house to the bunkhouse where Cobo was helping himself to what valuables Diego's men had left behind.

"Come quickly, Joaquin. Capitán Salezar wishes to see you at once."

"I will be there *uno momento*," Cobo said, not bothering to look around at the soldier.

"Por favor, Joaquin," the soldier pleaded. "Americanos are coming." Cobo whirled around.

"Why did you not tell me this first?" Cobo brushed past the soldier and hurried to the hacienda.

"Quickly, get on your horse and ride out and meet the gringos," Salezar said to Cobo. "They will not suspect you. Lead them here as if everything is okay. We will be waiting."

Joaquin Cobo did not wait for his horse to be brought around, instead leaped onto the soldier's lathered horse and galloped away.

"Hide yourselves in the house, on the roof and around the other buildings," Salezar told his men. "We will capture them alive, and hang them tomorrow in the plaza. After that, there will be no further resistance from these 'Liberation fighters,' " Salezar sneered.

Joaquin Cobo slowed the horse to a gentle trot to give the appearance that he was in no hurry. When he saw the dust cloud and the determined hard-faced men beneath it, Cobo's heart froze in his chest. What if he failed? These men would kill him as quickly as squashing a bug. He let them come closer and waved his sombrero in the air.

The riders swarmed around him in a thick cloud of yellow dust. Cobo had never seen such well armed and fearless gringos as these and he swallowed hard before speaking.

"Buenos dias," Cobo managed to say. He recognized Peck Overstreet and gave him his best smile. "Don Diego will be so happy to see so many brave Americanos."

"Yeah, well, I jest hope your boss has some grub on the fire. Ain't none of us et this day," Peck answered for them.

"Oh, sí, there is always plenty of food at Don Diego's."

"Well, let's get 'a going afore I melt in this heat," Peck said. Cobo turned his horse around and it was the longest ride he had ever made in his life with twenty pairs of eyes stabbing him in the back.

The group of unsuspecting trappers rode into the wide yard and stepped down from their horses.

"That porch shore looks invitin'," Skin said to Peck. "Danged if I can stay in the saddle fer too long at a stretch without kinking up."

"I will take your horses around to the corral," Cobo said eagerly, grabbing for as many reins as he could, while looking around him nervously.

"Hell, you cain't take them all, Pedro," Peck said, looking at the worried Mexican. Suddenly, Peck sensed something was wrong and in that instant soldiers poured out of the house and around both corners, quickly surrounding them. Salezar was two steps behind.

"Do not try to resist," he shouted. "No harm will come to you." Peck reached for his pistol, Skin Ledbetter and several others did the same. For a few tense moments, the mountain men stood toe-to-toe glaring at the Mexican soldiers with fire in their eyes. More soldiers crowded around until all thought of escape was wiped from their minds. The Americans lowered their guns and the soldiers quickly stripped them of their weapons. Had they known of the tragedy at Mora, they might have elected to fight it out.

"Guess we are gettin' too old, Skin," Peck said sadly, "to let a bunch of fancy dressed Mexicans sucker us in."

"Silence!" Salezar screamed, his demeanor changed now that he had disarmed the trappers. "Bind their hands and feet," he ordered. His eyes searched through the crowd for McClendon.

"Where is McClendon?" Salezar demanded.

"Who?" Overstreet asked stupidly. A soldier came up behind him and bound his hands tightly behind his back. Peck ignored the pain as the rope cut into his wrists, shutting off circulation.

Salezar stepped down from the veranda and stopped in front of Overstreet, his eyes glaring hard at the one-eyed trapper. Peck stood his ground, completely fearless. Salezar knew this; it sent him into a rage, and he slapped the old trapper on the side of the head, drawing blood from a split lip.

"You will not be talking so smart when we hang the lot of you tomorrow for all of New Mexico to see." Salezar's eyes flashed across the faces of the rugged men and found none that seemed concerned by the announcement.

"That what you done to Don Diego?" Peck asked.

Salezar's lips curled in a cruel smile. "Don Diego died with his blood running down my saber." He didn't bother to mention that the defenseless rancher had already been shot.

"Guess we can call off the weddin' then," Skin Ledbetter piped up. Salezar saw it was useless to try to cow such men, and he abruptly returned to the porch.

"March them into town," he ordered his soldiers. "Perhaps they will find the heat and the dust amusing as well." Salezar returned to his chair and picked up his wine glass, smiling. Fifty soldiers prodded the trappers with the points of their bayonets. The trappers could only take small steps and some began to swear heavily. Salezar laughed behind them.

"You should cover the five miles by tonight, gringos, if you don't die first from the heat. Adios, until tomorrow. Now I must ride to Taos and console my fiance over the loss of her father." Salezar continued to laugh as they stumbled awkwardly across the hot ground.

"Damn his greasy hide," Peck whispered to Skin Ledbetter.

"Hope old Zack is more alert then we was, but I doubt it, with two women 'a fawning over him," Skin replied.

"Zack ain't one to let his guard down no matter what's occupyin' his time," Peck said defensively.

"Silencio!" a soldier said, cuffing Overstreet upside his head and knocking his leather hat off. The Mexican wouldn't let him stop to retrieve it and Overstreet walked the remainder of the day bareheaded under a broiling sun.

CHAPTER 21

The trembling horse with head held low walked slowly down the dirt street of Taos carrying a man who was slumped over, unmoving, in the saddle. One arm hung useless, and dark blood, dried by the heat of the desert air, covered his hand. Men watched silently from the street as the horse walked by, none moving to help the wounded man. Billy Williams had ridden the punishing forty miles through Vigil Canyon and across the rugged Sangre de Cristos by the light of the moon. The last fifteen miles he had turned north and given the animal his head as he drifted into a weary pain-ridden sleep. Halfway through town, the horse simply stopped walking, too exhausted to go any further. The animal lifted his head and looked around as if asking to be relieved of the burden on his back.

Father Fray Escalante was hurrying back to the mission when he spotted the animal. He saw the man and the bloodied arm.

"*Madre Dios*," he muttered under his breath and hurried towards the animal.

"Be careful, Father," a man called from the shade of a

building. "That horse could be loco." Escalante ignored the warning and caught the horse by the bridle, patting the animal on his glistening neck.

"Whoa, boy," Escalante said, soothingly as he worked his way back to the unconscious man. It was one of the white trappers he had seen in town several weeks back. He checked to see if the man was still breathing. A moan escaped the man's lips but he never opened his eyes. The best thing he could do right now was to get the man off the street and away from prying eyes so he could check his condition.

Escalante led the tired horse behind the mission and found McClendon tying his horse to a post.

"Señor McClendon, a man is badly hurt."

In two steps Zack was beside the unconscious man, lifting him from the saddle. The man cried out as McClendon banged his injured arm.

"Be careful," Escalante cautioned, "it looks like he has been shot in the arm."

"Open the door for me," McClendon ordered the padre, his face grim after recognizing Billy Williams.

"Take him to my room," Escalante ordered and led the way. McClendon laid the wounded man on the bed while Escalante poured water into a basin to clean the wounded arm.

"Got any whiskey, Padre?"

"I have wine."

"Get a bottle while I take a look at his arm," Zack said, cutting away the filthy material with his big knife. Escalante hurried away.

"What happened?" Carmelita asked as she came into the room.

"Billy's been shot in the arm. Lost a lot of blood, but don't think it's too serious a wound," Zack said carefully examining the ragged hole in Billy's arm. "Bullet's gone clean through."

"Here, move out of the way," the woman said, pushing Zack aside. "I have cared for gunshot wounds before." Escalante came back with a dusty bottle.

"Mescal. It has been here a very long time. Thought it might be better than wine."

"You're right, Padre," Zack said taking the bottle and pouring a little into a glass. "Here," and he handed the bottle to Carmelita who saturated the wound with it. Billy cried out and came awake, looking around with unfocused eyes.

"Lay still until I bandage your arm," Carmelita said softly. Billy tried to focus on the woman.

"This heaven?"

"Ain't a trapper alive likely to ever see heaven," Zack cut in. "Take a sip of this, Billy," and he held the glass of mescal to the wounded man's lips. Billy drank it gratefully. It seemed to clear his head.

"That you, Zack?"

"It's me, boy, what happened?" Billy's face crumpled, tears forming in the corners of his eyes. He looked at Carmelita and felt embarrassed by his show of emotion. The woman pretended not to notice as she soaked clean bandages with the alcohol and bound the arm. He turned back to McClendon.

"They all dead, Zack . . . nineteen as good a men ever set a trap. Cheyenne caught the first bullet. Never knowed what hit him." Gradually, McClendon pulled the story of the terrible massacre from him. Zack's features flattened into a tight band across his forehead, his lips a thin line as he listened to the desperate struggle by men outnumbered three to one. With the massacre of the mountain men, it looked like it was going to be up to the small group of men he had pulled together plus whatever Don Diego and Chaves managed to come up with.

"Find Billy something to eat will you, Padre?" McClendon turned to the woman. "Carmelita, this is Billy Williams, a trapper friend of mind. Would appreciate it, if you could look after him while I'm gone."

Williams started to get off the bed. "Hell, Zack, gimme a minute and I'll be ready to ride again."

Carmelita pushed him back down on the bed, "you are not able to ride, Señor Billy. You need rest as does your horse."

207

"Zack, find me a horse. I can ride, you know I can."

McClendon shook his head, "Carmelita is right, you need rest. Tell you what, you give it a day and if you feel up to it, head on down to Don Diego's ranch. It's just north of Santa Fe, four or five miles. That's where the rest of us will be holding up 'til we figure out how to pull Salezar's teeth for good."

Billy Williams accepted Zack's statement of fact. He could use a little rest and there was the pretty Carmelita fussing over him. He gave her a weak smile. Billy looked at McClendon, who stood tall and menacing in the small room.

"I'll join you tomorrow," he promised McClendon. Escalante came in with a bowl of stew and a thick slice of bread.

"This will lift your spirits, and then you sleep, no?" Carmelita took the bowl from Escalante and began feeding the wounded man.

McClendon started from the room when Carmelita called to him. He stopped and looked back at her.

"You be careful, Zack."

McClendon nodded. "Take care of Pauli," he said, and then he was through the door with the padre at his heels.

Billy looked at Carmelita. "Who is Pauli?" he asked taking a bite of bread.

"My son," the woman said simply.

"Oh," Billy said a little crestfallen. "Does your husband ride with Zack?"

"I have no husband. Salezar killed him before we could be married." Billy could see the smoldering hate for Salezar mixed with the pain, and he regretted asking. Then the woman's face hardened. "If Ignacia was living, he would be proud to ride by your friend, McClendon's side against Damasio Salezar."

Billy wasn't surprised by the statement, and he managed a small chuckle. "Don't know a man in them mountains wouldn't ride beside Zack even if it meant riding straight through the flaming gates of hell."

"I am not so sure that is not what's facing anyone who rides against Salezar," Carmelita said with a pensive look.

"Padre, keep an eye peeled. Expect things will start happening fast where Salezar is concerned." Zack was checking the cinch on his saddle. "Just make sure you keep the women inside the mission and stall Billy for as long as you can. But with Billy, expect that'll only be one or two days at best. The kid's got a lot of sand, and he and Cheyenne Jack were partners."

"I will do my best, but as you know, Doña Magalena and Carmelita are headstrong women." He lifted his hands helplessly.

"What was that you were saying?" Magalena asked, stepping through the door.

Father Escalante smiled at Zack. "*Vaya con Dios,* old friend," he said, and he disappeared back into the mission. Zack and the woman stood there a few seconds, looking at one another. Concern was etched on Magalena's face.

"Carmelita told me of the massacre," she said softly. "I am sorry for your friends." She moved next to him. Zack caught wind of her perfume, and it reminded him of high country wildflowers in early spring. Zack resisted the urge to crush her in his arms.

"Would appreciate it if you'd give Carmelita a hand looking after Billy," was all Zack could think to say. She reached out and laid a gentle hand on his leathered chest.

"You will be careful? Tell my father to have nothing to do with Damasio Salezar. I am afraid for my father when Damasio learns the truth about me."

"Don Diego is a smart man, Magalena. I wouldn't be too concerned with Peck and the others there." She came into his arms and he held her close for a moment before pulling away to look at her beautiful face.

"Listen, I don't know if this is such a good idea . . . what

209

I mean, you have everything . . . look at me, I can't tell you where my next meal will be coming from, much less how I'm going to pay for it. Me and Peck Overstreet been traipsing 'round mountains most of our life. Got nothing to offer. . . . Expect old Peck is right. We'll both die wandering across the land, looking to see around the bend of the next river or across some mountain range.''

Magalena merely smiled, pulled his head down, and kissed him gently on the lips. Zack's resistance vaporized, and he held her tight, reveling in the taste of her. She pulled back, yet stayed in his arms.

''You have more to offer a woman than you realize, Zack McClendon.'' Her voice was soft and husky. Her eyes in the harsh light of midday were dark and smoldering. Zack could almost feel their heat as she looked deeply into his own.

''Best get to riding,'' he finally said, not really wanting to let her go.

She kissed him once more and stepped back. ''Be careful,'' she said once more. ''Damasio will stop at nothing to get what he wants.'' Zack climbed into the saddle and looked down on the woman with soft eyes.

''Now that I see what I want, it's Salezar best look out,'' Zack said, his voice taking on a hard edge. Magalena watched as McClendon rode away, broad-backed and ramrod straight in the saddle. If anyone could cause Salezar's downfall, it would be this big gringo with the eyes of a cougar. At that moment, a lot of other men were pinning their hopes on Zack McClendon as well.

Black Mesa was nothing more than a dark smudge behind him with McClendon clinging to the Rio Grande as it flowed southward slowly eating its way through the red layers of earth. Since leaving Taos, Zack had encountered only one other living soul in the desert heat, a Mexican peasant leading a slab-sided burro who had seen better days. He said his name was Luis Covarrubias. They shared a tortilla and a chunk of dried goat meat that McClendon found tough and stringy. The Mexican said he had a little patch of land deep in the broken country to the west of the river. It was lonesome at times but the Mexican said his life there was good. He and his wife had enough to eat and a few pesos for something extra from time to time, and he worked for himself. He showed McClendon the fine pottery of water jugs, plates and other items he made from the reddish-brown clay of the area that he was taking to Taos to sell. This he did once a year, living all winter and spring on the proceeds. A beautiful water pitcher painted sky blue with a band of dark red, circling the neck caught McClendon's eyes. The glaze caught the sun, reminding Zack of shiny stones in a Rocky Mountain stream. McClendon gave the old Mexican a five-dollar gold piece instructing him to deliver it to Doña Magalena at the mission.

"But this ees two much money, señor. It is only worth three pesos," Luis Covarrubias protested, trying to return the gold coin. McClendon refused, stepping into the saddle once more.

"Just make sure you give it to the lady."

"I will, señor," Luis promised, bowing gratefully to the American. "You can depend on Luis, that's ees a promise." McClendon touched his hat and took the buckskin to a steady lope, leaving the Mexican smiling broadly at his good fortune.

Luis Covarrubias slapped the tired burro on the rump, "Let's go and you be careful, little one. We must not break this special gift." The burro started forward at his usual pace, his long ears flicking back and forth at the sound of Luis's happy voice.

An hour later, McClendon stopped to water the buckskin and found himself studying a cloud of dust to the south that clung low to the horizon. Through the quivering heat waves McClendon estimated the number of horses at well over fifty. Without really knowing why, McClendon had already ruled out the possibility that it could be Peck Overstreet and some of Don Diego's men. After all, why would they be headed back to Taos? Had they been forced to abandon the ranch by

Salezar? He stepped into the saddle, keeping his eyes on the riders, who were still two miles off but coming hard at him. An uneasiness settled over him as he rode cautiously forward.

At a distance of a mile, McClendon caught the flash of metal in the sun and pulled up. A blaze of color struck him in the eyes and he knew he was looking at Mexican soldiers. McClendon looked around him. At this point, the only safe place to escape was into the broken country leading into the mountains. To cross the Rio Grande would only put him deep into the flat desert of cactus and sagebrush—not an ideal place to lose pursuers. He began moving away from the river the same time he was spotted by the soldiers. There was a distant shout, and McClendon put the spurs to the big horse, who lunged forward into a strong gallop. He had to be careful riding fast over ground he did not know. A fall now could be devastating to him or his horse.

McClendon took his eyes from the rough ground for a moment to see if he was being pursued and was startled to see the soldiers riding hard to cut him off from the protective folds of country to the east. He threw caution to the winds and gave the buckskin his head as a puff of smoke leaped in the distance followed by a pop. The shot fell short. There were more popping sounds, but McClendon leaned across the neck of his horse, concentrating on the increasingly rough ground. The open canyons yawned back at him at a distance of three hundred yards. He prayed his horse didn't stumble now or that the narrow canyon ahead of him didn't turn out to be blind. Either way, Zack figured he would be dead.

He chanced another look behind him to find the soldiers had closed the distance considerably and were nearly in rifle range now. He was further shocked to see Salezar leading the pack on his large white horse. A bullet droned by him like some fat bumblebee. He urged more speed from his horse as slugs bounced off the naked rocks around him.

McClendon swept into the mouth of the cedar-dotted canyon at full speed, feeling his horse shudder. For a moment raw fear clutched his throat at the thought of falling now. He would be shot to pieces by Salezar's men in seconds. The big horse regained his stride and with a final burst of speed was lost to the pursuing soldiers. The canyon walls grew steep and protruding rocky outcropping narrowed the canyon floor even more. Above him, on both sides, sandstone and granite formations pushed upward for hundreds of feet, their colors of dull gray and vivid magenta intermingling with the dark greens of cedar and pine.

Behind him McClendon could hear the thunder of hooves echoing loudly against the narrow walls. Without warning the buckskin stumbled and went down hard, throwing McClendon over his head to the rocky ground. Zack hit on his back, tumbled once, and, despite the pain, regained his footing instantly. He ran back to the downed horse, noticing the blood on the horse's stomach and hindquarters. Zack's features hardened, and he slipped the thong holding his rifle from the saddle and brought it to his shoulder as the soldiers burst into view. He felt the anger rise up inside him as he unhorsed the lead soldier, who was no longer Salezar. Apparently the officer had not been so willing to ride recklessly into the canyon. The roar of McClendon's big bore rifle sounded like a cannon in the narrow-walled canyon. The soldiers drew up immediately, milling around their fallen comrade, who was beyond caring. Where there had been two eyes, the dead soldier now had three.

McClendon used this time of confusion and hesitancy on the part of the soldiers to grab his possibles sack and start up the rocky wall of the canyon. If he intended to survive this, he had to get some altitude between himself and the soldiers. He could hear their voices clearly as he climbed. Sweating heavily from the exertion and the heat, McClendon was two hundred yards up the wall before Salezar rode up and forced his men deeper into the canyon. They came with caution at first, but as soon as they spotted his dead horse, there were shouts of joy and laughter. They knew the gringo would never leave this canyon alive without a horse to ride.

Zack hunkered down behind a wagon-sized boulder and watched with smoldering eyes as the soldiers spread out across the canyon, trying to cut his trail. He reloaded his rifle without thinking. And then a familiar voice floated up to him on the heated air.

"Hey, gringo, give yourself up," Damasio Salezar shouted, "I have your men in jail. You can hang with them tomorrow. As you can see, I have over seventy men with me here. There is no way for you to escape." The words stung McClendon and forced the truth on him. Salezar would not be here now if he was lying. The heated silence was broken by dislodged rocks as the soldiers scrambled over them looking for his trail. McClendon felt the hate in him take over, yet he stayed hidden. If he chanced a shot at Salezar now they would riddle him with bullets. He looked upward at the steep slope. He had to get higher, out of their rifle range, yet still in his. Zack began crawling upward towards a slab of rock a hundred yards away. He thanked God his leather clothes were weathered almost to the same color as the surrounding rocks. He was within thirty feet of the huge slab of sandstone when a shout went up from down below. Immediately there was a burst of rifle fire that fell short. He almost wanted to laugh, glad that it was Mexicans shooting at him. According to Peck, when a Mexican became excited, he almost always shot too soon and too short, never allowing for distance and angle of ground.

The bullets weren't even close, and McClendon scrambled the short distance to the ledge and pulled himself up and over. In doing so, McClendon nearly rolled over a rattler who was sunning himself. There was a warning buzz before Zack swept the snake into the air with the point of his long rifle. He lay down on the flat rock and sighted down the barrel. There was no way they could shoot him now without flanking him, and he had no intentions of letting them do that. The big gun growled and a Mexican soldier climbing the wall screamed and pitched backward, bringing loose rocks down on those below him. Mexicans ran for cover ahead of the tumbling rocks.

McClendon smiled and reloaded the weapon from powder and shot out of his possibles bag. He could hear Salezar screaming orders at the retreating soldiers. McClendon allowed a cold smile to settle over his face as he tried to draw a bead on the prancing figure on horseback. The gun roared once more and Salezar left the back of the white horse as if shot from a cannon. McClendon's half-spent big bullet put a huge dent in the Mexican's chin-strapped metal helmet at a distance of over eight hundred yards.

The dazed Mexican officer scrambled behind some rocks while his soldiers stood by, shocked that their leader had been nearly killed. The badly shaken Salezar removed the chin strap from the helmet with unsteady hands and pulled it off. There was a quarter-inch dent in the metal the size of a fifty peso coin.

"Get down, you fools!" Salezar screamed at his men who dropped to the rocks like flies as McClendon's gun boomed once again. A Mexican some distance away from Salezar had his chest ripped open by the slug. He flopped over screaming, spilling bright blood across the dull rocks. Silence fell over the heated canyon. Those soldiers who were in the process of climbing the steep wall plastered themselves to what little cover was available and stayed there. None wanted to draw any of McClendon's deadly shots.

Salezar wiped stinging sweat from his brow, trying to ignore the ache in his head caused by McClendon's bullet. He considered his next move. It would be dark in two hours, and he wanted to be in Taos by nightfall.

"Sergeant!" Salezar called. Dutifully, Sergeant Sagasta zigzagged his way over to where the Mexican officer was hiding.

"Sí, Capitán," Santiago Sagasta said, breathing hard.

"Take twenty of your best men and remain here. When it starts to get dark, you should have no trouble flushing this man out. And when you do, show him no mercy, understood!"

"Sí, Capitán!" said Sagasta, but he did not like the assignment one bit. The gringo in the rocks was much dangerous and

215

a deadly shot. He hated to think about stalking such a man in the dark.

"I will take the rest of the men with me and proceed into Taos as I planned. If I find resistance, we will destroy the town."

Santiago Sagasta merely nodded his head, knowing full well there weren't enough men left in the tiny community to offer any organized resistance. It was the women the vain Salezar was after; nothing less would do.

"Bring me my horse," he said to Sagasta, who did as he was ordered, expecting to be shot any minute while Salezar barked orders to his men. Slowly they left the rocks, and, keeping the upper wall of the canyon between them and their horses, they made their way back down the canyon.

Standing behind the neck of his horse, Salezar shouted up at McClendon. "Gringo, I go to Taos now, but I leave you twenty men to keep you company. I promise to take care of Doña Magalena and my little puta, Carmelita, while you are busy here." Salezar laughed derisively as he led his animal away.

"Salezar!" McClendon screamed. But the Mexican was now out of earshot. McClendon settled back down on the giant slab, feeling the prick of white-hot anger race through his veins. There was no way he could stop Salezar from reaching the women now. Why hadn't he planned things better? He was mad at himself for allowing his thinking to become clouded first by Carmelita and then later by the smoky-eyed Magalena. If things had remained strictly business maybe things would not be in such a mess. Whatever else, he was stuck here until dusk. After that he had to manage to slip away from the waiting soldiers, steal a horse and ride to Don Diego's. He had to get Peck and the others out of jail, and suddenly he knew how he would do it.

CHAPTER 22

"I'm beginning to hate this town," Peck Overstreet remarked, his one eye glowering through the bars at the guard who sat in a straight chair ten feet away. Exhausted and dust-covered from their forced march, most of those with Peck simply dropped to the bare floor and fell asleep as soon as they were herded into the stockade.

Skin Ledbetter lay against a wall next to Peck and seemed to be suffering the worse from the blistering march due to the recent leg wound. Peck filled the bowl of his pipe and handed Skin his tobacco pouch.

"Town ain't too bad, Peck, it's people like Salezar and Armijo who make it miserable for everyone else," Skin said, lighting his pipe. "That ain't half-bad terbacker."

"Any hope this Armijo fellar will dehorn Salezar before we go under?" Peck asked gloomily.

"Nary a chance. Armijo unhitched Salezar from his chain and ain't got the juice to rehook him."

"Jest hope Cheyenne Jack gets back with enough men to

help Zack before Salezar shows up in Taos," Peck said worriedly. The guard laughed loudly. Both men looked through the bars at the Mexican, wondering what was so funny, not realizing he had been listening to their conversation.

"What's eatin' you Pedro?" Zack asked.

The guard laughed again, rocking back in his chair. "Don't you know?"

"Know what, you crazy Mexican," Peck snapped. Overstreet hadn't had any coffee since early that morning and he was growing more irritable by the minute.

"Thees Cheyenne Jack you speak of, he and eighteen others are dead."

"What?" both men said in unison, the shock of what the Mexican was saying, plain on their face.

The guard looked delighted to be the one to break such news. "Lieutenant Gomez and his men trapped the gringos north of Mora and wiped them out to a man. Unfortunately, Gomez was killed by a stray bullet."

Peck felt numbed by the news. His forgotten pipe still clenched tightly in his teeth, died out. He turned to look at Skin Ledbetter.

"Zack ain't got a chance against sixty, seventy men," he whispered. "No way he can hold Salezar off much less spring us outta here."

"And that sets a new trap in the water don't it," Skin said solemnly.

Damasio Salezar rode proudly into the dusty streets of Taos, leading his column of soldiers as a fading sun disappeared behind the dark peaks to the west that marked the Continental Divide. Out of the corner of his eyes, he saw men scurrying for alleyways and into buildings. Salezar smiled to himself, pleased he could strike such fear in men. When he became governor, they would know what true fear really was. He held up his hand and brought the column to a halt in front of Juan

Ortega's cantina. He motioned to one of his men, who slipped from the saddle and hurried into the bar. He reappeared in a few minutes and said something to Salezar who ordered most of his men to secure the town. He turned towards the mission, taking a dozen soldiers with him.

His men kicked open the wooden doors to the church and Salezar entered, holding his pistol in his hand. Father Escalante was kneeling before the Virgin Mary and he looked around at the soldiers and stood up.

"What is the meaning of this?" he demanded. "This is a house of God, not a cantina."

"Precisely, Father. That is why we are here," Salezar said, motioning his men around him to begin their search.

"You cannot do this thing," Escalante said, blocking the soldiers' path.

Salezar looked at the padre with burning eyes. "Either step aside, Padre, or die," Salezar said simply.

Slowly Father Escalante did as he was told, and the soldiers rushed around him through a rear door to the sanctuary.

"I will lodge a strong protest to Governor Armijo and to the government in Mexico City for such barbaric action," Escalante said. Salezar shrugged his shoulders.

"As you wish, Father." Salezar's eyes fairly gleamed as his men came back, leading Doña Magalena and Carmelita, both tight-lipped and drawn. Carmelita had managed to hide Pauli beneath the bed when she realized soldiers were searching the mission. She and Magalena were standing in the doorway when the soldiers came down the hall.

"Ah, ladies, it is so good to see you again. I trust you have gotten to know one another better." Salezar smiled broadly. "After all, it is fitting for my future wife to know my mistress. That way, there can be no misunderstanding later, no?" He laughed loudly, enjoying their discomfort.

"What is the meaning of this?" Doña Magalena demanded, her voice cold and distant.

"Why, I came to fetch you home, of course," Salezar responded. Just then two soldiers appeared from the rear, shoving a sickly looking man ahead of them.

"We found this man hiding in the Padre's bedroom," one of the soldiers explained.

"Wasn't hiding," Billy Williams snapped.

Salezar caught the concerned look on Carmelita's face, and his eyes narrowed as he studied the man closely.

"What is your name?"

"Billy Williams," he said defiantly, looking Salezar in the eyes. "Late of Colorado and the high lonesome," he added for effect.

"You are a friend of this Zack McClendon, no?"

"Never heard of the man," Billy lied.

"You lie! All you gringo trappers are like brothers, willing to die rather than talk about one another," Salezar screamed.

"Please, this is a church, Señor Salezar," Escalante interjected, hoping to prevent further trouble.

"All the more reason to tell the truth," Salezar quipped.

"Ain't tellin' you nuthin' about Zack," Billy said, clamping his mouth shut.

"There is no need," Salezar said. "I know precisely where Zack McClendon is at the moment." He did not fail to see the sharp look Magalena threw at him. He smiled again, looking the tiny group over with cold eyes. "That is right, I know where he is and that most likely he is dead by now."

"Ain't no way old Zack's gone under," Billy said.

"Oh, but you are very wrong. I left him pinned down in a canyon with twenty of my best men stalking him. There is no escape this time, even for the legendary man you people call Straight Arrow," Salezar said, a sneer twisting his features.

"My father will have you shot!" Doña Magalena spit out.

"Such hot blood," Salezar remarked, "and to think of all those nights we wasted sitting on the veranda so proper and above reproach." He shook his head. "It was a good thing I had little Carmelita here to ease my suffering."

Carmelita flushed crimson, "I did it for the liberation fighters. Every time you touched me, I felt sick to my stomach."

The smile faded from Salezar's cruel face, and in two quick steps he backhanded the woman across the mouth. The stinging blow sounded like a pistol shot in the small room. Blood seeped from the corner of Carmelita's mouth yet she continued to stare defiantly at Salezar.

Salezar wanted to hurt them both as he himself had been hurt by their betrayal. Even now, a hot wave of embarrassment washed over him. He turned his cold eyes to the only woman he had ever loved.

"And I do not fear Don Diego's reprisal."

"What do you mean?" Magalena asked, her hand flying to her throat.

"The great Don is dead." Salezar saw the instant pain and welling of tears in Magalena's eyes and he laughed harshly.

"You killed my father?" Magalena whispered, not wanting to believe that even Salezar could do such a thing. Carmelita moved to comfort the woman.

"In a way. First he was shot by his trusted ally and friend, Joaquin Cobo. I only ran him through with my saber. His men are all dead as well."

Magalena collapsed into Carmelita's arms, sobbing.

"You bastard!" Billy yelled and started for Salezar only to be stopped by the soldiers' bayonets. "Peck Overstreet and the others will see you hang."

Salezar laughed once more. "That is another thing, gringo. I have them locked in my stockade. Tomorrow I will hang them. But for you, I think we keel you now." Billy's face drained of all color but he stood his ground.

"No wait, you must not do this!" Carmelita said, her eyes flying from Billy to Salezar.

"No? You want this man? How quickly they forget," he said, looking at the tight-faced Escalante.

"Ain't afraid of dying," Billy whispered. "Fact is, I shoulda

221

died back there with Cheyenne.'' Salezar looked at him sharply.

"So, you were with the others at Mora. Did others escape as well?''

"Go to hell, Salezar,'' Billy said gruffly.

Salezar laughed. "Take him out and shoot him now,'' he ordered his men.

"You can't do this,'' Father Escalante said, "in all that is holy, I beg you.''

"Pray, Padre, that I don't have you shot as well.'' Escalante straightened to his full height, his hands tightly clasping his Bible.

"Shoot me then in his place.''

Salezar shook his head. Even he wasn't quite ready to butt heads with the Catholic Church just yet.

The soldiers marched Williams from the tiny mission. Billy turned back at the door and spoke to the grieving women.

"Don't give up on Zack. It'll take more than a few Mexican soldiers to bring him down.'' And then he was gone into the night.

Father Escalante turned, knelt before the Virgin Mary, and began praying out loud for the soul of Billy Williams. The others remained silent, waiting for the shots that would end a young man's life on this planet.

When the rifles cracked a few minutes later, both women burst into tears.

"Now that is done, we will have a feast, no? My men are tired and hungry. Later, maybe, you and I will get to know one another a lot better since you are going to be my wife,'' Salezar said, touching Magalena's hair.

Magalena shrank under his touch, horrified by what Salezar was saying. "I would rather sleep in a bed of scorpions than have anything further to do with you Damasio.'' Her voice was cold and deliberate. Magalena still clung to the hope that McClendon was alive. She had a beautiful pitcher given to her by an old man who spoke of meeting a *mucho grande hombre* on the trail below Black Mesa.

Salezar merely laughed again. "The night is yet long, no? Perhaps you will change your mind."

There had been no exchange of gunfire between McClendon and the soldiers since Salezar had ridden away nearly two hours ago. He lay like a statue on the rock, unmoving except for his eyes, which searched every rock and crevice below him, marking each soldier's position. Soon it would be dark and McClendon wondered why the soldiers had not attacked.

As soon as he thought this, McClendon saw the soldiers starting to climb in unison in the fading light. McClendon smiled. A good tactic. He couldn't shoot them all at once; the others would have time to overrun his position.

The only trouble with a plan like that, no one wanted to be the one shot. He moved the big rifle to his shoulder and sighted on a Mexican who wore sergeant stripes. McClendon squeezed the trigger; yellow flame and black smoke leaped from the end of his rifle in the dying light. A cooling wind carried the smoke east. One second the sergeant was climbing and the next instant, he was tumbling back down the rocky slope. The other soldiers froze in place and began calling to one another across the rocky surface of the canyon wall.

McClendon sat up and calmly reloaded his gun while he watched two soldiers scramble to the bottom where the sergeant lay. Another thing he knew from experience; take out the leader and things generally went quickly to hell. It was time to make his move while the soldiers were undecided and confused. He had to have a horse. Without one, he was as good as dead.

A wide-eyed soldier rolled the prostrate body of Sergeant Sagasta over on his back and sucked in a sharp breath at the gristly sight. The lower half of Sagasta's face was completely missing where the big slug had torn through flesh and bone. Sergeant Sagasta was very dead.

"What do we do now, Pico?" another soldier asked who crawled over and looked at their leader.

The thin Mexican known as Pico studied on this for a moment. It was dusk dark now and he could barely make out the flat space of rock where the gringo was perched.

"I think we should leave. This hombre is a deadly shot and it grows dark."

"But what will we say to Capitán Salezar?"

Pico seemed irritated at being prodded into taking the lead now that the sergeant was dead. He was not even a private. The only private, Jaime Santulce, lay dead just several yards away, an early casualty of the gringo's gun.

"The capitán is not here facing this gringo's gun," Pico snapped. "Do you want to climb up there in the dark and kill him?" The soldier shook his head. Pico continued, "We tell Capitán Salezar that we left the gringo here to die. Without a horse, how he can live?" The other soldier didn't seem convinced.

"Thees gringo is deefrent, Pico," the soldier said reverently. "He is like something wild, half man, half lobo."

"He is a man, nothing more." Pico waved his hand. "Tell the others to climb back down. And be careful, this gringo loves head shots. I will bring the horses up." The other man nodded, glad to be leaving this haunting place of death. Every time he had moved, he felt as though the gringo watched only him. It made his skin crawl.

While the soldiers began their cautious descent, McClendon was already looking down on the single guard who watched over the horses. McClendon worked his way down the slope through the gathering shadows of night and slipped among the horses where the guard sat smoking. Just then Pico came walking up. The guard jumped to his feet.

"I heard a shot, did you keel the gringo?"

"That was hees rifle, stupido! Could you not tell? Sergeant

Sagasta ees dead. We leave here now before it ees too dark to find our way out of thees canyon.''

McClendon rose up out of the gloom, threw his leg over the nearest horse, yelling and firing one of his pistols as he grabbed the reins of the startled animal. The other horses broke forward and the guard and Pico had to scramble up the face of the canyon wall to keep from being trampled by the suddenly wild animals.

McClendon wheeled the stolen horse around and headed towards the mouth of the canyon at a brisk lope, leaving the unnerved soldiers to sort out the mass of confusion. He cleared the canyon just as a thin slice of moon pushed its way above the Sangre de Cristos, casting a weak paleness across the broken landscape. He pointed the horse southwest for Don Diego's hacienda at a hard gallop. He had no time to lose. Peck and the others were in jail; he would have to free them before they could try rescuing the women from Salezar. He only hoped they would be all right until then.

McClendon skirted the tiny settlement of Tesuque, a place mostly inhabited by Tewa Indians. The five-hundred-year-old pueblo was the sight where the first blow was struck in the Pueblo Revolt of 1680 by the Indians, who killed a Spanish civil servant by the name of Cristobal de Herrera. McClendon had found the Tewas unfriendly if not downright hostile when he and Peck had stopped by several years before. Most Mexicans and whites alike learned to leave them alone.

CHAPTER 23

A short time later, Zack saw the yellowed glow of windows that marked Don Diego's ranch. McClendon brought the worn-out animal down to a walk. When he got to the ranch, he would need to borrow a horse from Diego. The small-framed animal beneath him was about played out.

He walked the hard-breathing horse into the ranch yard and up to the house. Things seemed too quiet to suit him, and he looked around for signs of life. The outbuildings and bunkhouse stood dark and silent. *Where was everybody?* McClendon tied the horse to the hitch rack, went up the steps, and knocked on the door. A silhouetted figure passed by a curtained window.

"Open up Don Diego, it's me, Zack McClendon!" He heard boots crossing a planked flooring, and suddenly the door was yanked open. The big, barrel-chested Mexican Joaquin Cobo stood there in the doorway.

McClendon recognized the hired hand and brushed past him. "Where is Don Diego?" Cobo closed the door behind them

226

and went back to the fireplace, where he was in the process of building a fire against the evening chill.

"He rode into town," was all the startled Cobo could think to say at the sudden appearance of the wild-eyed trapper. Had Salezar failed?

McClendon looked around the room. The house seemed strangely quiet and no sounds came from the kitchen where he knew the cook spent most of his time.

"Where are the rest of the men?" Zack this time was watching the big Mexican closely.

"Rode in with Don Diego."

"Why did they ride into town?" Something wasn't right about the big Mexican and he had not even mentioned the obvious fact that Peck and the others were in jail.

"I do not know," Cobo said lamely. McClendon knew now the big Mexican was lying.

"Got anything to eat? Coffee? And, I'm going to need another horse. Mine was shot out from under me by Salezar's men."

"We have nothing to eat. The cook had to leave, his sister is very sick."

"Then I'll settle for coffee," McClendon said, stepping into the deserted kitchen. While he poured coffee, Zack looked around at the disarray. There were mixing bowls, opened containers of flour, sugar and other items lying about. The cook had left in a big hurry, McClendon concluded.

"What about you, why are you still here?" Zack asked coming back into the room.

Cobo shrugged as he bent down to add a bigger piece of wood to the fire now that it had caught hold. "I was told to stay here in case you came," Cobo lied, poking the fire with a thick iron rod.

For the first time, McClendon noticed the dark stain against the fireplace next to the Mexican who seemed to be trying to cover it with his body. Suddenly, it hit him. What he felt here was death.

The big Mexican seemed to sense the change in the trapper and he came up swinging the iron rod in a vicious sweep, aiming for McClendon's head.

Zack dropped the cup, ducked the deadly blow, and drove a fist deep into the man's stomach. The air rushed from Cobo's lungs but he recovered quickly as McClendon backed away from the Mexican who crouched for another swing with the rod.

"Drop it, Cobo," but the Mexican's eyes were glazed over with hate and he came at McClendon with a rush. This time Zack's hand shot downward to his pistol, and he was firing before the Mexican had taken two steps. The slugs ripped into Cobo's chest, three shots fired as one.

The Mexican absorbed the shots without falling and he stood there, swaying on his feet and looking down at the bright blood pumping from his body. When he looked back at McClendon hate still lingered in his eyes, but there was also the realization that he was dying. Cobo tried to raise the iron rod again, but it slipped from his weakening grasp and clattered to the floor.

"Where is Don Diego?" Zack asked the swaying Mexican.

Cobo tried to smile, but failed. Life was leaving him fast. "I keeled him, gringo," he whispered and crashed to the floor.

McClendon stood there a few seconds absorbing the news about Diego, thinking immediately of Magalena and how profoundly affected she would be. And at the center of all this was Salezar. McClendon's features hardened as he left the house and saddled a big-framed dun horse that was standing in the corral. Cobo's horse most likely, McClendon thought as he threw a Mexican rig on the large animal. He opened the corral gate, stepped into the saddle, and drove his heels into the dun's sides. The animal bolted forward at a dead run. There would be no more reacting to Salezar's actions. From here on out, Zack was going on the offensive.

When he slipped into the darkened streets of Santa Fe, McClendon was surprised by the ghostly feeling of the place.

The plaza, normally raucous and filled with activity, was dark and silent. The only human movement came from bands of soldiers patrolling back and forth. McClendon left the horse in a narrow passage between two buildings and moved quietly as a shadow towards his destination. To try and force his way into the stockade and free Peck and the other trappers would be suicide. He was left with only one choice, and Zack prayed he had picked the right one and the right night.

A shadowy figure appeared against the folds of lace curtains gently moving by the desert breeze that flowed into the darkened bedroom. Within seconds, the figure gained entrance, hugging the wall for a few minutes and listening to the rhythmic breathing of the two people on the bed. The room smelled of perfume and whiskey. Once his eyes were accustomed to the darkness, McClendon moved quietly to the edge of the bed, reached out and touched the sleeping man's shoulder. Instantly, the man came fully awake.

"Huh—what is it?" Armijo asked, thinking it one of his soldiers who guarded the outside door. He changed his mind upon hearing the ominous clicking of a pistol. Armijo sat up quickly and was about to scream for his men when he felt the cold steel pressing into the side of his temple.

"One word and you're dead," McClendon hissed. Doña Gertrudis Barceló rolled over in her sleep and mumbled for her lover to lay back down.

A match flared in the darkness, and Armijo found himself looking into the coldest pair of eyes he had ever seen. McClendon touched the wick of the bedside lamp, and a flickering yellow light spread across the room. He threw the match to the floor.

"How dare you come here!" Armijo snapped, thinking the man was some Mexican peasant by his dress. Then he looked closer. "Who are you?" There was growing alarm in his voice.

"Out of the bed and put on your clothes," McClendon ordered. The woman was awakened by their voices, and her eyes grew wide at the sight of a man standing there holding a gun. Unconsciously, a scream formed in her throat as she sat up in bed, half exposing herself to the man's cold eyes.

"You scream and lover boy here is dead," Zack said softly, waving the big pistol at Armijo who was busy getting into his clothes.

"Do as he says, please," Armijo told the woman, who finally realized she was uncovered and quickly pulled the sheet up to her throat.

"Who are you?" Armijo asked as he slipped into his shoes.

"McClendon, Zack McClendon," came the cold reply. Armijo's eyes filled with terror.

"Damasio spoke of you. You are the one wanted for murder," Armijo managed to say. The woman only stared wide-eyed at the man towering over Manuel Armijo.

"Salezar set me up with that one, although I've killed a few of his men today and almost nailed him as well." Armijo shrank further from the big trapper.

"What could you possibly want with me?"

"You have any soldiers still loyal to you?"

"Of course I do!" Armijo snapped, getting a rein on his unchecked emotions.

"I want your word you won't interfere when Salezar and I butt heads. Then you and I are going over to the stockade and release my friends."

"You must be joking?"

"Death is no joking matter, Armijo, and you of all people should know this." The governor paled somewhat.

"And you trust me to keep my men out of this affair?"

"All I can do is ask, the rest is up to you. But if you decide differently, you'll be crushed just like Salezar will be tomorrow." McClendon's words had a final ring to them and Armijo fully believed the tall trapper meant every word he said.

"What about after?" Armijo asked.

"Got no quarrel with you . . . yet. Expect some of your

people may have though. Salezar overstepped his bounds with me when he ordered some of my trapper friends bushwhacked in Mora. Had Don Diego murdered as well. That's enough for me to act." Armijo was shocked by the news Don Diego was dead, and he grew worried.

"I'll admit Salezar has been a problem of late, but I had no idea he had carried things so far. Don Diego was a close personal friend."

"Look around you man! Haven't you noticed what this town has turned into?" McClendon said harshly, his eyes flaming hot. "Or is ill-gotten money and fornicating all you care about?" Armijo turned crimson. Nobody had ever dared talk to him in such manner, but he kept quiet now.

McClendon backed over to the open window and pushed aside the curtains. He motioned for Armijo with the gun.

"Let's go, it's past time for talking." Armijo obediently came over to the window. "One other thing. Tell your ladylove to keep her mouth shut. I see any guards making a play and you'll be the first killed," McClendon promised.

"Please, Doña Barceló, say nothing of this," Armijo pleaded. "I will do as the grin—, as McClendon asks. Everything will be okay."

"As you wish," the woman said, looking at Armijo with soft eyes. "But you," she said to McClendon, "if you hurt the governor, I will see you hang." McClendon grinned at the fiery woman.

"Why do I get the feeling hanging is everyone's favorite form of punishment around here?" he asked, and then they were through the window and gone in the night. Doña Barceló rushed to the window, taking the sheet with her, but the night was empty when she looked out.

"How many guards at the stockade?" McClendon questioned Armijo.

"I—I do not really know. Two maybe three, no more."

"Just remember, when we get there you even breath the word double-cross and I'll shoot your frijole basket loose."

"Do not worry, Señor McClendon, you have my word. I will do my best to keep my soldiers from joining Salezar, but I must tell you, some will."

"Fair enough," McClendon said as they crossed the quiet parade ground of the Palace of the Governors and entered the hallway that led to the stockade. No guards had been outside, yet McClendon knew that less than twenty yards away Armijo had at least a hundred men in the barracks.

Armijo led the way down the hall and opened a wooden door that led to the cell. Three soldiers jumped stiffly to their feet at attention upon seeing the governor. McClendon shoved Armijo deeper into the room and drew a bead on the surprised guards.

"Hold it! Don't any of you so much as breathe deep."

"Do as he says," Armijo said to his men, who dropped their weapons at McClendon's insistence. Peck Overstreet, roused from sleep by the sudden noise, was astonished to see McClendon standing there holding a gun.

"Ain't you a sight fer this old eye of mine," Peck boomed, waking the others who came up rubbing their eyes.

McClendon grinned at his friend. "You, unlock the cell," he ordered one of the guards. The Mexican hesitated.

"Do as he says!" Armijo screamed at the guard. The man almost jumped out of his shoes, fumbling nervously with the keys.

Peck and the others filed out, banging one another on the shoulder. Relief was etched clearly on their faces.

"Told you Zack couldn't be brought down by no greaser," he said to Skin Ledbetter and Ingram.

"In the cell," McClendon ordered the guards and Armijo.

"There is no reason to lock us up. I gave you my word," Armijo said.

"That may be, Armijo, but like you say, some of your men might not listen to you and we don't want to have to watch our backs right now. Got bigger things to worry about."

Peck peered hard with his one eye at the squat Mexican. "So this little squirt's Armijo, huh?"

"In the flesh," Zack said, locking the cell behind the Mexicans.

"Why don't we jest render him to grease while we got the chance?" Skin Ledbetter said.

"Gave him my word," Zack said.

"All that means is, we'll hafta fight him and Salezar together," Peck said, wishing he could get his hands on the little man for a minute. Armijo shrank back from the bars as if half expecting McClendon to turn the two trappers loose on him.

"That may be, but it's the chance we take." Peck walked over to the bars and looked hard at one of the guards.

"How come you ain't laughing now, Pedro," Peck said to the one who had told them of the massacre at Mora. Sullen-faced, the guard turned away.

The released men moved out into the hallway and waited for McClendon to speak. Zack looked over the faces of men who had seen a lot of living and dying. If there was going to be a fight, he could think of no better group of men to have around him.

"We're facing a pretty grim situation," McClendon began. "Salezar probably will have close to a hundred men under his command after he picks up those that desert from Armijo. I take it you know Don Diego is dead along with his men as well as Cheyenne Jack and the others. Only Billy managed to make it to Taos after he was shot."

"Billy gonna make it?" Skin asked.

"Left him at the mission with Father Escalante. Carmelita Torres is looking after him." McClendon told them of his gunfight with Salezar and his men in the canyon and how later he was forced to kill Joaquin Cobo when he came at him with a fireplace iron.

"Then Billy is done fer soon as Salezar hits Taos," Peck said. Nobody had a mind to refute the statement.

"What about the women? Surely Salezar would not stoop so low as to harm them?" Lafe Ingram said.

McClendon looked worried on this score. "We can only

McClendon looked worried on this score. "We can only hope the man possesses some decency, but remember, he was spied on by one and scorned by the other. Hard to say what will happen, but Carmelita and Doña Magalena might surprise Salezar. Those are two tough ladies." He hoped he sounded more convincing than he felt.

"We got to find our weapons," Ezekiel said.

"They locked up in that office down there," Skin said, pointing down the hallway.

"Let's go then and be as quiet as you can. We alert Armijo's soldiers now, we'll never get out of here alive," Zack reminded them. They found the door locked but Zack put his shoulder to the flimsy door and it popped open. After they had sorted through the pistols, knives and rifles and made sure they were still loaded and primed, the group slipped across the parade ground without alerting anyone.

"Where to now?" Peck asked McClendon as soon as they were safely away from the Palace of the Governors. They were standing in the shadows between the blacksmith shop and the livery.

"We got about three, maybe, four hours before daylight. Salezar won't waste any time getting back here to carry out your hanging, so you can add another two hours or so to that. For now we'll take over the hotel and post a couple guards while the rest of us grabs some sleep."

"Hotel suits me jest fine," Peck said. "They got a kitchen and that means coffee."

CHAPTER 24

Carmelita had endured a long night of sheer terror, physical abuse and violation at the hands of a furious Salezar. When he learned McClendon had escaped, killing Sergeant Sagasta in the process, Salezar became even more abusive. Through it all, her resolve never faltered, her spirit was never diminished by Salezar's attacks. Carmelita simply detached her mind from what the crazed Mexican officer was doing to her body. And when she failed to respond properly, he beat her even more. When Salezar finally collapsed across the bed, exhausted, Carmelita had gathered her torn clothes to her and crawled to a corner of the room where she finally gave in to the pain and sobbed quietly.

Now in the predawn darkness, a bleary-eyed Salezar climbed heavily into the saddle. A cold wind cut across the plaza like a sharp knife, causing the soldiers to hunch over in their saddles. It had been a short night for all of them, and now they had to endure the punishing ride back to Santa Fe.

A door opened to the mission, and Doña Magalena came out

dressed in a riding habit and mounted the horse a soldier was holding for her.

"I trust you slept well?" Salezar said, his voice emotionless and cold.

"I slept not at all, Damasio," Magalena fired back, "for I spent the night thinking of the many ways to kill you for what you've done to my father and to Carmelita."

Salezar responded with a harsh laugh, holding no humor. "You should be thankful it was Carmelita I choose last night, no? But there is tonight, after I'm done with this gringo McClendon. I will first let him watch as I hang his men, then I will hang him as well."

"You ride to your death and so do most of your men," Carmelita spit out. "Zack McClendon *is* a legend because of his deeds, not because he talks about them like you do. Cutting the ears off dead Texans who couldn't defend themselves is not much to brag about."

"Oh, so you still have a little fire left in you after all. It ees too bad you did not show more of it last night, *puta*. Maybe, I hang you next to this McClendon you seem so fond of." Without waiting for a reply, Salezar jammed his four-inch rowels deep into the flanks of his horse and left Taos at a brisk lope. From a darkened window, a man watched the soldiers leave in a cloud of dust. He breathed a sigh of relief and returned to his bed to wait for daylight to come.

Doña Magalena was horrified at the discolored, swollen face of the woman who rode quietly beside her when it grew light enough to see. She could only guess at the bruises Salezar had inflicted on Carmelita's body. Magalena wanted to speak words of comfort to the abused woman but she dared not risk it with Salezar riding so near them.

Salezar drove them hard before allowing a stop to rest the horses, fifteen miles below Black Mesa. The two women walked down to the river's edge and out of earshot of the soldiers.

"How is Pauli?" Carmelita asked in a small voice.

"He is fine but he misses you terribly." Magalena put out a hand and touched Carmelita's damaged face. "I am so sorry for last night."

Carmelita's eyes flashed fire and hardened. "He will pay . . . for that but mostly for what he's done to Montoya and the gringos who came to help." Her eyes softened somewhat, "I, too, am sorry about Don Diego. He was a good man." Magalena nodded.

"Do you think Zack will be able to get his men out of jail?" Magalena asked.

"Yes. Salezar underestimates McClendon and he will pay for this mistake today when we ride into Santa Fe."

"*Vamonos!*" Salezar shouted, and everyone checked their cinches and mounted up. Salezar waved them on and the yellow dust cloud followed them south as they skirted the Rio Grande.

Before he settled down to catch an hour or two of sleep McClendon had ordered several men, led by Ezekiel Smith, to break into the only mercantile in town and take whatever they needed. The Banks brothers slipped into their gunshop and brought back all the guns and ammunition they had there. McClendon closed his eyes for an hour, but sleep would not come for thinking of the two women and what Salezar may have done to them.

He watched restlessly as dawn came to the quiet streets of Santa Fe. Even the soldiers were gone and McClendon wondered if Armijo had pulled them back, away from the fight that was sure to come in a few hours, or whether he had merely redeployed them in the surrounding buildings to join the fight when Salezar showed up. Tackling Salezar head-on was one thing, but if Armijo's soldiers joined in the fracas it was all over.

Peck came in through the back leading Manuel Chaves and smiling broadly.

"Look who I run into," Peck said, stopping by the coffee

pot. Since taking over the abandoned hotel last night, Overstreet had taken over kitchen duties and seemed to be enjoying himself.

"Señor McClendon, I am sorry I and my men did not foresee the attack on Don Diego's hacienda. Maybe we could have saved Diego's life."

"Not your fault. Guess we both underestimated Salezar. How many men do you have we can count on?"

"Twenty-five, but I'm afraid more than half are not very good with guns," Chaves said apologetically.

"We take what we can get. Why don't you deploy some of those men who aren't used to handling guns along the roads and trails you think Salezar will most likely use to come into town."

Chaves grinned, accepting the cup of coffee from Overstreet. "This I have done already. The remainder are scattered about in the various buildings you see before you. None will act until they hear your guns."

"That's good, Chaves," McClendon said. "Like a man that thinks ahead. Now if we only knew Armijo will keep his promise, we might stand a chance of pulling this off."

"My uncle will bide his time until he sees how things go. If it appears Salezar is winning, he will throw his forces against us." Chaves shrugged. "What can I say, my uncle is a survivor. If we win, he will want to be our friend, but deep down he will only wait until he is sure of winning and turn on us like a savage animal. These things I know," Chaves said simply.

They both sipped their coffee for a time and watched the night shadows pull back from the street, retreating between the adobe buildings. McClendon studied on this matter of Armijo. He was the only loose end to the equation. Chaves broke in on his thoughts.

"I am also sorry to hear that your friends were killed at Mora. We could have used their help badly."

"Only Billy Williams made it through to Taos. Expect Salezar put him to the blade first thing," McClendon said gloomily.

"What of the women?"

"Don't know for sure, but even a man like Salezar must have a little decency when it comes to women."

"Don't be too sure of that, amigo," Chaves said.

"You don't suppose he would use the women as a shield, do you?" McClendon was horrified at the thought.

"Salezar is too vain a man to hide behind a woman in full view of the town, even if it would benefit him in the end," Chaves assured him. McClendon wasn't comforted by Chaves's words.

"I must be off," Chaves said, standing up. "I need to check my men. Then I go visit my uncle."

McClendon turned away from the street to look at Chaves. "Armijo may not welcome you with open arms. What's to prevent him from throwing you in jail 'til this is over?"

"We are blood, amigo, do not worry," Chaves said lightly, although his eyes reflected his concern.

"What do you hope to gain by seeing Armijo?"

"To solidify his pledge to you."

"What makes you think he'll stand by just because you asked him?"

"Because, I am going to take his brother along with me as insurance. Then maybe he will listen."

"Just be careful, Chaves. Armijo may be your uncle, but I got a feeling with what's about to happen here, this time blood may be a lot thinner than water."

Chaves gave McClendon a thin smile, "With my uncle, it has always been."

Peck and Skin came up beside McClendon as they watched the Mexican move silently from building to building, conversing in low tones with his men. Finally, Chaves disappeared down an alley.

"Think he's got a chance with Armijo?" Skin asked, more out of curiosity than concern about saving his own hide.

239

McClendon smiled faintly. "He's all we got."

An hour passed and the day broke clear and bright. With the sun came the infernal heat. Even with all the windows opened in the hotel, a hot breeze sought out all the cool spaces, and before long the waiting men began to curse the heat as well as Salezar.

Rather than break up his small force, McClendon had decided to keep them together in the only two storied building facing the plaza. That is, all except one. Ezekiel Smith had taken his long gun and climbed into the church tower at the end of the street. His orders had been made plain by McClendon. Concentrate on killing Salezar, nothing else. McClendon hoped Salezar would not suspect them of putting the church to such use, but they were slim hopes. One never knew with a man like Salezar.

Whether out of cruelty or a desire to exert his power over them, Salezar stopped at the deserted ranch of Don Diego's. It was all Magalena could do to keep from breaking down when she entered the vacant house.

"Fix me breakfast," he ordered Carmelita. "The gringos won't mind hanging a little later than I promised them." He saw the stricken look on Magalena's face, and for a second, Salezar felt a twinge of remorse for the Don's death. Her pain was all too real. He came over to her where she sat at her father's desk, touching things as if the act would somehow bring her closer to her father. Salezar knelt down by her chair, removing his dented helmet.

"Magalena," he said softly, "your father was killed by mistake. Joaquin was to detain him until I arrived so I could talk some sense into him." He reached for her hand, but the distraught woman drew it quickly away from him.

"There is nothing you can say to me," she said woodenly. "This time, you have picked the wrong man to attack."

"Listen, I will let McClendon go if it pleases you . . . if you will still marry me."

Magalena stared at the Mexican officer, horrified. "Marry you! You ask me that in my father's house where you had him murdered. I would rather die next to Zack McClendon then to have you touch me again!"

Salezar stood up, his defenses back in place. "You may wish you had changed your mind when I am governor."

"Never!"

"Perhaps," Salezar said, turning to the kitchen, "when I am done with these gringos you will see things differently." Magalena lay her head in her arms on her father's desk while hot tears stained the green blotter.

While Salezar ate the meal Carmelita prepared for him, one of his soldiers rushed in with the news they had found Joaquin Cobo's body near the corral, covered with a tarp.

Carmelita had managed to talk Magalena into eating a little something to keep up her strength. The two women were seated quietly at the far end of the long table that was kept polished to a mirrorlike finish.

Salezar laid aside his fork, picked up the glass of brandy he preferred to coffee, and looked down the table at the women. "Seems your McClendon has murdered Joaquin Cobo on his way to Santa Fe."

"That what you call it, when the man who shot my father is killed?" flashed Magalena. Salezar raised the glass of brandy to his lips and tasted the sweet liquid.

"Don Diego always did keep the best liquor in all of New Mexico." He raised the glass in a silent salute.

"Enjoy it, for it will be your last," Magalena said.

"Ladies, you should not pin all your hopes on one gringo. What help can he expect to find in Santa Fe? Old men and farmers who know nothing of guns?" He laughed. "I have seventy well-trained soldiers, tempered like the finest steel by many bloody fights."

241

Carmelita lifted her bloodied eyes to Salezar. "We will prevail in our struggle. The old men . . . even the women. They will meet you in the streets with rakes, knives and even sticks when the time comes."

"Sticks, rakes? Against my men?" Salezar threw his head back and laughed at such lunacy. He got up from the chair and, taking his brandy, strolled down to where they sat.

"Let me tell you what will happen today . . . no, in one hour. First we will crush the resistance. No mercy will be given to anyone who resists." He turned his burning eyes on Magalena. "Next, we will exterminate the gringos." He walked behind them, looking up at the huge pillars supporting the ceiling. "When that is done, I will personally report to Manuel Armijo and put a bullet into his brain." He came back into their line of vision, his face red from the brandy. "So you see ladies," Salezar continued as he leaned across the table, holding them with his demonic eyes, "in less than two hours, I will be the new governor." The thunder of horses in the yard interrupted Salezar. He walked into the living room and pushed aside the curtains.

The women seemed to be thinking the same thing, that a lot more was riding on the outcome of the impending fight with McClendon than had first appeared. Salezar as governor! If that were allowed to happen, their very way of life in this valley would be over. Only the big trapper, McClendon, blocked this crazy man's path. Salezar came back into the kitchen and refilled his glass.

The front door opened in the other room and hurried footsteps came into the kitchen. Magalena and Carmelita's eyes were glued on the soldier who stepped briskly into the room.

"*Buenos dias,* Capitán," Lieutenant Delgado said, snapping a smart salute at his superior officer, who dispensed with the formality with a casual wave of his hand. Delgado started to continue, but hesitated upon seeing the women.

"It is okay, Lieutenant," Salezar replied, lighting a *cigarrito.* "The ladies are my guests and I have nothing to hide from them.'' He smiled down the table at the two women, who sat stiffly in their chairs, fully expecting more bad news.

Delgado began to speak, ''I have brought with me thirty men from the regiment to help you fight these gringos. I feel certain others will desert Armijo after they have had time to think about it.''

Salezar puffed rapidly on the Mexican cigarette. ''You and your men will be rewarded for your faithfulness, this I promise. Together, we will easily crush McClendon to pieces.'' Delgado looked uncomfortable. ''What is it, man? Is there more news?''

''Sí, Capitán. The gringos were released from jail during the night by this McClendon.''

Salezar banged his fist on the table. ''Every time I hear this gringo's name, the news is bad. What else?''

Delgado wanted to smile at what he was about to say next, but the look on Salezar's face changed his mind. He stole a glance at the women at the far end of the table to gauge their reaction to what was being said, but their faces remained inscrutable.

''McClendon forced Armijo from Doña Barceló's bed at gunpoint. After the gringos were freed, he locked Armijo in the cell where he stayed until this morning.''

''It's too bad he wasn't kept there. Our job would have been made easier.''

''The gringos have barricaded themselves in the hotel. Chaves has another ten, fifteen men scattered about the plaza, nothing we can't handle,'' Delgado said confidently.

''And what of Armijo now?''

Delgado shook his head, ''this is the part that is amazing to me. Armijo has given his word to this McClendon that he will not interfere in the fight. Less than an hour ago, he told this to Manuel Chaves in my presence.''

''So, the old sly devil plays the game of the coyote,'' Salezar said, crushing out the cigarette carelessly on the polished table, scarring the wood. He looked at the women. ''Do you not see?'' The women remained silent. Salezar poured more brandy for himself from the bottle on the table.

"Armijo is a wise man, Delgado, do not forget this. But I know how he thinks. Therefore we will outflank his every move, every plan.'' Lieutenant Delgado merely nodded his head, not really understanding what Salezar was getting at, and he began to worry how much of this talk was brandy.

"He thinks he cannot lose. If the gringo wins, which is impossible, Armijo loses nothing and he sends them on their way back home. But even if we win, he is hoping McClendon and his men will inflict such damages that Armijo will have no trouble doing away with us in the end.''

"Then what are we going to do, Capitán?'' Lieutenant Delgado asked.

"The unexpected,'' came the reply as Salezar tilted back his head and drained the contents of his glass.

CHAPTER 25

A molten sun climbed high above the mountains to the east, while dust devils danced weirdly across the desert in the shimmering heat. And still there was no sign of Salezar.

"How do you figger it?" Peck asked the sweating McClendon, who never left an upstairs window that faced west, away from town. McClendon watched as two dust devils merged into one that walked its way to the thin line of blue that marked the river.

"Could be they got a late start from Taos," Zack said, breaking off a piece of trade tobacco to put in his mouth. He really didn't feel like chewing, but it gave him something to do other than stare out at a bleak landscape where nothing moved in the heat.

"What about the soldiers we saw left more'n an hour ago? They join up with Salezar, he'll know we're no longer in jail and there goes our element of surprise."

McClendon spit through the open window. "That 'id be my guess."

"You jest full of information, ain't you?" Peck glowered at his friend. Zack stiffened, his eyes narrowing as he tried to identify the moving object through the glimmering heat. Peck followed his gaze.

"Aw, that ain't nothing more'n a greaser ridin' some donkey," Peck said after a few minutes, totally disgusted at the heat and the long wait. "Ain't even a lizard out there with him." McClendon agreed with Peck's assessment, but he continued to watch the peasant grow larger. There was something vaguely familiar about the man coming straight at them.

"Keep an eye out this window," Zack said, getting up from the floor. "I'm going to have a talk with that man."

Peck Overstreet shook his head. "A waste of time. Pedro ain't got nothing more on his mind than tortillas and siesta."

But Peck, it turned out, was very wrong.

McClendon stepped out the back of the hotel after stopping by the kitchen for a dipper of cold water. He carried the water down the back steps. The Mexican altered his course slightly and rode straight for McClendon. Zack felt sure he knew the man and when he drew closer, he put a name to the face. It was Luis Covarrubias, from whom he had purchased the beautiful water pitcher.

Luis stopped before McClendon and slid down from the burro. He gave McClendon a shy smile. "*Mucho caliente,* no?" the Mexican said, accepting the dipper of water from the trapper. He smelled of dust and animal sweat.

"It's hot for a fact," McClendon agreed. "What brings you this far south?"

The Mexican handed the dipper back to Zack, his coffee-colored eyes reflecting the seriousness of his mission. "I am sorry to bring such sad news, but your friend who was staying with Father Escalante was shot by Salezar's men last night and the two women abducted." McClendon's features tightened. He regretted now not riding back to Taos after stealing the horse last night.

"Do you know where the women and Salezar are at now?"

"Sí. I just left them now at Don Diego's. I am here with a message from Salezar."

"What's he saying?" Peck called from the upstairs window.

"Come on down and bring what men is up there with you," McClendon called. "Let's go to the lobby and get out of this sun," he said, turning back to the Mexican. "That way the rest of the men can hear what you have to say as well." McClendon led the way into the darkened lobby where the temperature was a few degrees cooler.

When everybody had gathered around, McClendon introduced the shy Mexican who looked with big eyes at the well armed and grim-faced men. He didn't care how many men Salezar had, these trappers looked like death waiting to happen.

"You got the floor, Luis," Zack said. The Mexican cleared his throat.

"Capitán Salezar has asked me to tell you he is willing to agree to a compromise if you will only declare your neutrality and leave New Mexico."

"Hell, that ain't compromisin' " Ezekiel Smith shot back. "As fer me, I can leave here anytime I get ready, so's he ain't offerin' a thing we ain't already got." Others murmured their agreement. Zack held up his hand.

"Hear the man out first. Go on, Luis."

"If you agree to this offer, he will release Doña Magalena and the other woman . . . I forget her name."

"Carmelita Torres," McClendon prompted.

"Sí, she is the one. After their release you are to take the women and leave New Mexico and promise not to interfere when he attacks Armijo."

"So that's his game," Peck said. "With us outa his hair, guess he figgers he's got enough firepower to try Armijo on fer size."

"Sooner trust a Durango scorpion to keep his stinger sheathed while he's in my drawers," Skin Ledbetter added. Of

247

those present, he had lived the longest in New Mexico and had been witness to a lot of atrocities Salezar had committed in the last few years.

"Did he say what he would do if we refused his request?" Zack asked, trying not to let things get out of hand.

Luis Covarrubias nodded his head silently, then said, "If you attack him, he could not guarantee the women's safety." Luis hesitated and added, "Señor McClendon, thees woman, Carmelita, has been badly injured. I saw her face through the window when Salezar did not think I was looking. Her eyes, they are blackened and one is closed tight." McClendon felt his anger rise as the men around him began talking in loud voices. There was no doubt as to what their answer would be to Salezar's proposal. He could only hope Magalena hadn't met a similar fate.

"How long did he say he would wait for a reply?" McClendon asked Luis.

"You are to come alone and unarmed by two o'clock today. You will remain there until your men, also unarmed, are escorted to the Arkansas by his soldiers and released. Only then will you be permitted to leave with the women."

McClendon smiled tightly. "Looks like what he's offering us don't include much give on his part, does it?"

"Only thing to do is ride out there and lay siege," Peck shouted above the talk. Others nodded their agreement.

McClendon shook his head. "That's just what he's hoping we'll do. Ain't enough cover to protect us. Remember, they'll be the ones in buildings, not us."

"Then what we gonna do?" Skin asked, exasperated.

McClendon looked around the group of men and saw no give in any of them. They were willing to fight to the death and under any condition. The men could not have been more shocked by McClendon's next words.

"Expect the only thing left to do is give myself up."

* * *

"McClendon will never agree to such a ridiculous compromise," Magalena said to Salezar. They were seated in the huge den of the ranch house. He had allowed Carmelita upstairs to change her torn clothes, but only under guard.

Salezar allowed her a salacious smile. "He will agree, because all gringos have consciences where females are concerned. They want to do what is right and just. To save you and my little whore," he nodded his head, "he will come."

"But what if he doesn't?" Magalena pressed. "You said yourself, McClendon was not like most gringos."

"You listen too well, I think," Salezar said, his hot eyes raking her lithe form when she walked over to her father's bookcase, scanning the shelves for something to read. He watched the steady rise and fall of her ample bosom and the heat in him became too much. With her back turned to him, Salezar moved up behind Magalena.

"You are a beautiful woman, Magalena," Salezar breathed heavily. Magalena was startled to find the Mexican officer standing close behind her. She tried to side-step him but he blocked her path. He was so close now she could smell the brandy on his breath.

"Please, let me by," she said. She had turned to face him and he quickly pinned her arms to the bookcase with his. His eyes betrayed his thinking. The more she struggled, the closer he pressed against her. Finally he smashed his lips down on hers with a savage lust. Magalena held her breath, nearly gagging from the taste of him. He continued to press against her, allowing one hand to roam freely over her body. She willed her mind not to think of what was happening to her and stopped struggling.

Salezar took it as a sign of surrender and his ardor grew even stronger, but when he stepped back enough to reach for her blouse, she slapped him hard across the mouth. His reaction was instantaneous. He grabbed her by the front of her blouse and ripped the material as if it was paper, exposing her undergarments.

"No more," he said thickly, wiping the blood from his mouth, "will I treat you like a lady. You will be my new whore, do as I say, when I say." His face was engorged with blood as his eyes took in her half-exposed bosom.

"I would rather die first!" Magalena screamed.

"Leave her alone!" Carmelita shouted from atop the stairs. The guard standing behind her seemed embarrassed by his commander's actions. Carmelita flew down the stairs at Salezar. He looked over his shoulder and shouted for the guard to stop her. He still held tightly to Magalena. But the guard was too slow and Carmelita came at Salezar with blood in her eyes. He turned to meet the new challenge just as the door flew inward and Lieutenant Delgado stepped into the fracas.

"Stop that crazy woman," he screamed at Delgado who took two steps and intercepted Carmelita, catching her up in his powerful arms. Carmelita kicked and screamed at Delgado for a few minutes until she realized it was useless to struggle against his powerful grip. Magalena stepped away from Salezar, pulling up the front of her blouse to cover herself.

"Excuse me, Capitán, but the old peasant returns. Perhaps he has news for us," Delgado said. It was a minute before the fires died down enough in Salezar for him to think straight again. Delgado released the woman without being told and Carmelita rushed to Magalena's side and helped her straighten her clothes as best she could. Magalena was shaking uncontrollably from the attack, and Carmelita held her close, trying to soothe her.

Salezar saw the open disapproval of his officer and he lashed out at him.

"What are you still doing here? Bring the peasant to me!" he said, getting himself under firm control once more. He ignored the two women completely.

"He is not alone."

"What do you mean he is not alone?" Salezar demanded, straightening his clothes.

"See for yourself, Capitán," Delgado said. Salezar strode

over to the window and looked out. In the distance he could see tiny specks growing larger on the horizon. They were not so far away that Salezar couldn't recognize the old man on the burro and the soldiers who rode behind him. He thought for a minute before turning to Delgado.

"More deserters from Armijo?"

"Sí, Capitán. At least thirty more."

Salezar smiled broadly. "This will be easier than I first thought. If Armijo was smart, he would surrender his powers to me while he still can and prevent bloodshed."

"I will bring the old man here as soon as he arrives." Delgado bowed stiffly to the women and left.

Salezar turned to the two women. "Do not just stand there; change your clothes," he ordered Magalena. "Did you not hear, we have a guest coming with news from the gringo, McClendon." Salezar went over to the side cabinet and poured himself another drink. The prospect of being governor soon filled him with an excitement he had never known before. He raised the glass in a silent salute to McClendon and Armijo whom he promised quick though not painless deaths. He laughed out loud at his good fortune and poured himself another brandy. There was no doubt about it, Don Diego had the finest sipping brandy in New Mexico.

CHAPTER 26

Most of Salezar's soldiers were scattered among the out-buildings of the ranch, while ten or more lounged in the shade of the veranda out of the building heat. Having been prepared for action for several hours now, the inactivity had dulled their readiness for battle and none moved from their positions while they watched the old man on the burro draw closer.

Only Lieutenant Delgado, as he came out of the house, swept the approaching men with a critical eye. The old man seemed somehow larger now, but Delgado did not dwell on this small discrepancy, for part of his brain worried more about the sudden change in behavior in Salezar. Just when he should be leading his men to Santa Fe and victory, he was busy getting drunk and molesting women like some common outlaw. For the first time he felt a vague uneasiness settle over him. One of his men distracted him.

"When do we ride, lieutenant?" the soldier asked.

"Soon, Carlos, soon," Delgado responded, shading his eyes with his hand to watch the approaching soldiers. Although at the present time he had no idea when they were leaving. Salezar wasn't in a hurry, and that worried Delgado more. An opportunity should be seized the moment it presents itself.

"How many more men do we need to whip the gringos?" Carlos persisted. "Even now thirty more arrive."

"Capitán Salezar will order us against the gringos when he feels the time has come, not a minute sooner!" Delgado said with irritation. He, too, was restless and thought they should have ridden directly from Taos to Santa Fe. Stopping by the ranch served no purpose that Delgado could see. By now the gringos would have been dead and Armijo removed from office. Carlos dropped his head and stared down at his boots. Delgado placed a hand on the man's shoulder.

"I am as anxious for battle as you are, amigo, but we must wait until the capitán gives the order." The soldier nodded his head in response. Together they watched as the approaching horsemen did not slow down so their dust could settle. Delgado's irritation grew over their thoughtlessness. The old man was on the burro, riding a dozen yards ahead of the soldiers and whipping the little donkey until the animal was running flat out. Delgado was a little puzzled by the old man's actions. The soldiers watched from the veranda, but none were alarmed by the fast approach.

The little donkey came to a skidding halt before the waiting group. Delgado frowned as the old man got off the burro with surprising speed and came up the steps towards him. The rest of the soldiers thundered into the yard under a cloud of eye-stinging dust.

"Why do you punish your burro so, old man?" Delgado asked. The man kept his head low beneath his wide sombrero as he came up to Delgado, never speaking. He still wore the same dingy clothes and threadbare serape that barely seemed to cover his body now. When the old man gained the veranda, Delgado felt a surge of fear as the sombrero tilted slightly upward, exposing a cold pair of eyes. Instinctively, Delgado took a step backward. The lounging soldiers did not see the

253

look of concern on the officer's face, for they had already turned their attentions to the arriving soldiers who were busy dismounting in the settling dust.

The man in the dingy peasants clothes pressed Delgado, who stepped further back at the same time reaching for his sidearm. The old man locked a steely fist around Delgado's arm and came out with his own weapon from beneath the serape.

Delgado finally found his voice. "It's a trap!" he screamed at his men. Several jumped for their rifles as the soldiers in the yard pulled their guns.

Delgado struggled to free his gun arm but was pushed hard against the door. A chopping blow to the side of his head and the officer dropped like he had been hit with a hammer. The man in the serape threw aside the big sombrero, stepped over the prone officer and threw open the door just as a blazing gun battle erupted from the veranda.

The two women were seated on a couch holding each other when the door burst open, and a familiar figure stepped quickly in as gunshots raked the ranch house. Carmelita was the first to respond.

"Watch out, there is a guard by the fireplace!" Carmelita shouted, jumping to her feet. The guard and McClendon fired simultaneously, but the rattled guard did not hold his rifle steady and the shot went wide, gouging a hole in the door frame. McClendon's bullet ripped into the guard's chest and sent him crashing against the stones.

Salezar managed to get his own weapon out as he grabbed Carmelita around the neck and began pulling her towards the kitchen, using her as a shield. He snapped a shot at McClendon but the brandy spoiled his aim. McClendon ducked behind a large chair, holding his fire for fear of hitting Carmelita.

"Do not let him escape!" Carmelita screamed, struggling against the Mexican officer. With a cruel grimace, Salezar backed into the opened doorway leading to the kitchen and shot the woman in the back. Carmelita screamed. Her eyes sought McClendon as she slumped to the floor.

In an instant, McClendon was on his feet. He fired his pistol as Salezar was disappearing through the door and saw the Mexican flinch. The fire fight on the veranda was now hot and heavy, and tinkling glass marked the flight of stray bullets. McClendon cursed loudly as he ran over to Carmelita, who lay crumpled on her side.

Peck and several others burst into the room.

"Salezar!" McClendon said, pointing towards the kitchen as he bent over the bleeding woman. Peck jumped through the kitchen door with gun in hand.

The lounging soldiers on the veranda were shot to pieces in a matter of seconds by the trappers and by Chaves's men dressed as soldiers. But now the fighting grew more intense as the surprised soldiers began firing at them from the other buildings, forcing the small group to seek refuge inside the main ranch house. Outside, a dozen or more soldiers formed a line out front using fallen animals and two wagons they had pulled up to use as breastworks. They began laying down a withering fire of hot lead.

Like a flash, Magalena snapped out of her daze and rushed over to the fallen woman. A strangled cry rose from her throat at the sight of blood pouring from Carmelita.

"That bastard will pay for this!" he said under his breath as he tore open Carmelita's clothes to get at the bleeding wound. The bullet had entered her back and exited her chest just below the ribcage. Her eyes fluttered open, and Carmelita smiled weakly at the hard-faced McClendon.

"I am sorry, Zack, if I messed things up." McClendon brushed aside stray hair that covered half her face, and his features softened.

"Hush that kind of talk," was all he could say. Magalena knelt beside the woman and took her hand in hers.

"Just remain calm, Carmelita. Everything will be okay." The dying woman turned her head and looked at Magalena.

"Promise me you will take care of Pauli," Carmelita

pleaded, her eyes showing a mixture of sadness and increasing pain.

Magalena squeezed her hand reassuringly, "Do not worry about Pauli, I will see to him. We need to get you a doctor." She lifted her eyes to McClendon, who was watching helplessly. He shook his head. Tears formed in Magalena's eyes.

Peck came running in from the kitchen, grim-faced, his one eye shining hard. He shook his head, looking down at McClendon.

"Salezar made it out the back. Left a trail of blood, though. Opened the kitchen door and I got a greeting from fifty rifles sounded like."

"Get the men scattered out. Upstairs as well. We don't know how badly Salezar is wounded. They just may decide to rush the house." Peck nodded and moved off to tend to details.

"Pauli is fond of you Zack," Carmelita said, her voice growing weaker.

McClendon bent closer. "Say the word and I'll raise'm like my own." Carmelita managed a small smile through the burning pain.

"Pauli would like that very much . . . and so would I." She coughed once and cried out from the pain it caused. "You will tell him how much I love him?" McClendon nodded, his eyes holding hers for a moment.

"You're one hell of a woman, Carmelita. I won't let people forget your sacrifice."

Carmelita found strength in his words and her eyes blazed with hate one more time. "Promise me you will see Salezar dead . . . for Montoya and Ignacia. Promise me!"

"If I got to track him clear to hell," McClendon promised, his features flat and hard once more. Carmelita closed her eyes, stopped breathing, and died with a peaceful look on her face. Magalena fell across the dead woman, sobbing.

McClendon stood up and, for the first time, allowed himself to concentrate on the steady rattle of gunfire in and outside the house. At least Don Diego had built the ranch house solid and with adobe walls three foot thick. What they had to do was keep enough men at the windows to keep Salezar's men from rushing them. McClendon edged over to a window where Peck was keeping watch on the front.

"Woman dead?" Peck asked. McClendon nodded without speaking. "Salezar has a lot of accountin' to do."

"I'm not forgetting about Bull Stanton either," Zack added, peering out the window at the dead bodies of soldiers scattered across the veranda. There were several dead ones lying in the yard as well as among fallen horses killed in the crossfire.

"That's John Atwell over there," Peck pointed to a sprawled figure of a man. "Other two are Chaves's men."

"Where is Chaves?"

"Handlin' the fight from upstairs," Peck said. "Figgered to roam around down here, coverin' things as they developed. Got the Banks brothers coverin' the windows in the rear." The bulk of the fighting was coming from that side of the house facing the corrals and outbuildings. Cap Singleton and two others covered a front window next to Peck and Zack. Since the kitchen had no windows, Peck had simply bolted the door and hauled the long table up against it.

"Keep an eye peeled, I'm going up and look the situation over."

"What about her?" Peck asked, indicating Magalena, who was covering Carmelita's body with a tablecloth taken from a side drawer in the pantry. McClendon, squaring his shoulders, went over and helped her arrange the cloth over the dead woman. McClendon noticed her red-rimmed eyes. He wanted to take her in his arms and make the world right again, but he knew that for her, things had changed forever. He wasn't even sure if they could hold out against Salezar.

"Why did Damasio shoot her?" she asked.

McClendon shook his head, "you know him better than most but I figure it had something to do with how she made him feel. You can't ever tell what a vain man will do on impulse." They stood there, looking down at the covered body.

"Carmelita stopped Damasio from abusing me, just minutes

before you came," she said in a small voice. "I . . . I didn't even have time to thank her." Her shoulders lifted in a sob and McClendon found himself standing there in the middle of a gun battle, with the woman crying softly on his chest.

"Carmelita was a rare person," Zack said softly, "She gave her life so others would someday live free from men like Salezar. You thanked her aplenty by saying you would look after the boy." She pulled back to look at him.

"You really think so?"

"Stake my life on it," Zack said, wiping away a tear from her flawless skin. He thought of Carmelita's battered face and his voice hardened. "Salezar has seen his last sunrise . . . hope he took time to enjoy it."

"McClendon!" Chaves shouted from upstairs. "You best come up and have a look." She clutched his arm, looking up at his face.

"I gotta go," Zack said, pulling away. "Want you to get behind that staircase until this is over. It looks to be the safest part of the house."

"Be careful, Zack, I wouldn't want to lose you now." Zack didn't know what to say. He had nothing to offer someone like Magalena. For all his knocking about, he owned no property, precious little money and a cloudy future in the trade business. He mumbled something and headed upstairs where Manuel Chaves stood waiting.

"I'm sorry about Carmelita," Zack said to the Mexican.

"More of us will die before this is over," Chaves said, his face drawn and solemn. He led the way into the bedroom where Zack and Carmelita had spent the night. Zack looked at the bed and felt a strange chillness pass over him. She had been so warm, so willing . . . a bullet sang through the room like a mad hornet and McClendon automatically ducked. In a half-stance, Chaves motioned McClendon to the window. A crackling of gunfire drew him closer and he looked out across the corrals, bunkhouse and barn at a sea of soldiers. Some had even taken the time to dig a shallow trench near the corrals and were steadily pouring a directed fire at the windows.

"Be careful, gringo." Chaves grinned. "They may shoot your head off." McClendon ducked back as a slug gouged a path along the deep-set window. Zack looked over at Chaves.

"Anybody been hit?"

"None so far up here, but we left two of our dead out front."

"Did you notice the activity near the barn?" Chaves asked.

"Not enough to do any good," McClendon smiled faintly and looked around the edge of the windowsill. A tall Mexican was giving orders to others, who scurried back and forth. In the shadows of the opened barn door, a wagon seemed to be receiving most of the tall Mexican's interest. *Now what were they up to?* Zack ducked back down, looking at Chaves.

"What do you make of it?" Chaves asked. A sudden thud, a sharp inward breath, and a Mexican at the next window fell backward to the floor, shot through the throat. McClendon checked the charge on the muzzleloader Peck had given him just minutes before.

"What we need is a little respect," Zack said, standing up suddenly to fire through the window. The big gun was deafening in the small room. The whole act took less than three seconds. Zack ducked back down and began reloading the big gun. The men at the other window howled with delight.

"You killed one by the barn. Look how the others did in the dirt like badgers," Chaves exclaimed.

Zack stood up and peered from the window. It was true, the shooting dropped off sharply as several men crawled towards the fallen Mexican. He shoved his rifle barrel through the window. Those looking up saw the gun and dove for cover. The shooting stopped altogether. Chaves grinned at McClendon.

"That ees a most powerful gun, señor."

"It'll do the job in a tight spot," Zack said, looking for a target. A Mexican officer appeared from the barn and started lashing with a riding quirt at the soldiers who were not fighting back. He was screaming loudly at them. His thin voice carried up to them on a hot wind. Those receiving the lashing began firing again.

McClendon sighted down the weapon, taking more time to aim this time, and shot the Mexican officer through his left ear, the big lead ball exploding deep within his brain. Once again, the soldiers dove for the dirt while the Mexican straightened, took a feeble step and pitched head-long into the shallow trench where the soldiers were hidden. They immediately rolled the dead officer to the front of the ditch where they used his body to reinforce their breastworks. McClendon thought it a fitting end.

"Look!" Chaves said, pointing to the barn. McClendon was busy reloading his rifle and he glanced up from what he was doing. A wagon piled high with hay was being rolled from the barn by a half dozen soldiers. He caught a glimpse of a familiar figure hovering near the shaded barn door. Salezar stood there with blood on his uniform and his left arm in a makeshift sling. At least he had drawn a little of the Mexican's blood, McClendon thought grimly.

"Looks like Salezar plans to heat things up for us," Zack said. They pushed the wagon, with its tongue tied up off the ground, towards the corral and the line of trenched soldiers.

"Get Peck and Zeke up here now," Zack commanded. Chaves jumped for the bedroom door and was gone. They had to stop the wagon from reaching the ranch house. This section he was standing over had been added to the original adobe building and was heavily timbered and exposed. It was the most vulnerable part of the house, and Salezar knew it. After all, how many times had he been to the ranch courting Doña Magalena? By now he must know every inch of the place. The yard grew deathly quiet as the soldiers held their fire waiting for the wagon to be lit.

McClendon heard heavy footsteps coming up the stairs and a few seconds later Peck and Ezekiel Smith, looking all the more dried up than his usual condition, came through the door.

"Hear Salezar's planning a barbecue in our honor," Peck said lightly, as he joined McClendon by the window. Zeke went over to cover the other window.

"That wagon rams this side of the house and we're in big trouble," Zack said. "When they fire the hay, we got to concentrate our fire on those pushing the wagon. Forget about the others for now. We got to stop that wagon."

"Could pick one er two off right now," Peck said.

"No, that's just what Salezar wants and when we stop to reload our rifles, that's when he'll give the orders to fire the hay. McClendon turned to Chaves. "Tell those in the downstairs bedroom to concentrate on the wagon. Let one man fire and while he's reloading, the other man can fire his weapon. That way, we ain't bumping into one another for window space." Chaves nodded and left.

"We've lost four more men," Peck said, checking his weapon for the third time and laying out his powder horn, lead shot and wadding in a row next to the window. "Dern Mexicans have pulled up several wagons and ox carts near the front and it's gettin' mighty hot down there with all that lead flyin' 'round. Ain't a piece a window glass left, or fer that matter a chair that ain't sportin' bullet holes."

"Magalena?"

"Got her tucked behind that stairwell real good. It'd take a cannon to blast through those thick timbers before she'd even get a nick."

"Salezar may be a lot of things but he's not dumb. He'll keep up attacks on two fronts, wear us down and send in the burning wagon. And if he manages to fire the house, we're gonna have a rough time of it for sure."

"You do know how to paint a bleak picture," Peck said gloomily. "And jest think, we coulda taken old Broken Hand's advice and be guidin' pikers 'long the Oregon Trail about now with only a few redskins to worry us. Instead, we got half of the Mexican Army aiming to fry our bacon before the day is done."

McClendon kept watch on the barn for a chance shot at Salezar but the wily Mexican never exposed himself for more than a second or two at a time before ducking back. And why should he risk his life at this point? He had superior numbers and stood to gain everything once he crushed them. Zack had a feeling Armijo would fold like cardboard if Salezar came calling.

"What are you doing here?" McClendon heard Chaves say. He glanced over his shoulder and was shocked to see Magalena coming through the doorway.

"You shouldn't be here. It's much too dangerous," McClendon said, going over to the woman who stood there holding her father's rifle.

Magalena looked at him coolly and said simply, "I want to help, to be with you. My father taught me how to shoot and right now you need everybody at a window." McClendon could see there was no use arguing with her. She had suffered as much as anyone, and had every right to be here.

A fusillade of bullets echoed up the stairs from down below. They heard a strangled cry and knew someone had been hit. Salezar was opening the ball once more by trying to draw their fire away from this side of the house.

"Get ready boys, looks like the shindig is about to commence," Peck hollered to those in the next bedroom. McClendon returned to the window quickly and looked out. Magalena knelt beside him and waited for his instructions.

"I'll cover the other window with Zeke," Peck said, looking down at the woman, who gave him a warm smile. He picked up his things and dropped down beside Zeke Smith, who was nervously chewing a wad of trade tobacco the size of a fist. It was his way of dealing with a moment of crisis. His mouth may have been working nervously but Peck knew the rest of the old man was rock steady.

Zeke Smith shot a load of brown juice through the window and gave Peck a tobacco-stained grin. "A fellar jest never knows when he's well off."

"Whatcha driving at, old coon?" Peck eased the barrel of his rifle out the window and waited for Zack's signal. The firing downstairs was intense now.

"Why all them shining times we done lived through. High livin' at its best and us too danged dumb to know it at the time."

"They fired the hay," Zack warned the others. Magalena started to get up but Zack pushed her back down. "You'll get your chance as soon as I unload my gun," he promised.

In preparation for pushing the wagon forward there was sporadic firing along the line of trenched soldiers. Suddenly, a high-pitched scream floated up to them from the opened doorway of the barn and McClendon knew Salezar had given the command. It was also the exact moment Zack chose to shoot the lead soldier by the smoking wagon. Peck shot the front man on the opposite side, grinned at Zeke and told him to make it count. Zeke shot a soldier who was trying to half hide beneath the burning wagon for protection. His body lay between the wheels of the wagon and forward progress stopped.

Against his protest, Magalena fired her rifle at the line of men along the trench, not knowing if she had inflicted any damages. By now the line of soldiers were pouring a steady stream of fire into the bedrooms. A yell came from Magalena's bedroom, and Zack knew they had lost another man.

He turned back to the window with his loaded rifle as several soldiers scrambled forward and dragged the dead man from between the wheels of the wagon. The wagon started rolling again. Yellow-orange flames leaped several feet into the air from the burning hay. The thick smoke offered some protection to those shoving the wagon, but two more were killed before the wagon had gone a dozen paces. Yet the wagon rolled steadily forward. The soldiers in the trenches kept up such a steady stream of fire that it was impossible to stay at the window for more than a few seconds at a time.

Magalena screamed and Zack whirled around, thinking she had been shot only to see a soldier coming into the room with his weapon raised and pointed at Chaves. With no time to warn Chaves, Zack pulled his pistol and shot the Mexican in the face, but not before he fired his rifle. Chaves let out a strangled cry and dropped to the floor. Magalena crawled over to him and checked his wound. He had taken the rifle shot in the shoulder.

"They've breached the house!" Zack yelled to the others as he leaped to the open doorway and dragged the dead soldier out of the way so he could close it. Glancing down the stairwell, he saw two more soldiers coming up the stairs. Zack shot them both, stepped back into the bedroom and slammed the door shut, throwing the bolt.

"We ain't gonna stop the wagon!" Peck warned.

"Damn!" Zack blurted out, racing for the window. The wagon was now a mass of hot flames and coming fast for the house, less than twenty yards away now. Gray-black smoke completely encircled the burning vehicle.

McClendon looked beyond the burning wagon and saw the soldiers rise up from the trench and run forward with their bayonets fixed. There must have been forty of them—too many to meet head on. There was a banging at the door, and McClendon fired one of his pistols through the door. The banging stopped. Suddenly the house shuddered slightly beneath their feet and all knew without looking that the burning wagon had made contact with the house. Immediately, smoke began pouring into the bedroom, choking everyone and stinging their eyes. They could hear the deafening yells of the soldiers below who were sure of victory now.

"Stay down on the floor," Zack shouted as he crawled back to the window. All was lost now and he knew it but Zack was determined to take Salezar with him. That's what he lived for now as he searched with tearing eyes among the running soldiers for the paunchy officer. He could hear the crackling fire as it ate hungrily at the seasoned timbers. Very soon, when the floor beneath them grew too hot, the whole room would explode into flames.

Zack felt a soft hand on his arm and looked around as Magalena crawled up beside him, her eyes red-rimmed and tearing. She pulled at him, forcing Zack to abandon the window for a moment. She clutched his neck tightly and he held her close for a minute. She coughed heavily and struggled to breathe through the thick smoke. Zack pulled back from her.

"Save yourself," he said, "Salezar won't harm you." She shook her head.

"I'll not leave you," she said coughing hard.

"Listen, Magalena," Zack pleaded, "we are stuck here. Salezar already has control of the downstairs area. In a few minutes, it will be too late for even you to leave. Please go."

"I choose to die here with you rather than face Salezar again," she said calmly. Zack hesitated for a moment, then pulled her to him tightly.

"God, another time . . ." was all he managed to say.

"Zack, you still there?" a voice out of the gloom asked. It was Peck and his voice was filled with wonder.

"We're still here, Peck, what is it?"

"Take a look out the window if you can."

McClendon scrambled to his feet, bringing the woman with him. Through the dense haze of smoke he saw something that startled and amazed him all at the same time.

"Don't that jest beat all?" Peck called to him, coughing hard against the dark smoke.

"I can't believe it," Magalena said reverently. "It's just like Carmelita said would happen." Zack noticed for the first time, the only sounds now were coming from the burning fire.

"Carmelita said this would happen?" Zack asked incredulous.

"She knew what her people were capable of doing when pressed too far," Magalena said.

The scene seemed unreal to Zack. There must have been a hundred people . . . old men, women and even little children, all crowding around the soldiers with nothing more than sticks and hoes in their hands. Even the children were armed with sticks. The soldiers just stood there, unmoving, no longer firing their rifles. Officers screamed at the men to keep firing and even shot one or two, but then the soldiers turned on them and used their bayonets on them.

"Let's get outa here before we all cook," Zack said, taking the woman by the hand.

" 'Bout time you gave the order," Peck said. "Here, Zeke, give me a hand with Chaves."

Zack clawed his way to the door through the dense smoke, and, throwing the bolt, kicked the door wide open. In one hand he held his pistol, with the other he kept a tight grip on the woman. They stumbled out of the smoke-filled room and met no resistance. Two men staggered from the adjacent room.

"Anybody left in there?" Zack asked. One of the coughing men was Lafe Ingram, who shook his head. "Then let's get out of here."

The living room was a complete shambles. There was death everywhere they looked. Not a single trapper had left his post, and that was how they died. A group of peasants were busy carrying the dead from the burning structure. From the looks of slain soldiers, Zack figured the trappers had given a good account of themselves. He asked Ingram to make sure Carmelita's body was brought outside.

Once outside, they all stopped and breathed deeply of the clean air. Even the hot air felt cool and sweet after the ordeal upstairs. Peck and Zeke propped Chaves against the wheel of a wagon among the dead that littered the yard. The Mexican coughed weakly, and there was a large bloodstain on the side of the Mexican uniform he was wearing. An old woman came up with a bucket of water and gave him a drink.

"Take care of Manuel, will you Magalena? We got to find Salezar." Zack said. His face blackened by smoke and gunpowder looked wild in the glare of the overhead sun. Black smoke rose sickeningly from the rear of the beautiful ranch house as the fire ate its way deeper into the structure.

"Be careful, Zack," the woman said, turning her attentions

to the wounded Chaves. "Salezar will be more dangerous now than ever."

Peck and Zeke hefted their guns and followed close behind McClendon. Out of a fighting force of thirty-five men, only four were still standing. They had lost a number of close friends today, and Zack was determined to see those responsible paid for it with their lives.

They didn't have far to look. A subdued Salezar and three of his officers plus a big brute of a fellow were being held in the barn by a group of old men who had stripped guns from dead soldiers. The milling soldiers had either thrown down their arms or were holding the weapons like useless sticks, with dazed expressions on their faces.

When the three trappers stepped into the shade of the barn, an old man came over to them. He looked vaguely familiar.

"Señor McClendon, I am Rauel Montoya." Now Zack saw the resemblance.

"I'm sorry about your brother," Zack said, looking past the Mexican at Salezar.

"We are from Los Lunas and had to walk the whole distance. Had we known of the troubles, we would have come sooner."

"I'm only glad you came when you did. Are you responsible for this?" Zack said, waving his hand around him. The old Mexican smiled.

"We are all old, amigo, but we are not too old to fight for what is right and just." And then he winked at McClendon, "it also doesn't hurt to have the Blessed Virgin on your side."

McClendon turned to Peck, "You know what we got to do." Peck nodded and moved away. Zeke looked puzzled.

"What you up to?"

"Best give Peck a hand, then you'll know." Zack replied.

CHAPTER 27

The big brute, Mateo strained mightily at the ropes binding his arms, his dark eyes bulging in their sockets. Rauel Montoya looked at the huge man with hooded eyes.

"I am told you are the one who beat my brother to death." Mateo stopped struggling and looked down at the wrinkled old man.

"If I get loose, I'll do the same to you, old man," Mateo warned, twisting his huge arms against the ropes. If he expected Montoya to show fear, he was wrong.

The old man stepped closer and spit in Mateo's face. Mateo reacted immediately and lashed out with a foot which Montoya easily sidestepped. Drawing his knife he stepped closer as if to thrust it into the big man. Mateo tried to back up but tripped, falling heavily to the ground. Rauel Montoya smiled wickedly at the brute.

"Maybe I don't let them hang you. Maybe I cut you up into little pieces and feed your miserable soul to the dogs." Mateo lay there on his back, saying nothing, staring up at the old Mexican who kept stroking the big knife. For the first time in his violent life, Mateo felt raw fear.

Under heavy guard, from the deep shade of the barn, Salezar and his three officers watched the proceedings with alert eyes.

Rauel Montoya, still clutching the knife, turned to Salezar. "You have brought grief and bloodshed to this peaceful country for the last time today, Damasio. It is time to pay for your crimes." Salezar looked pale and drawn and only stared at the old man as if not comprehending what he was saying to him.

Peck came up driving a wagon pulled by four spirited animals he and Zeke had taken the liberty of borrowing from dead soldiers. A wounded Chaves was sitting in the wagon next to Peck while Zeke rode in the back. Peck turned the animals expertly at the barn and eased them back until the wagon was halfway inside before setting the brake. Zeke jumped down from the back of the wagon and disappeared into the gloom of the building. In a few minutes he was back with a wide plank that was a good two inches thick. He laid the board across the back of the wagon near the rear while Salezar and the others watched closely.

Zack had finally gotten a count of the dead; sixty-three soldiers and thirty-one resistance fighters, seventeen of whom were American trappers or mountain men. A lot of good men had gone under today because of Salezar's greed for money and power. The ranch house had been quickly gutted by the fire and now the blackened adobe walls were the only reminder that a house once stood there.

When some of the peasants had passed the penned hogs, they found part of Don Diego's remains where Salezar had ordered him thrown. Zack kept this fact hidden from Magalena, and he had them bury what was left of the old Don in the family cemetery.

With the fight gone out of them now, most of the soldiers either drifted back to Santa Fe quietly or simply milled around, looking lost now that Salezar was no longer giving the orders. More than twenty, all of them unarmed, gathered at the barn along with twice that many old people.

McClendon came up from the corral with Magalena and Lafe Ingram beside him. He held five ropes in his hands he had formed into nooses. At the sight of the ropes, Salezar rose from his seat, his mouth falling open.

"You don't mean to hang us?"

McClendon gave the frightened officer a cold smile. "Seems to be your favorite way of dying."

"You can't do this! I demand a trial, a chance to defend myself." Salezar's face was suddenly livid now that he was fighting desperately for his life. His junior officers never lifted their bowed heads as if in silent prayer, while Mateo looked ready to bolt. Zeke and Skin trained their guns on the big man.

"Like you gave Antonito Montoya or my father?" Magalena asked coldly. "And poor Carmelita?"

"Salezar, my only regret is we can't hang you separately for each of your crimes. Bull Stanton was a friend and so were the others you had ambushed at Mora. By rights we ought to drag you through the cactus for a couple days and leave you for the buzzards," Zack said, throwing the ropes over the thick rafter, one at a time. He centered them over the wagon gate.

"I have money . . . lots of it," Salezar said, out of desperation. "You can have it all. I'll clear out of New Mexico."

"Notice you ain't offering to save your officers here as well, Salezar. That's been your problem all along . . . not caring for anyone but yourself. But don't worry about your money. A lot of people, relatives of folks you've had murdered, will make good use of your ill-gotten gains."

Salezar looked around at his disarmed soldiers. "I am still your captain. Kill this madman now!" Salezar shrieked, saliva forming on his loose lips. The soldiers looked at Salezar with impassive faces. A few of them simply turned away.

"Cowards!" Salezar screamed after them, completely out of control now.

McClendon gave the nod to Zeke, and he and several others helped get the doomed men into the back of the wagon where Zack stood waiting. The three officers meekly took their places on the plank, a defeated look on their faces. Zack adjusted the rope around each of their necks.

It took several men to manhandle Mateo to the back of the wagon. Even then brute strength on Zack's part was necessary to slip the rope around his thick neck. Mateo began whimpering like a child as his legs were securely tied. Zack looked into the killer's glazed eyes.

"Funny how men who dish out pain and suffering like a meal at suppertime is the first to beg for mercy." McClendon looked down at Salezar. "Okay, let's go, Salezar." Ledbetter prodded him with his gun. Even then Salezar threatened to rebel, flailing his injured arm around like it was suddenly well. Ledbetter had a time trying to get the half-crazy officer to cooperate. It was Ingram who finally helped subdue Salezar and get him in the back of the wagon.

McClendon adjusted the noose around the officer's neck while Zeke tied the man's feet. Salezar seemed calm now and ready to accept his fate. McClendon leaned over next to Salezar's ear.

"Just so you'll know," McClendon whispered, "once we done hanging you I'm going to feed you to the coyotes. You don't deserve burying after what you did to Don Diego and Carmelita." Salezar slumped against the rope, his face drawn and frightened.

"See you in hell, gringo," he managed to say, his dark eyes full of hate for McClendon.

"Expect there's a few good men down there waiting for you to join them," Zack said, smiling. McClendon stepped down out of the wagon.

Peck straightened up in the driver's seat, pulled the brake handle free and poised the whip. Chaves looked over his shoulder at the doomed men. There was a look of satisfaction on his countenance.

Magalena stepped over and took the buggy whip from Peck who looked at Zack for guidance. McClendon didn't know what to think but said nothing. Magalena walked around the end of the wagon and looked up at the glassy-eyed Salezar.

"I want you to know who it is sends you to hell." Her eyes held nothing but hate for the man who had murdered her father.

Salezar looked down at the woman, his eyes bright with fear of the unknown. "You are a stupid woman, Magalena. We could have had everything together."

"I will have everything . . . only with Zack McClendon."

Salezar's face filled with anger. "Damn you McClendon!" he screamed, looking over at McClendon.

"Say your prayers, boys and make it quick," Skin Ledbetter said, looking up at the five men.

The brute, Mateo, was still whimpering when Magalena stepped back to the front of the wagon and expertly cracked the whip across the rumps of the horses. The sudden pop in the heated silence sent the horses bolting from under the five men and it was all Peck could do to get the animals under control within fifty yards from the barn. He finally got them straightened out and turned back around.

Magalena stood there looking up at the swaying bodies for a full minute. Finally, she dropped the whip to the ground, her shoulders sagging with grief. McClendon was beside her in an instant, leading her away from the grim scene. It was finally over for everyone who had suffered at the hands of Damasio Salezar.

CHAPTER 28

The day was bright, cloudless, and punishingly hot by the time they said their goodbyes to Luis Covarrubias near Black Mesa. With a flourish of his broad hat and a wide smile Luis saluted them and rode away on the fine black horse McClendon had given him after his burro had been killed in the shootout the day before.

"That Luis is one proud Mexican," Zeke commented. He, Skin Ledbetter and Peck Overstreet were watering the horses from the Rio Grande while Zack and Magalena waited in what scant shade the towering mesa provided. Lafe Ingram had said his goodbyes that morning in Santa Fe and left for St. Louis with the other traders released from jail. Armijo also had agreed to return all their wagons and goods so they could dispose of them in the plaza before starting back.

"Ain't half as proud er as relieved as Armijo was yestedidy," Peck said. "Shouda been with us when old Zack laid down the law to him. Hell, he thought we wuz there to run him outa office, and once Zack commenced to telling him what changes he expected, Armijo even throwed in a few of his own." They led the watered horses over to Zack and the woman who was listening to their conversation.

"You woulda too," Zeke stated, "at least 'til we was outa sight. Armijo and Salezar are a breed . . . only things they're after is money and power. Won't take long, he'll be back to his old tricks. Not all at once, mind you."

"Then why in the devil didn't we jest go on and salt his hide as well?" Peck asked, looking at Zack.

McClendon didn't answer directly. He looked at the woman beside him, who smiled back at the big trapper. Zack scanned Black Mesa near the top, beginning to feel at home in the strange beauty of this lonesome country. He could see why men like Ezekiel Smith and Skin Ledbetter chose to stay here.

"There's been too much killing of late," Zack finally said quietly. "We all need time to heal, some more than others." Magalena reached for his hand and gave it a light squeeze as if thanking him for understanding her grief. "Besides, I figure in a year or two things will come to a head between the Mexican Government and the Texans over their struggle for independence. That happens, the Arkansas ain't likely to stand long as the northern border either, and where we standing will be U.S. Territory."

"Dawged if he don't sound like he's runnin' fer office, don't it?" Peck asked the other two trappers. McClendon seemed slightly embarrassed. "Guess that means we stayin' in New Mexico." Peck looked at his partner.

"Let's get on to Taos," Zack said as an answer.

They found Taos wide open and busy once more now that Salezar was no longer a threat. McClendon figured good news traveled fast as bad sometimes. They rode by two new graves and Zack guessed both parties must have lost the fight.

Magalena and Zack dropped off at the mission while the others continued on to Ortega's cantina. Zack promised to meet them there in a few minutes once the boy was told about his mother. One thing was for certain, Pauli wouldn't have to worry about his future. Zack had extracted from Armijo all of Salezar's money. A good portion he kept for the boy. The rest he distributed to the poor who had suffered a loss. Even Armijo had volunteered ten thousand in gold of his own money, yet McClendon suspected the sum was a mere pittance to a man like Armijo.

Zack helped Magalena from the saddle and saw the tired lines around her eyes. The last few days had been terrible for her. Not only had she lost her father and her home, but loyal friends as well. Zack vowed one of the first things he was going to do was rebuild the beautiful ranch house.

Magalena saw the worried look on his face. "What is it, Zack, Pauli? I can handle it myself if you wish."

Zack shook his head, "you've been through enough already alone. From now on, we do things together."

She hugged him close. "I'd like that very much."

In the end, Zack stood off to one side with Father Escalante while Magalena told the boy as gently as she knew how about his mother. His little body shuddered under the news as he manfully fought back tears. He didn't want to cry in front of the kneeling woman, though his chest felt on the verge of exploding. His pain-filled eyes locked on McClendon and he flew into the big trapper's arms, a sob tearing from his tiny chest. Zack picked the boy up, holding him close.

"It's okay to cry, Pauli," Zack whispered in his ear and he felt the little body convulse as the tears began to flow. He carried him from the church out into the bright sunshine. In a few minutes, Pauli wiped away the tears and looked at Zack.

"Am I going to stay with you now?" he asked in a shaking voice, his chest still heaving. McClendon hadn't had time to do much thinking along those lines, but he knew there was no way he could just walk away from the boy now. And what of Magalena? Of course there were unspoken feelings between them, but they hadn't really made any hard and fast plans.

Magalena came up and slipped her arm into Zack's and answered for both of them. "You will be staying with both of us, Pauli. Would you like that?"

The boy's face brightened and for a brief second Zack saw Carmelita's flashing eyes underneath. "Oh yes. Will I have my own pony to ride?"

"You betcha," Zack said, feeling a little euphoric himself with the woman pressing close to him, yet not knowing how he was going to manage it all without money. He knew without thinking that St. Louis was out. He wasn't about to leave the woman or the boy for that long no matter if he had to start raising goats for a living.

McClendon left the boy with Magalena to gather up his things and rode down to the cantina to tell Peck what he had decided—not that, he figured, Overstreet would be all that surprised. He found them lounging over beers at the bar. Peck waved him over.

"Here is the man responsible fer Salezar's quick departure from this earth," Peck boomed. An immediate cheer went up and several Mexicans pounded Zack on the back as he made his way to the bar. A beer appeared before him as if by magic.

"A toast," Zeke said, lifting his glass and the crowd roared their approval.

Peck smiled at Zack. "Drink up, partner, beer is on the house fer us today." Zack raised his glass in a salute and downed the contents in one long swallow. The crowd loved it and another beer appeared at his elbow.

"Even checked to see if old Kit would join us fer a cold one," Skin said, "but he's off guiding this Fremont fellar fer most of the year."

"Wal, it's his loss," Zeke said, downing half a glass in one swallow.

"Maybe so, but I hear tell, Fremont's payin' Carson a hundred a month what most of us been doing fer free," Skin responded.

"Fitzpatrick been tellin' me and Zack guidin' Eastern folks

276

West, is the coming thing," Peck said sadly, thinking they could stand a few months guiding wages right now.

"I fer one ain't hankerin' to fill up this country no faster'n it already is, especially with city folk," Zeke pronounced, "and I don't care what wages they payin'."

"Ain't nothing like pore man pride," Skin said, shaking his head.

"Look who jest walked in, will you?" Peck said, wiping away the foam from his bushy beard on the back of a sleeve. Zack turned his attentions to the doorway and found the scraggly-bearded Sylvester Houseman standing there. The man still had that worried look about him, and when he saw McClendon he veered over to the far corner of the bar.

"Got something to tell you," Zack said to Peck.

Peck grinned, taking a swallow of beer. "Let me guess. We ain't going to St. Louis."

"How did you know?"

"Hell, ain't hard to figger, even fer me. That black-eyed beauty's got you by yore pod fer good and they ain't no use denying it. What I cain't figger is how we gonna make a living."

"They's a lot of wild mustangs to the west of here could be rounded up. Fact is, been giving it some thought of late myself," Skin spoke up. McClendon turned that over in his mind for a moment while Peck and the other two trappers discussed the merits of such an endeavor. They had one more beer before stepping into the baking street of midday.

"Would you look at that!" Zeke said, pointing up the street. Through the searing heat, they saw the stumbling form of a man coming directly at them. The man, or what was left of him, leaned heavily on a crude stick he used as a crutch. His tattered clothes hung from his gaunt frame like rags on a scarecrow. His feet were bundled in filthy rags and he looked ready to collapse with each painful step.

"Fetch a beer," McClendon ordered Zeke who hurried inside to tell the others. McClendon, Overstreet and Ledbetter left the shaded overhang and hurried towards the gaunt figure. The first thing Zack noticed about the half-dead man was his intense eyes. They seemed to be the only thing about the man that wasn't dying. As they drew close the man tried to speak, but no words came out of his mouth. He sank gratefully into McClendon's strong arms. The stench was unbearable as he and Peck carried the half-conscious man over to the shade and eased him down.

"Piker's about gone," Peck commented.

"Been in them mountains fer a spell by the looks of him," Skin said.

Zeke hurried back with the beer while patrons from the cantina spilled into the street to get a look at the poor unfortunate. Sylvester Houseman tagged along in the excitement of the moment. McClendon lifted the skinny man's head and allowed a little of the beer to trickle down his throat. The man gripped McClendon's hands with surprising strength and drank greedily.

"Whoa now, friend. Not too much," Zack warned, pulling the glass away from the man's swollen lips. The cooling drink seemed to revive the man somewhat and he looked up at McClendon.

"Thanks, mister. Never tasted anything so good."

"What happened to you, friend?" Zack asked. The man rolled his eyes and shook his head as if the situation was totally hopeless. "Are there others out there?"

The gaunt man shook his head and opened his eyes once more. "Only me." His voice was laced with bitterness.

"Who are you?" Zack asked, wanting at least a name in case the man died.

"Lankford," the man whispered. McClendon straightened up. *Now where had he heard that name before?* Peck was busy thinking the same thing for he spoke first.

"Hell, ain't that the name, Houseman said was his partner?"

McClendon looked quickly at the feeble man whose face

had taken on a new life of its own. "You Tom Lankford?" Zack asked.

"How . . . how did you know? You've seen Houseman?" Suddenly things made a lot of sense to McClendon and he felt his anger rising. McClendon turned to the crowd.

"Houseman! You here?" The crowd of Mexicans looked around and slowly parted to reveal Sylvester Houseman standing there with a shocked look on his face.

"Guess you didn't expect to see your old partner again?" McClendon said, smiling thinly. Houseman took a step closer, still not believing his eyes.

"It can't be," he whispered. "Tom Lankford is dead."

"Seems like you didn't do such a good job killing him," McClendon said, his voice hard and dangerous now.

"I—I never tried to kill Tom." Houseman took a step forward. "Tell them Tom, tell them how I looked after you."

"You gave up on me too soon, Syl," Lankford said. "Guess I got the gold to thank for that." Houseman stepped backward, his eyes darting over the crowd, coming to rest on McClendon.

"He was dying, what else could I do?"

"Reckon the law will answer that question for you," McClendon said.

"No! I'm not going to jail," Houseman shouted.

"Watch him, boy," Peck warned.

"Tom, I still got part of the gold left. You can have it."

"It's too late for that now, Syl," Lankford said weakly.

"Ain't going—" and then his hand shot down for his pistol as he continued to back up.

McClendon's movements were a blur and flame shot out of his big fist. Houseman was knocked backward and landed in the dusty street, face up. A bluish hole appeared beneath his right eye. The back of his head was a puddle of crimson. McClendon holstered the smoking gun, noting the approving eyes of the crowd. There wasn't much worse a man could do then leave a wounded partner behind to die.

"Only wished I had the strength to do that myself," Lankford whispered. "It's the only thing been driving me on all this time." The man seemed to be drifting away, now that he had seen it through.

"Guess that explains why Yellow Weasel wanted you two dead. Gold is a mighty powerful draw and he could see his hunting grounds being overrun by prospectors."

"Want to thank you proper, mister." Lankford held out a feeble hand which McClendon covered with his.

"Zack McClendon. These two old coots are Zeke Smith, Skin Ledbetter and my partner, Peck Overstreet. Now you just rest easy and we'll get you a soft bed and something to eat. This time tomorrow, you'll be a new man."

Lankford smiled weakly. "Wish I could believe you but I know my time is close. Knew it when I stumbled into town. Got nothing left to build back to."

McClendon started to say something but caught himself. He couldn't lie to the man, not now. Lankford reached among the tattered rags and brought forth a wrinkled piece of brown paper. He handed it to Zack.

"It didn't do us much good but you fellows are welcome to it." McClendon unfolded the paper and looked at the rough drawing.

"We can't take—"

"No, you go on. Put it to good use. There's more than enough gold there to keep ten men happy for the rest of their natural lives," Lankford said. "All I got to give you for what you done for me." McClendon nodded and stuck the paper in his shirt pocket. An hour later Lankford simply closed his eyes and stopped breathing. McClendon paid two Mexicans to bury Houseman's body outside of town while he and Peck dug Lankford's grave themselves while Zeke and Skin looked on, smoking their pipes.

"Seems a shame a man has to die just when he has all the gold in the world," Peck said, sweating heavily. He shot the pipe smokers a poisoned look. The old trappers ignored Peck.

280

As far as they were concerned, burying Tom Lankford in the heat of the day didn't make a whole lot of sense to them. Man coulda waited until the cool of the day.

"It's where it's located that presents a problem," Zack said, throwing aside a shovel load of dirt and rock.

Peck stopped and leaned on his shovel. "Jest where is this gold mine anyhow?"

"About a mile up the Middle Fork of the Snake in the Elkhorn Mountains."

Zeke whistled. "That's some rugged country all right and crawlin' with Utes."

"Uh-huh. Ain't no easy way in or out. And Yellow Weasel will keep his eyes on that part of the country for awhile, I figure," Zack said.

Peck fanned himself with his leather hat, his eye gazing at the distant blue mountains and winked at Zeke and Skin. "Gives us time to rebuild the ranch house and get old Zack settled in by the fire with the little woman, before we take off."

"Just try and leave without me," Zack shot back. "Remember, I'm the one with the map."

WALK ALONG THE BRINK OF FURY:

THE EDGE SERIES

Westerns By GEORGE G. GILMAN

MEET THE DEADLY NEW BREED OF WARRIOR:

WARBOTS

THE SCIENCE FICTION THRILLER SERIES BY

G. HARRY STINE

#4: SIERRE MADRE (132-0, $3.95/$4.95)

#5: OPERATION HIGH DRAGON (159-2, $3.95/$4.95)

#6: THE LOST BATTALION (205-X, $3.95/$4.95)

#7: OPERATION IRON FIST (253-X, $3.95/$4.95)

#8: FORCE OF ARMS (324-2, $3.95/$4.95)

#9: BLOOD SIEGE (402-8, $3.95/$4.95)

#10: GUTS AND GLORY (453-2, $4.50/$5.50)

DEATH, DESTRUCTION, DEVASTATION, AND DOOM
EXPERIENCE THE ADVENTURE OF

THE DESTROYER SERIES

By WARREN MURPHY and RICHARD SAPIR